His Witness To Evil

by

Autumn Jordon

Evil's Witness
COPYRIGHT 2009 by Dianne Gerber
Published in the United States of America
Contact Information: www.autumnjordon@yahoo.com

Front cover design by Rae Monet

Please Note: This work was first released as Evil's Witness by The Wild Rose Press.

Kudos for Author Autumn Jordon

RT Reviews said of His Witness To Evil

John Dolton is the best character; his background and the sorrow he lives with make a good subplot. Readers will wish they were the ones offering him a shoulder to cry on.

Romance Reviews said of His Witness To Evil

This book has it all! From murders to lust and tension in their most extreme forms, to traitors and backstabbing, mystery and action-packed suspense, drama and high emotions, depression and happiness, and a hot romance strung throughout.

Other Titles By Autumn Jordon

In The Presence Of Evil

Obsessed By Wildfire

Dedication

To Jim, without your support and love,
I would not be who I am.
You are my hero.

~~~~

Chapter One

No matter how hard she tried, her efforts never seemed to be enough. Stephanie Boyd jabbed a burning log within the fire ring, sending sparks to jet into the night sky. Smoke coated her tongue and she clamped her lips tight—an action that had become a habit over the past few years.

Hearing a twig snap at her side, she looked up. Her son stepped farther into the forest's veiled darkness, outside the fringe of security cast by the campfire, and beyond the full moon's realm.

Bobby thought he could handle anything, but he was only ten. Like it or not, he needed her protection. "Bobby, don't go too far. I want to be able to see where you are."

He stopped among the hip-high saplings and turned. His thin chest deflated under his muscle-man T-shirt with his huff. "I don't want you seein' me pee, Mom."

"I'm not going to watch you."

"Em will."

His glare shot to her other side and landed on his seven-year-old sister sitting next to her on the log. Leaning forward, Em peeked in Bobby's direction. Stephanie bumped her daughter's elbow with her own. "Emily Ann, mind your own business. Your brother needs his privacy, just like you."

Em cupped her mouth. "Don't worry, Mommy. He won't go too far. I told him I saw a bear down by the river."

A phantom growl stalled Stephanie's heart. She scanned the brush surrounding Bobby and listened for threatening snarls. All she heard was the fire's crackle, the nearby river's babble and an owl's hoot.

With a narrowed stare, she turned back to Em. "You really didn't see a bear, did you?"

Mischief sparkled in Em's eyes. Proud of herself, the girl sat regally on the log and propped her teddy bear, Mr. Blakeslee, on her knee. Her freckles pushed together as she grinned, exposing the swollen pink gap where her front tooth had been an hour ago. "Bobby scared me today with a worm, so I wanted to scare him back."

"You two will drive me insane with your constant picking." Stephanie sighed, tossing the stick she held into the fire. She stood and brushed bark from her cargo shorts. "I can actually feel gray hair sprouting on my head. Tomorrow I'll have to rob my piggy bank, clip a coupon and buy some hair dye. Otherwise, the children at school will definitely call me old Nurse Boyd."

"Ah, mom."

Em's laugh lightened her frame of mind.

Walking back into the diminishing circle of light, Bobby slipped his pen light into his pocket and hiked his jeans up his slim hips. He plopped down on a stump and kicked up dirt with the beat-up tip of his sneaker. "This is so lame. Why couldn't we go someplace cool? There's nothing to do. Can't we go home now? I want'a watch T.V."

Stephanie's mood headed south, again. Thousands of tourists each year considered exploring the Appalachian mountains of Pennsylvania an adventure, but not Bobby. He played in the woods behind their home every day. "You've always enjoyed camping."

"That was before. When Dad was with us."

The divorce had been hard on all of them, but especially on Bobby. He worshipped Gene.

Her son's frown weighed her heart.

Stephanie masked her sorrow with a sigh, pretending it was exertion caused by lifting the Coleman cooler she'd borrowed for their trip. She lugged the container to her old SUV. She knew how her son felt. She wished she had the money to take them away on exciting excursions like their friends had this summer. To places like Disney World, but she couldn't even afford a day trip to Hershey Park, America's chocolate capital. Em's special diet, because of her allergies, took up a third of her take-home pay. After paying the mortgage, utilities, car insurance and miscellaneous expenses, she was lucky to save a few dollars a week.

She chewed on her bottom lip. Hopefully, next week Bobby and his friends would be off on new adventures, their summer vacations a distant memory.

The howl of a diesel engine jerked Stephanie from her musing. The squeal of brakes, crushing metal and shattering glass made her spin around. I-80 ran parallel to County Road and laid about five hundred yards through the forest. Whatever had happened didn't sound good.

Faster than she'd seen him move all weekend, Bobby raced to the edge of the clearing. Em, with Mr. Blakeslee in tow, followed.

"Bobby. Em. Stop! Stay where you are."

Bobby skidded to a halt. He danced with anticipation. "Someone crashed. Can't we go see?"

Trained as a nurse, she knew she had to try and help the accident victims, but she couldn't leave her children here, alone. "You're going to have to listen to me.

Understand?"

The pair nodded.

"Okay. Douse the fire, Bobby." She grabbed her first-aid kit and flashlight from the rear of the SUV, circled the spiral column of smoke and hurried past Bobby and Em. "Stay behind me."

Shining her flashlight, she stumbled several times as she moved through the thick forest. Thickets pulled at her socks and bit into her legs. Her fingers became sticky as she bent pine branch after pine branch away from her children.

"What do you think happened, Mommy?"

Em hung on tight to Stephanie's tank top hem.

"An accident. A big one," Bobby replied.

Em edged closer to her heels.

Stephanie touched her belt. Damn. She forgot her cell phone in the Blazer.

With his little pen-light illuminating his way, Bobby somehow forged ahead of them. A second later, he disappeared through the last stand of tall pines and yelled, "Cool!"

Adrenaline had Stephanie's heart pumping, her mind whirling, and every sense supercharged as she rushed out into the clearing and pulled up short on the ridge.

The full moon, grinning down at them, created a near dusk effect. She clicked off her flashlight and clipped it to her nylon belt.

Below them, a tractor-trailer had sheered off the guard rails and lay on its side in the gully between the ridge and the interstate. Its headlights peered off into the night at odd angles. The limbs of a huge pine draped over its nose. Shrink-wrapped boxes had pushed through the trailer's roof, producing a jagged gaping hole. One of the rear trailer tires still spun as if in an attempt to *keep on movin'*.

Two men, dressed in white coveralls, scrambled up the side of the overturned truck. The stockier man yanked on the cab's door until it gave way with a metallic groan.

Stephanie immediately stooped in front of Bobby and Em. In awe, their wide stares remained on the truck. "You two stay here while I go and see if I can help."

"Aww, Mom."

"Bobby, no argument."

Voices echoed through the narrow valley behind her.

Stephanie spun around as she stood. She hadn't taken notice before, but two vehicles were parked along the interstate just in front of the twisted guardrail, a utility van, with an advertisement she couldn't quite make out on its side, and a black car. Two men stood by the car's front fender.

"He's gone," the man who had pulled the truck's cab door open called up to them.

"Where would he go?" The taller of the two men answered in a deep voice thick with a Baltic accent. "Get inside, look for him, and bring him out, Mac."

"Yes, sir." Mac grabbed his partner by the back of his coveralls and yanked him away from the cab's edge. "Get in there, Dog."

Stephanie blinked. The guy's name was Dog?

Dog dropped to his knees as ordered, and vanished into the cab.

Stephanie's calves twitched. She had to get down there. The driver shouldn't be moved until he was examined. She understood it was human nature to try to help someone who was injured but these men were definitely not trained medics.

"Let's go see." Bobby jumped onto a path formed by

all-terrain vehicles. Under his sneakers, bits of shale crunched.

"No way." Stephanie grabbed his thin arm. "You stay here. The truck might explode into flames."

Flashing amber lights cut the darkness. A few seconds later, two squad cars veered onto the shoulder behind the parked vehicles, blocking the breach in the safety barrier.

Good. Someone had reported the accident. The officers had responded quickly. They must've been patrolling the interstate, she reasoned. At least she'd have some professional help.

"Dad," Bobby called to the cop climbing from the cruiser.

Every cop car carried his dad. "He's not your dad."

"Yes, he is." Bobby twisted and ripped free from her grasp.

"Bobby Boyd, get back here."

He ignored her and scampered down the steep path, sending dust swirling into the light breeze.

Stephanie cursed under her breath and hiked the first-aid kit's strap onto her shoulder. She studied the cop skidding down the incline. It was Gene.

Her jaw clenched. The only luck she seemed to have anymore was bad luck. This area sat on the very edge of Laurel Dam's jurisdiction and, of course, her ex-husband had to be on duty and the one to respond. Along with Morse.

Morse ambled along the guardrail toward the men standing by the car. The old sheriff never got his hands dirty. He flung his arms in the air and shouted, "What the hell happened?"

The taller man replied harshly with words she didn't understand.

"Speak English, damn it," Morse retorted, his words carrying clearly on the night air.

"It is about time you came here. We have a problem now because of your lateness."

"Humph. They know each other," she mumbled. Stephanie zeroed in on the tall man. From this distance, she didn't recognize him.

She checked Bobby's location and saw he now slid to the bottom of the steep embankment on his rump. She exhaled loudly. The quicker she got down there and helped Gene with the accident victim the quicker she and the kids could get back to having fun. Or maybe she'd do as Bobby wished and they'd just pack up and go home.

She yanked a dead limb from the brush and stabbed it into the ground. "This is where we go back, Em. Stay right by me."

They started down the rocky trail. Below, only Bobby's head and shoulders bopped above the high grass as he ran toward Gene, calling, "Dad. Dad."

Beside the trailer, Gene stopped cold. He saw Bobby and, after a quick glance toward his commanding officer, Gene raced to his son. After reaching Bobby, he searched the area, apparently looking for her.

The moon faded behind a cloud as he quickly headed toward her and Em. When he was within yards, Gene pushed Bobby toward her.

"Damn it, Stephanie. What are you doing here?" His jaw locked waiting for her answer.

Anger flamed in her gut. She pulled Bobby to her side. "I came to help." Her heart pounded beneath her tank top as she stepped around him, pulling Em with her. Bobby followed close behind.

"We were camping, Dad," Em answered her father

over her shoulder.

The smell of diesel fuel floated on a breeze and she warily scanned the truck.

Gene scrambled in front of them and blocked their path. "We don't need your help."

"Bobby, take Em and go wait over by that tree." She pointed to her left.

"Stay where you are," Gene ordered them.

Stephanie's free hand curled into a fist. Tension coiled her muscles. "I'm not here to steal your limelight, Gene. You can be the macho cop hero. But I am the medical professional. Just let me do what I can to help the driver."

She attempted to sidestep him again, but his callous fingertips clamped around her wrist and held her in place. Her heated glare met Gene's wild gaze.

"I don't have time to explain," he said in a hushed whisper, leaning into her. Gene nodded toward Bobby and Em. His gaze drove into her resolve. "Take them away, now. You were never here. Understand."

She yanked her arm from his clasp. Uneasiness, not anger made her step back.

"Officer Boyd." Their family name echoed along the ridge. "The people. Who are they?"

"Nobody, Victor. Just some campers. They heard the accident. I told them to leave," Gene answered the foreigner, who scaled down the embankment after Morse, followed by another man.

Victor hopped onto a sandstone boulder and stared down at them. His cropped hair was a golden blonde, a contrast to his olive skin and dark eyes.

Inch by inch, she committed the man to memory, from his head, past the oversized belt buckle, to the tips of his boots, which reflected the moonlight. "Who is he?"

"No one. Forget him," Gene growled.

"He knows you."

The shorter man peeked around Victor.

"You should bring them here," Victor ordered Gene.

"No. They're just campers."

Victor moved to the left, exposing the man who appeared to be his shadow. The man kept his face down as if he was trying to stay hidden. He held his head just so and repeatedly pushed his glasses back onto the bridge of his nose.

Suddenly a thrashing noise came from the truck's cab.

"Dog got him. The son of a bitch is still alive," Mac shouted from atop the tractor. "Get him out here, Dog."

Stephanie sidestepped Gene and rushed toward the truck. Gene caught up to her and latched onto her arm. "Stephanie."

"Let me go!"

"No."

The driver emerged from the cab, gasping and moaning. Kneeling on the cab, he held his arm against his ribs. Mac yanked him to his feet.

Bent slightly at the waist, the man was unsteady.

Dog rose from the belly of the cab and grabbed the driver's other arm, forcing him to stand upright.

Stephanie's eyes narrowed as she assessed the driver's condition. Blood flowed from a gash above his left eye.

She tried to tug her arm free, but Gene held fast. "What is the matter with you? We need to get him down from there."

Suddenly the driver elbowed Mac in the chest, flinging him to the cab's edge. He hooked Dog with his fist. Dog tripped and landed across Mac. From behind his back, the driver pulled a gun.

Two shots pierced the night.

"No!" Victor shouted, jogging down the embankment with his short shadow behind him.

Gripping his stomach, the driver staggered a step before falling from the truck and crashing to the ground.

Stephanie's scream wedged in her throat while her children's cries echoed off the gully walls.

The driver's white T-shirt swiftly turned dark.

She stared at Sheriff Morse who pointed his smoking gun to the stars.

The short shadow cowered away from the sight, whining, "Oh, my goodness. Oh, my. No, no, no. This is not happening."

"Shut up, you bean counter," Morse ordered.

The man cringed.

Why did Morse shoot the driver? The driver had pulled a gun. Why? What the hell was going on? The questions shot though Stephanie's fogged mind like rapid fire.

At her side, Em whimpered.

Stephanie turned and scooped her daughter into her arms. Immediately, the crook of her neck moistened with little girl tears. "Don't worry, baby. We're out of here."

"Stay where you are." Victor's dark gaze zeroed in on her.

From on top of the truck, Dog and Mac aimed their weapons in her direction.

Her knees shook as she backed up a step.

Gene stepped forward and held a hand out, telling her to stand still.

"Mom," Bobby cried. Trembling, she pulled her son to her side and wrapped her arm over his back. His heart pounded against her thigh.

One by one, Mac and Dog jumped down from the cab.

Dog kicked the driver's head. It lolled to the side.

Damn. Why hadn't she listened to Gene? She glanced at his back. Because he was her ex, that's why. The past year had been nothing but a war between them.

Dog and Mac now watched her every move. How would she get Bobby and Em away?

"Have you gone crazy in the head?" Victor ripped into the sheriff.

"He was going to shoot us."

Victor crossed to where the driver lay. He stared down at the dead man only for a second before shifting his eyes to the old sheriff.

Stephanie saw the pistol on man's belt, at the hip and quaked, knowing he had the power to end lives in a second too.

Victor stalked the short distance to Morse and literally stood nose to nose with him. "Your mama raised a fool."

The old man's eyes bugged out. "I ain't no fool."

"Your actions prove you're an imbecile."

The shadow stepped up to Victor's side. "This wasn't supposed to happen. No one was going to get hurt."

"It happens," Victor stated coldly without relinquishing his stare from Morse. Then Victor nodded in their direction. "Because of this imbecile, we now have more to deal with."

Stephanie's mouth went dry.

Morse's features hardened. "Stop calling me an imbecile. You're the one who told me to intercept the truck at ten. It's ten and the Goddamn truck is down in a gully."

Victor shook his head. "Nah, I said nine forty."

"I haven't lost my hearing." Morse closed the distance between him and Victor.

The pair's heated argument drew Mac's and Dog's

interest. Their lips curled up.

Gene took a snail step back and mumbled out of the corner of his mouth, "Steph, back away slowly."

"I—" She stared at him. She couldn't breathe, much less move. Her feet were frozen in place.

She heard a snap and glanced down.

Gene slowly slid his gun from his holster. "Do it. Bobby. Em, now. Don't go home."

Stephanie eyed the trailer. If they made it to the back before they were noticed, maybe they'd have a chance. The wood line was a good fifty yards away.

Slowly, Stephanie stepped back, pulling Bobby with her.

"Where the hell do you think he was going to go?" Victor shouted and glanced in their direction. "Now we've got witnesses to get rid of."

A few paces behind Gene, Stephanie stopped as the man's merciless gaze fell on her. They were going to die.

Gene stepped in front of her. "They're not going to say a word, Victor."

"How do you know this, Boyd?"

"I just do."

"She's his ex-wife. And they're his kids," Sheriff Morse offered quickly, eager to direct Victor's anger to Gene.

"Why the hell didn't you speak up right away?" Victor glared at Morse.

"I mmmm…" Morse backed up.

"Did you think it was not important?"

Gene glanced over his shoulder and, for a brief moment, looked at her before shifting his gaze toward the forest. He stared at Em and Bobby as if for the last time and turned back to face the other five men.

"Boyd. How about you? You did not think it was important to tell me this is your family?"

"She won't say a word. Trust me. I know."

Listening to Gene's plea, Stephanie's fear abated for a moment and her heart broke again over all they'd lost. She clung to the soft, warm flesh of her children while tears blurred her vision. She didn't want Em and Bobby to die. She didn't want to die. And she didn't want Gene to die.

"She's your ex. Even if she was your wife, I couldn't take the chance," Victor said.

"Let them go," the shadow pleaded, pointing toward Bobby and Em.

"I cannot."

"I won't give you anymore information if you hurt them."

Victor spun on his heel and grabbed the shadow by the neck. The smaller man struggled for a breath as Victor's fingers clenched his windpipe. "You have no choice. If you do not, your children will feel my fury. Do you understand?"

His eyes bugged. The man managed a quick nod.

"You used your head. Good." Victor tossed him back.

Gasping, the shadow landed on his ass and quickly scurried away from Victor spider style.

Gene aimed his gun at Victor. "You're not going to hurt them. If you try, you'll have to go through me."

Victor's spine stiffened. His glare smoldered like an enraged Satan.

The urge to turn and run made Stephanie quake inside. She knew running was no longer a possibility. Gene couldn't take on all of them. They'd be gunned down within seconds.

"Don't be stupid, son." Morse put up his hand,

stepping forward.

"Shut up. I'm not your son, and I'm not going to let them hurt Stephanie and my kids." Determination made Gene's tone dangerous.

She stared at the back of the man she'd once loved with her whole heart and then had hated with her whole heart. He stood tall with his shoulders squared. He was laying his life on the line for Bobby and Em. And for her.

Gene was doing his part to save their children. She had to do hers.

The shadow crawled on his knees toward the embankment.

Mac's and Dog's full attention was on Gene.

If she kept herself in between the men and the kids, maybe, just maybe her children would live. She couldn't think about her fate or Gene's.

She inhaled and let Em slip to the ground, keeping her close while Gene's stand against the man began to heat.

She squeezed Bobby's small hand. He looked up at her; fear dulled his beautiful blue eyes. She nodded toward the back of the trailer and motioned with her hand for them to stay below the high grass. She mouthed, *car, slow.* Behind her back she pulled them together and placed Em's hand in Bobby's. She waved them off, hoping Bobby and Em wouldn't run but would back away slowly while she and Gene distracted their enemies.

Somehow she had to help Gene and draw attention away from them. Taking a deep breath, Stephanie swallowed her fear, gathered her nerve and eased her flashlight from her belt.

"Gene's right," she exclaimed, stepping forward. Her legs shook with each step, but she kept moving away from Bobby and Em. "You can trust me. I won't say a word."

She reached out and touched Gene's arm. He didn't look her way, but she knew by the way he leaned slightly into her touch that they were making their peace with each other for the sake of their children. "We didn't see a thing. And we won't tell anyone."

"I don't want to kill no kids, Victor." Mac danced in place ready to dodge Victor's wrath.

"You will do as I say," Victor snarled.

She looked at the dead driver. His lifeless stare pleaded to her for justice.

"Don't trust her," Sheriff Morse ordered, turning his gun on her.

Stephanie refused to flinch under Morse's scrutiny.

Gene moved in front of her. "Frank, what the hell are you doing? You've known Stephanie all her life."

"There is too much at stake, Gene. She saw me kill that guy. I'm not going to jail." Morse's tongue skimmed his lips. "Why the hell are you trying to protect her anyway? You two have been fightin' like junkyard dogs for years. You complain every day she's milking you dry. This is your chance to be rid of your mistakes."

"Steph was never a mistake to me," Gene's voice rose in response. Then it softened. "I was hers."

Tears threatened to blur her vision and she blinked them away. She squeezed Gene's arm and glanced at her ex-husband's profile. He remained focused.

"Touching," Victor said. "But, sorry, no. They must die here."

Stephanie gasped. Morse's hand shook as his trigger-finger pulled back.

She switched on her flashlight and swung the beam onto Morse's face.

Gene shot off a round.

Morse dropped his gun, clutching his neck.

"Oh, damn," the shadow shouted and scampered up the hill.

Loud pops. A flash.

Something whizzed by Stephanie's head, flirting with her hair. She dropped to the ground. A jagged sandstone bit into her hip, but she ignored the pain and fumbled to snap off the light.

Motionless, she clutched the rocky ground. The tall weeds towered above her, their flowering heads silhouetted against the night sky speckled with stars. She held her breath, listening, waiting for death to find her.

"Run," Gene ordered as another blast pounded the air. He dove behind a log.

Stephanie peeked above the thick grass. Mac and Dog fired their weapons as they separated in an attempt to surround them.

Victor snatched up Morse's gun and fired several shots in Gene's direction using both his gun and Morse's.

Gene bellowed, gripped his shoulder and reeled backward.

She aimed her flashlight again. Gene recovered in time to fire twice. He missed Victor but he hit Mac, sending him flying to the ground.

A dark cloud moved across the night sky, masking the full moon, giving them precious seconds to regroup. She glanced toward the wood line and prayed the kids had made it to the safety of the forest.

Stephanie crawled on her belly toward Gene. Gun shots bit the dirt behind her, missing her by inches.

The light. They had aimed for the light. She snapped the flashlight off again and rapidly made her way to Gene's side.

He crouched on his heels, using the log and high grass as cover. His blood-soaked shirt stuck to his arm. "You need to get out of here, now," he whispered.

"I can't leave you like this." A red stream flowed down his forearm. He was losing a lot of blood, fast.

"Steph, for once, listen to me. I can't hold them off forever. Bobby and Em, they need you."

"Gene—"

"I'm sorry. For everything. Go. Please."

She bit her lip, fighting the bile rising in her throat. Gene was right. If she was going to live, she had to run, and now.

She switched on the flashlight and tossed it in the air, just above the tall grass, away from them.

Shots rang out, following the beam.

Her fingers became wet and sticky as she touched Gene's arm for a brief moment. She pushed off like an Olympic sprinter, dodging left and right. She made it to the rear of the trailer. Her legs felt like a pair of limp noodles, making it impossible to dig in, get traction and give her some speed. She focused ahead, ignoring the racket building behind her. Her lungs stretched painfully as she sucked in the humid air in gasps. Keep moving. Don't stop. Don't give up, played over and over in her mind.

The moon moved from behind its cover, exposing Bobby and Em. They'd done as she'd hoped. Backing quietly away had given them the precious distance they needed to make their escape. They scampered up the embankment and disappeared into the pines where she had marked the way back to camp.

Rapid gunfire and cries pelted the air, coming closer. Stephanie didn't look back. She had to escape. She had to live for Bobby's and Em's sake.

Shale slipped under her hiking boots as she scurried up the path. Her fingers clawed at the jagged, loose ground, ripping her nails and skin. Her heart pounded, waiting for a bullet to pierce her body.

Finally, she pushed into the forest. Limbs slashed at her bare arms and clawed at her legs. She wanted to stop, let her heart slow, but there wasn't time. She pushed forward.

Suddenly all she heard were the snapping of twigs under her own feet and the pounding of her heart. She slid to a stop. Holding her chest, she swallowed cool air and listened.

Nothing. No screams. No gunfire. Not even a flap of a bat's wing.

A moment later, like the cry of an angry animal, she heard Victor roar, "Boyd, I will find you."

~~~~

Chapter Two

After receiving the call, it took Agent John Dolton exactly forty-three minutes to reach the crash site.

A legion of blue and red lights danced across the northbound lanes of I-80, casting an unnatural glow on the faces of a growing crowd. The August day had been stinkin' hot, but now the late night temperature had dipped below sixty and the spectators stood shoulder to shoulder with their hands shoved deep into their pockets like they had been plunked onto the frozen tundra.

State, County and local officials, with their eyes fixed straight ahead, rushed to carry out their orders. Overhead, two helicopters whacked the air while their unsteady white beams scanned the dark scene below.

An uneasy feeling of being watched snaked up John's spine. Were the thieves standing among the crowd?

He scanned the group of onlookers one more time, noting which television station filmed them before peering over the steep embankment at the tractor-trailer resting on its side like a two-toned silver dinosaur, its crown ripped open by a century-old pine. Emergency personnel crawled up its side and into its cavities like maggots on a corpse.

"What a fuckin' mess," he mumbled. Even though there would be pictures of the scene from every angle, John mentally rolled up his sleeves and began to jot down notes of every detail.

"Dolton."

John turned. Ben Stover, the FBI's head of field operations in Northeast Pennsylvania, made his way through the sea of emergency response personnel. The five-foot-eleven agent still carried the money-belt belly.

"It's been a while." John gripped his old friend's extended hand.

"Two years, since we were huntin' up in Potter County. How are you?"

Ben's words, spoken with reverence, unearthed memories. Ben knew without his wife and daughter he lived each day with half a heart, existing. John released Ben's strong grip. "Still doing what I have to do."

"Good man."

John turned to the accident scene, blinking away the pain.

Beside him, Ben stretched his neck, hampered by a white collar noose. "I heard about Luke. Damn shame. He was a good man. I'm sorry."

John simply nodded. The recollection of Luke bleeding out in his arms during their failed sting to capture these thieves closed in on him. He pushed the remembrance away, cleared the emotion from his throat and changed the course of their conversation. "Still haven't given up smoking those cigars, have you?"

Ben smiled around the unlit butt clenched between his teeth. "I'm workin' on it. I gave up the smokin' part."

John chuckled. "I hear ya. Baby steps."

"You remembered." Ben laughed. "Careful baby steps get you somewhere. Charging like a bull, all you do is crash. So, now that I made you smile, back to business. With I-80 and I-81 runnin' through here, I wondered when I might get a crack at these guys."

"This is my fuckin' case."

The smile surrounding Ben's cigar disappeared. He looked over the embankment. "I heard you. But you're in my fuckin' territory now, and I intend to give you all the help you need." Ben turned back to him. "Fill me in."

John pursed his lips, not sure he should share info, but his gut told him, even after years of separation, he could still trust Ben with his life. "At first these bastards snatched one load a month, but now things are escalating. This is the third heist this month and it's only the twentieth. The sons of bitches are getting greedy; nearly four million dollars over the past year in damn quarters. There's no fuckin' way of tracking serial numbers when there aren't any."

"Sweet. So, they have their game plan down to a science," Ben said. "That's good. Now all we need to do is figure it out."

"Right. The whole damn U.S. Treasury Department is on alert."

"I bet everyone's running around, looking over their shoulders and watching their asses."

"You got that right. No one knows who they can trust. Someone has to be on the inside, feeding transport information to the thieves. With a million tractor-trailers on the road, they can't be getting lucky every time. Hell, the Treasury drivers don't know if they're hauling currency or supplies. These thieves are only targeting quarters. We ran checks on all of the drivers that have been heisted and they're clean."

John visibly saw Ben wrap his mind around the information before he stepped into the break between the guardrails. "This time was different, though. Something went wrong. They didn't get the load. Their mistake could be my break. I just have to figure out what happened."

Below in the gully, an officer approached the van trailer's rear door. The bolt scraped along the frame as he forced the handle up and out of lock position. He jumped back as the door crashed to the ground. Cartons toppled out, spilling quarters "Shit."

"The area is going to be a Goddamn treasury site for tourists with their metal gadgets."

"I hear ya."

While the officers below deliberated what they'd do with the money, the activity around Ben and John escalated. The state police on the scene started moving the on-lookers back as another tractor-trailer was backed along the guard rails.

"What a mess," Ben said. "This section of I-80 east bound is going to be closed all day, if not two. Because of the steepness of the embankment, the money will have to be unloaded and manually passed from man to man up the embankment to the trailer. It's going to take hours before a crane can be brought in to lift and tow the vehicle up to the highway."

"Where's the driver? Did you get anything from him?" John asked.

"Dead."

John arched a brow. "They've never killed before. Maybe this is just an accident?"

Ben's gaze locked with his. "Doubt that. The man was shot. And, we have three more victims. The driver's wife-- they were a husband and wife team out of the Chicago area-- and two local cops."

John's gut clenched. "They walked into it?"

Stover nodded in the direction of two stilled ambulances. "It looks that way. They're all under the paper over there. The wife went through the windshield. We found her twenty feet in front of the truck. She sheered off some good-sized pine limbs."

Ben led John through the regiment of local and state cops.

John's gut knotted tighter as they approached the corpses. It was his job to examine all evidence, which included the lifeless bodies.

"I jumped right in and got my people working. First reports show no indication that the driver and his wife were involved with the heist. Class A American citizens."

Slowly, Ben folded back the beige paper exposing the sliced face of the woman. Her right eye hosted a jagged wedge of tinted glass.

John winced. "Why in the hell don't they take that out?"

"Can't. You know that."

John ignored Ben's slight smile at his reaction and turned away. He'd seen death a thousand times. He delivered it himself in the name of justice, just like Ben. But he had a feeling this woman was an innocent bystander.

Ben dropped the paper. "The husband was shot in the chest. The cops, one was shot in the neck, the other looks like a freakin' pin cushion. He's got more holes in him then I could count. Some close up. Looks like someone wanted to make sure he was dead."

"Vengeance? Turncoat?"

"That's we need find out. We're checking backgrounds on both."

"Excuse me, sir." A Pennsylvania State Trooper approached them. "Are you Agent Stover?"

"Yeah," Ben said warily around his cigar.

The officer's gaze shifted to him.

"This is Special Agent Dolton." Ben flicked his thumb at him. "You can talk. What'd you got?"

The trooper nodded. "I've just received information from our local office. They're holding a woman and her two children. She says she was here. She's claiming she saw everything."

****

As always, when a case broke, John's heart raced as if he was having great sex. And sex was a distant memory.

The state police barracks was a small building located in a rural area off a main artery half way between the PA Turnpike and I-80. From the soft glow of several lights, John could tell a few dozen homes now dotted the surrounding hills that he remembered once had been farmland. It had taken them twenty minutes, at response speed, to reach the station. Too long.

He jumped from Ben's car the moment he parked and crossed the lot. As he pushed through the barrack's glass doors, Ben chomped on his heels.

John went straight to the front desk and identified himself as the agent in charge of the investigation. While the officer paged his commander, John turned and noted Ben's disgruntled expression. This was Ben's territory, but he was the lead agent on this case and if any questions were going to be asked, he was going to be the one to ask them. He'd worked too hard over the past twelve months following whatever leads came his way, and had lost his partner. He wasn't going to take a second seat now.

A few seconds passed before the desk officer buzzed them through a set of double doors and directed them down the hall to his commander's office. Before John could knock on the door, it opened, and he came face to face with a towering brick wall dressed in a lieutenant's uniform.

The officer quietly closed the door behind him, blocking John from his witnesses.

"I'm Lieutenant Zohara."

Always the gentleman, Ben stepped around him and extended his hand to the officer.

Formalities edged John's nerves. And while Zohara relayed the witness's statement, John peered through the tilted mini-blinds into the lieutenant's office. He studied the woman inside who sat on a couch, sandwiched between two kids.

A checklist ticked off in John's mind. She was small, maybe a hundred-twenty-five pounds. Her arms and legs were scratched and bruised. If he had to guess, he'd say she was about five-six. A few light brown strands had pulled free from her pony tail and framed her tan face. The way she held her head, watching her children sleep, he couldn't tell the color of her eyes.

Suddenly the little girl woke and scrambled into her mother's lap.

Mesmerized, John watched the woman Zohara identified as Stephanie Boyd cradle her daughter, smoothing her hair and whispering into her ear—just like Julie had done with Katie.

Fury, as familiar as the air he breathed, flickered fresh in John and he fingered the rubber band he'd worn on his little finger for the past two years.

He punched the anger away.

He couldn't deal with his demons now.

"They watched while their father was murdered," Zohara said, pulling John back to the conversation.

"What?"

Zohara turned to him. "I thought my officer at the scene would've told you. Officer Boyd, their father, was one of the responding officers killed."

"Ah, shit," Ben said. "That will put them into therapy for a long time."

"Every cop's nightmare." Zohara nodded.

John's finger worked the band, fighting the rash of memories that threatened his sanity. "One of them."

Ben gaze softened. Ben knew the details of Julie's and Katie's deaths and that John had lived through a nightmare of his own.

John cleared his throat and focused. "I need to speak to her."

"Of course. I'll bring her to the interrogation room." Zohara pointed further down the hall. "Third door on your left. Make yourself comfortable."

"And the kids?" John asked, knowing he needed to hear every account of what happened.

Zohara dropped his hand from the door's knob and exhaled. "It seems after the driver was killed the rest of the scene is a blur to the kids—at least consciously."

"Let them sleep," Ben suggested. "The evil they've witnessed, they deserve a few hours of peace. We can talk to them later."

"Okay. Sure," John decided, thinking about his own little girl, Katie.

The moment Zohara slipped into the room and spoke to her, Stephanie Boyd's grip tightened on her children and through the glass her gaze met John's.

Her shockingly green eyes reflected every troubled emotion she harbored.

She was a mother like Julie had been.

Stephanie Boyd was scared. She wanted to protect her children. And she needed help.

He winced only slightly as the band snapped against his skin. This time he was not going to fail.

~~~~

Chapter Three

Stephanie glanced over her shoulder again. Even though she was only going a short distance down the hall, leaving Bobby and Em was not what she wanted to do right now. She wanted to cling to them.

She ran her hands up and down her arms as she followed Zohara through the tiled corridor. The sweater she wore did little to fend off the chill that swept through her whenever she recalled Gene's frighten expression.

What if she and the kids had been followed?

Stephanie's step faltered.

She was being silly. They were in a police station for God's sake. Em and Bobby were safe. A woman officer remained on guard in the room with them. And Zohara had assured her they were surrounded by dozens of armed officers.

Bobby and Em were okay. *They would be okay*, she repeated again in her mind.

Zohara stopped at a metal door and peered through the little glass. Before twisting the knob, he gave her a reassuring smile. He swung the door wide.

White fluorescent light, brighter than the hall lights above, spilled across her.

Her heart pounded while she adjusted the oversized sweater Zohara had retrieve-d from the trunk of his car for her to wear. She inhaled deeply, fortifying her strength before she stepped forward.

Battleship gray walls and the air conditioning that swished on above her did little to refresh the tiny area's oppressive air.

"Stephanie Boyd, this is FBI Agent Stover." Zohara made the introductions after following her into the boxy room.

Agent Stover, seemingly calm, sat at the card sized table, twirling a stub of a pencil between his fingers. An unlit cigar hugged the corner of his mouth. His suit jacket hung on the back of the chair and his white shirt sleeves were rolled up as if he was about to get to work.

"And this is Special Agent Dolton." Zohara indicated the man who stopped in mid-pace and faced the large pane mirror.

The gun hugging the center of the man's back made Stephanie shiver.

He turned and his coal-colored eyes traced over her, chasing the chill from her and replacing it with heat.

She openly returned his assessment. Except for the gun, he didn't look like an FBI agent. He wore his brown hair longer than she thought allowed by the FBI, curling at his shirt's collar. His square jaw was shadowed with dark stubble. His casual blue shirt pulled across his chest and looked as if it came from the dryer and not the dry cleaners. His worn jeans were faded at the knees and near the lower area of the zipper.

"Would you like to sit down?" Agent Stover shot up from his chair.

Stephanie shook her head, trapping her lip between the teeth for a second.

"We understand you were at the accident scene on I-80 tonight. We need to ask you a few questions." Agent

Dolton stepped up to the table, reached across and handed her his business card.

Accident? Her pulse raced as she peered at his card. Her thumb brushed across the raised gold FBI logo.

"You know as well as I do there was no accident. Why is the FBI involved?" Stephanie looked from agent to agent and then to Lieutenant Zohara.

The three men surrounded her. Their focus trained on her. Did they know Gene was involved in whatever the hell happened tonight? Did they think she was guilty too?

Stephanie fought to keep her breathing even and not to pull her gaze away from theirs while she waited for one of the men to speak up.

Dolton sighed. "You're right, Mrs.—"

"It's Ms."

"Okay. Ms. Boyd." A smile played on his lips. "It wasn't an accident."

Giving into the need to run, she backed away from Officer Zohara.

"I think Ms. Boyd is feeling a little out numbered. Stover, what do you say, before we get started, you go with Lieutenant Zohara and get us coffee. I know I could use some." His gaze shifted to her. "And you look as if you need it too. Am I right?"

The realization that the FBI was investigating whatever Gene and Morse had been involved in had given her a jolt, but she was exhausted. She needed the caffeine. Stephanie drew a quick breath and nodded.

"No problem. How do you take it?" Stover rose and rounded the table.

"Black is fine."

"You got it. Okay, show me where the pot is, Zohara."

When the door clicked closed behind her, she quickly glanced over her shoulder before she asked, "How's Gene? No one will tell me anything."

Agent Dolton looked at her quizzically, "Gene?"

"Officer Boyd."

His glanced at the floor and she knew Gene was gone before he even said, "I'm sorry for your loss."

Finally, someone had the balls to tell her the truth.

Yes, they were divorced, but Gene had been her first real love. They had history. Pain curled her fingers into fists, crumpling the agent's card.

"Please. Sit down." Agent Dolton circled the table in quick strides and pulled the chair out for her.

She stuffed the wadded paper into her shorts' pocket and sank onto the hard plastic and buried her face in her hands.

Gene was dead. He'd died saving them. She clamped her eyes closed, fighting the tears that threatened to fall.

Stephanie heard scraping and knew the agent had moved the only other chair in the room around the table and taken a seat next to her.

He sat silently for a moment, giving her time before he said, "Ms. Boyd. I know this is a difficult time for you, but I need to ask you a few questions."

Stephanie dropped her hands to her lap while lifting her face to the ceiling. She inhaled deeply. Dolton's musk scent filled her nostrils along with the unambiguous stench of a hundred guilty men and women who'd sat in this chair before her. She looked at him warily. "Why is the FBI involved?"

"We believe while in the process of responding to an accident, your husband—"

"I'm sure you know what happened tonight wasn't an accident. And, Gene was my *ex*-husband." She held her chin high—a habit she'd formed in the past year when making it clear their divorce was her doing but not her fault. "We separated over a year and a half ago. Our divorce was decreed in May."

Dolton leaned back in his chair. "Right. Well, we believe Officer Boyd and Sheriff Morse stumbled into a situation and were ambushed."

Stephanie stared at her lap. She knew that wasn't what happened. Gene and the sheriff had been mixed up in *the situation*.

If it wasn't for the fact that she and the kids had shown up, Gene would probably still be alive. Maybe even the driver, but she had her doubts.

Gene was dead. In her heart, she'd known it as soon as the gunfire had stopped and silence had reached her. That was why, over the past several hours, her thoughts had turned to her own survival.

She was the sole supporter of their children.

She was the only witness to the scene. If she told Agent Dolton Gene died a hero, at least Em and Bobby would get survivor benefits and Gene's life insurance. If he died committing a crime, they'd get nothing.

Gene had saved them. By keeping his involvement in the crime a secret, she'd be helping their children, saving Gene's parents embarrassment and Gene would be buried with honor. Her children wouldn't be the children of a criminal.

She glanced at Dolton. Would she hamper the FBI's investigation by not telling the truth?

What about Victor? Stephanie's throat went dry with dread. She hoped he was dead. His look had told her she was dead before he'd even given the order. If Gene hadn't killed him, would Victor come after her and Bobby and Em?

"What kind of situation?" she asked wanting to know exactly what Gene had been up to.

"I'm sorry but I can't—"

"It has to be something pretty big for you, the FBI, to be involved," she cut him off. "If you need my help, I want to know what I'm getting myself into."

Stephanie began to tremble under Dolton's scrutiny. She folded her arms across chest and refused to look away.

"Fair enough," he conceded. He straightened in his chair, pulled Stover's pad in front of him, cleared his throat and continued, "You saw the scene. In the past, the driver would've been forced to the side of the road. The tractor-trailer would've been hijacked. In a few days, we'd find the truck ditched off a back road, the load missing.

"Tonight, apparently, this driver had no intentions of giving up his rig. In the process, he got himself and his wife killed."

Surprise straightened Stephanie in her chair. "I didn't see a woman."

"She was thrown through the windshield upon impact."

Stephanie shivered with the stark image in her mind. She hoped the woman had died instantaneously and not suffered while listening to her husband's death.

"You said, '*in the past.*' This has happened before?"

"Yes."

She tilted her head slightly and studied the agent. "What was in the trailer?"

"Quarters."

Her brows rose in disbelief. "Money? How much?"

"Thousands."

"You're kidding." She shifted on the seat.

"No."

"Why wasn't the tractor-trailer escorted?"

"The Federal Reserve transports coins undercover. The routes of the vehicles are highly guarded, but somehow that security has been breached. Over the past three months, nearly a million dollars of untraceable change has been stolen."

"A million," she repeated slowly, trying to imagine the mountain of coins and wondered how much of that huge pile would've been Gene's take.

"Ms. Boyd." He pulled her attention back to him. "Why were you there?

His dark stare leveled on her, reading her.

He did think she was involved in some way. She dipped her head slightly so he wouldn't see her swallow the lump forming in her throat and then met his dark eyes. "I hope you're not thinking that I was a part—that I'm a thief. Bobby, Em and I had to run for our lives. Look at my legs." She stood and rounded the table intent on showing the agent the red welts where the briar bushes had clawed her as she'd ran through the forest for her life.

His gaze trailed up her thighs, her body and met hers. "I noticed them before."

"Good," she replied, trying to keep her voice from shaking as she took her seat. "Look. The kids and I were camping off County Road. We go there often, to fish. It runs parallel to I-80. We heard the crash and ran to see what had happened. We were only there, a hundred yards away, for a moment before Gene and Sheriff Morse arrived. It all happened so quickly."

"Quite a coincidence you're there at the same time an accident occurs."

"Do you say that to all your witnesses?"

"Not all of my witnesses have ex-husbands killed at the scene."

"It's not my fault Gene was a cop in this town." She refused to look away. She was right and he knew it.

After a few seconds, seemingly to let her sweat, he asked, "What kind of vehicles did the thieves drive?"

Stephanie tried to relax back onto the chair while Agent Dolton fired the usual preliminary questions at her but it was impossible. By the time she'd given detailed descriptions of the men involved, including the very tall foreigner, Victor, her muscles were tight, like a bunch of rubber bands ready to snap. She'd been on the edge of her seat all night. Even now, sitting in a room with an armed FBI agent, she had this irresistible urge to run. But to where? Gene had said *don't go home*. Would Victor be waiting for them? Is that what he meant?

"Okay. Now. Try to recall. Step by step, what happened?" Agent Dolton pressed her, bringing her thoughts back to the here and now. "Every detail is important."

She let go of the chair's seat, flexing the circulation back into her fingers. "Bobby ran to his father. I chased after him and—" She closed her eyes against the bloody image her memory painted.

"What happened?"

Knowing once she said the words she couldn't take them back, she opened her eyes and stared at the federal agent. "I saw the two men pull the driver from the cab. He tried to get away, but Morse shot him."

"The sheriff?" The surprise twist shot John Dolton forward in his chair. "He was involved?"

She nodded, swallowing hard.

"And your—Officer Boyd?"

She shook her head before she could change her mind. "No. I don't think so. Gene seemed startled too. He drew his gun. The man who was in charge—Morse called him Victor—he ordered the sheriff and the others to kill us."

Recalling the chill of Victor's stare, caused her to openly shiver. She pulled the sweater up over her shoulder and ran her palms over the goose bumps lining her thighs. She never wanted to face him again. But if Victor was alive, he would find her. Her only hope would be to hide somewhere safe. But where? And for how long?

She needed John Dolton's help.

"There was another man. Morse called him a bean counter."

"Bean Counter? Did they call him by any other name?"

"No." She rubbed the throbbing pain stabbing her forehead. "The whole night was a nightmare. I just want to forget it." She sighed heavily.

"You're doing fine," Agent Dolton said calmly in an attempt to reassure her. "I can see you're exhausted, but the more information we gather now, the sooner we can follow up on the leads. You'll feel better after you have a cup of coffee. But then again, I remember Stover's coffee." His serious expression lightened with a smile.

She couldn't help but smile too. The anxiety melted from her neck muscles. "Okay."

"What happened next?"

"The shooting started. Gene shot Morse first, in the neck."

The agent's head snapped up.

Had she said something wrong? Maybe he didn't believe her.

"I don't think Gene wanted to kill Morse," she added quickly. "They'd been friends and worked together for over ten years. Morse had stopped by our house often. The men of the Laurel Dam police force shared everything; marriages, births, deaths…" Stephanie sighed. "Why did Morse do this to us?"

"I don't know. Apple gone bad?" he offered.

"I guess," she replied on the tail end of a sigh.

"What happened next?"

"Gene shot one of the other men in the stomach. I saw him fly back against the truck and go down. The scene was horrible—like something out of an explicit action movie. Gene yelled for me to run—with Em and Bobby. We did. Bullets whizzed past us." She was talking fast and couldn't slow down. "I've never been so scared. Thank God the grass was waist high. It gave us some cover."

She hesitated a moment and dropped her gaze to her folded hands on the table, avoiding the agent's eyes. A tear fell to her cheek and she swiped it away. "That was the last time I saw Gene. The shooting lasted—it seemed like forever. We were running through the forest when it stopped."

She'd done it. She'd lied.

Her hands slid from her lap to the chair's edge and she hung on, trying to steady her nerves while she waited for the agent reviewed his notes. She looked at his left hand. His thumb worked what looked like a blue rubber band circling his little finger and she wondered why he wore it.

"You said there were four men besides the officers?" he finally asked.

Relief washed through her. Agent Dolton seemed satisfied with her story. "Yes. The leader, Victor—"

"Did Victor have a last name?"

"No. I only heard him called Victor."

Agent Dolton scratched a note on his pad. "Who else?"

"Mac, Dog and the bean counter. Did Gene get them all?"

"Only the bodies of the driver, his wife and the officers were found at the scene."

"You mean Victor and his men are all still alive? Gene didn't kill any of them?" Fear's icy fingers grabbed Stephanie's lungs and she found it hard to breathe. She had to get to Em and Bobby. She shoved back from the table, stood and spun.

At that very moment, the door burst open, hitting the wall with a bang.

Stephanie jumped back against the table. Her knuckles paled as she clutched its edge.

"I'm sorry. I didn't mean to startle you," Stover said around his cigar. He held two steaming mugs of coffee.

John stood and rounded the corner of the table, putting himself between Stephanie and Stover.

Her eyes were green, shimmering pools. Her full bottom lip trembled. As if in an attempt to cover up her anxiety, she let go of the table and wrapped her arms around her waist.

John understood her fear. He'd been in hell many times. Tonight was her first trip. But she made it through alive. That alone said something about the woman.

His gut told him there would be more havoc in her life before this was over. Victor and his men knew Stephanie Boyd and her children were alive. They'd come after her.

If he were in their shoes, he would.

He wasn't going to let her or her children out of his sight. No matter how much the presence of the little girl reminded him of his Katie, causing his heart to break.

He placed his hand on Stephanie's arm. The oversized sweater she wore slipped off her shoulder. Immediately his gaze went to her exposed skin and heat shot right to his groin. Quickly, he pulled his hand away and stepped back from the attraction between them. Stephanie Boyd was a witness he had to protect. He had to keep his head on straight in order to ensure she and her children stayed alive.

John cleared the unexpected desire from his voice. "Your children are safe. You don't have to worry about them, Ms. Boyd."

"He was going to kill Em and Bobby." Her voice quaked. "They saw him. I saw him. We know what he looks like."

Her plea, loud and clear, pulled at his heart.

~~~~

Chapter Four

It was nearing two a.m. when Victor lowered his tinted window to half mast and swung his Porsche into the driveway. The engine's purr cut to a low growl as he eased off the accelerator only slightly before the armed guard waved him by with his automatic. His men knew he would die before he brought an intruder into his family's realm, so there was no need to stop him and search either him or his car.

A hundred yards further, a second guard swung the iron gates wide and he passed through without delay. He shifted gears. The car roared. The tires hugged the tarmac as he rounded each curve, climbing.

His grandparent's home was a fortress. A twelve-foot stone wall and an electric charged fence surrounded the entire twenty mountaintop acres. Guards and dogs walked the perimeters between the two twenty-four-seven. The stone home, built in the shape of a pentagon, lay hidden away from the world, even from the eye in the sky, by a dense forest. Even the courtyard hosted huge oaks providing cover.

The men of many colors who had breached the sanctuary's security, some with the help of his turncoat cousin, never saw the outside world again. His grandmother's treasured roses fed well off their rotting flesh.

Rounding the last curve, his family's two-story home came into view. The house was dark, except for a soft glow cast against the window of his papa's library.

Victor eased up on the accelerator. He wasn't looking forward to facing Papa. The man was known for his ruthless temper when business affairs didn't go according to plan.

Morse was a fortunate man to have been killed instantly by Gene. And Gene, he too was lucky.

Mercifully, he'd had Gene finished off instead of dragging his pussy whipped ass back here to Papa.

A spasm rippled Victor's crotch. Papa would have had the man hung up by his balls. The memory of his cousin's scream before Papa had granted mercy still haunted him.

Pulling up to the front door, Victor jammed the car into park and cut the lights and engine. He sat in the darkness a moment while his heart warmed, thinking of the times as a child he had competed with his many cousins for his papa's attention.

A smile pulled at Victor's lips. He had been Papa's favorite. Papa had been more than a grandfather to him. Papa had taken his father's place after the man had died taking a bullet for Papa.

He didn't like disappointing his papa. His father never had. Somehow he would make up for the mistakes of the idiots he supposedly controlled.

The front door opened, casting a bright path over the stone steps. Shermin, Papa's personal guard took a stance within the threshold. The sleeves of Shermin's black T-shirt stretched over his muscular arms as he crossed them over his barrel chest. His huge shadow darkened the channel of light.

Shermin waited for him.

Victor exited the car. He felt the smooth material of his slacks drop into place as he stretched his long legs. Out of his peripheral vision he saw the drapes of the library ease back.

Papa watched him.

He reached inside the car, across the console, grabbed his calf's leather coat from the passenger seat and stuffed his arms into the sleeves.

"Victor, your papa is waiting," Shermin called out, impatience evident in his tone.

Victor drew a deep breath, adjusted his belt buckle and exhaled. His breath curled in the crisp air in front of him. He chose his steps carefully—either too slow or too fast, and Shermin would look upon him as a coward.

No matter what his cousin, Lev, thought, or any of the others, one day he would control the family's business and no man would remember him as a weakling.

When Victor reached the top step, Shermin looked down his nose at him. The guard stood nearly six-nine. Shermin eyed his new hair color and smirked. "You're late. Your papa waits on you in the library."

Victor liked the blonde color. When it grew out he would look like the actor that played Billy the kid. "I came as soon as I took care of business."

"Humph."

Victor raised his chin and met the man's cold stare head-on. "You have something to say to me, Shermin?"

Shermin shook his head and stepped to the side.

Feeling his power, Victor pushed by him.

"Your papa does, however," Shermin said to his back.

Victor let the words pass by him, but made a mental note that even though Shermin would die for his papa, he could never trust his back to the man.

His steady footsteps slapping the marble floor echoed off the high ceiling as he crossed the foyer. The walls closed in on him. He walked through the hall toward the wing where the family business was conducted. As he was taught as a child, he knocked softly on the library's door and waited, hands folded and head bowed, until he heard his papa call, "Come inside."

Victor licked his suddenly dry lips before turning the etched knob. He entered Papa's office and softly closed the door behind him.

Dressed in his nightshirt and royal red robe, Papa sat at his desk. He looked tired, but Victor knew not to be deceived by Papa's slack shoulders and head that slightly shook the moment the old man's eyes lifted to meet his gaze.

"What's with the hair?" Papa asked extending a crooked finger at him.

"I felt like a change."

"Why? Are you not proud of who you are?"

"Yah, I'm proud." Victor puffed his chest.

"Then change it back to the color your mother gave you. Take a seat. Tankson woke me." Papa shook his head and got right to business. "He said the delivery he was expecting tonight did not come. What happened?"

"Morse was late," Victor answered, remembering to keep his chin high, as he crossed the oriental carpet and stood in front of the massive desk, hands clasped military style. "There was an accident."

Papa picked up a pen from the desk and twirled it between his fingers, clicking it every other turn. "And how did this accident occur?"

"The tractor went beyond the designated mark. Seeing Morse was late, Mac tried to get the driver to pull over. The rig's driver lost control and went over an embankment."

"I want to see Morse. We have made him a very rich man. He should be grateful."

"You can't."

"I can't."

Papa's tone set Victor back on his heel and he quickly explained. "Morse, he is dead."

"Dead?" The pen stopped its travel between Papa's index and middle fingers. "How did this happen?"

Victor sighed and dove into the recount of the night. When he finished, Papa's jaw was clenched and gray glare gleamed with anger. Victor fought not to step back.

"Why was Randall with you?"

Making Randall ride with him tonight had been a mistake. He knew that now. "Randall was threatening out."

"And you thought making him a part of the dirty work would do what?"

Papa was right. Randall was already involved up to his eyeballs. He was a traitor to his country. There really wasn't a reason to have Randall there tonight, other than he had wanted to show his power over the man.

Beads of sweat popped out on Victor's upper lip.

"You wanted Randall spineless and completely under your control?" Papa offered.

Papa understood. Relief washed through Victor as he nodded.

"We will not be able to replace Morse and Gene so easily."

"I know. I tried to reason with Gene but he would not hear what I was offering," he lied. He had not liked Gene from the moment they'd met. He had no qualms ordering Mac to put a bullet through his eye.

"Family is the most important. You know that."

"You are right, Papa. I should have brought them here and we could have dealt with them together."

Victor grew anxious again under Papa's scrutiny. He disguised his worry by taking a seat and making a chore of brushing a piece of lint from his dark slacks. He needed to appear totally confident in his actions. Papa had yet to decide who would succeed him. Victor couldn't see any of his cousins taking Papa's place. He was the only one capable of running the family.

"This woman can identify you and Randall?" Papa asked interrupting his vision of power.

Victor blinked.

"Stupes."

The act had been too much.

Papa threw the pen he held at him, hitting Victor in the chest. It might as well have been a dagger because the pain in Victor's heart was as such. His fingernails dug into the soft wood of the chair's arms.

Papa rose, knocking his chair to the floor with a thud, and rounded his desk with the speed of a much younger man.

The door behind them swung open.

"Get out, Shermin. I will call you if I need you," Papa shouted.

Victor heard the door's lock click.

Papa towered over Victor, holding his hand out, ready to slap him if he gave the wrong answer to his next question, "Where is Mrs. Boyd?"

"I don't know—" He stopped in mid-sentence, knowing one didn't say *I don't know* to Papa. "She and her

children ran into the forest while Gene held us off.
Afterwards, Mac searched the area and found their
campsite, but they were gone. Mac is staking out their
home. We will find them."

"And what did you do? Why are you not out looking
for her?"

"I drove Randall to his house. I thought it best I came
home and tell you myself what had happened. I will call
Tankson and let him know we will have his shipment to
him tomorrow."

"How?"

"I have things under control, Papa. Trust me."

"Pssh," Papa chortled. "You have a lot to learn, Victor.
A man must earn another man's trust."

"Have I not always done as you've asked?"

"Yes, son, but a man has to do the right things without
being asked. He must think." The old man tapped his
temple.

Papa's phone rang and he snatched the receiver up
before it rang a second time.

"Ya." Papa's focus remained on him. "I know. Victor
is here with me now."

Papa's face paled before heating and matching the
color of his robe as he listened to the caller. A chill ran up
Victor's spine and he adjusted his coat.

Papa's back straightened. "Where? Is there a way to
her?"

Victor strained to hear the caller's voice but the way
Papa clutched the phone to his ear, he could not. He shifted
forward in his seat.

"Nah. Be careful." Papa dropped the receiver. "Mrs.
Boyd has been found."

Victor's blood rushed. "Where?"

"She is at the state police. Your cousin is there. Hopefully we will have Mrs. Boyd and her children soon."

Victor shot from the chair. "I will bring them here."

"No, you will take care of Tankson as you promised. Get him his load of quarters. We have a sweet deal going with the man. I do not want it blown. Pasha will take care of Mrs. Boyd and her children. You must protect the family."

"I will not fail you, Papa."

Uri Zosimosky slapped his grandson's shoulder. "I hope not, son."

Victor rose and crossed to the door before Papa stopped him.

"Son."

Victor turned. "Yah,"

"The next time I see you, your hair will be the color of your birth. Yah?"

"Yes. Papa."

~~~~

Chapter Five

Ben circled the room one more time before he grabbed the chair, swung it around and straddled the seat opposite John. He picked up his coffee and asked, "So, Morse was in on it. How about her ex?"

John ignored Ben's question and continued to stare at his notes, tapping his pen at each point. Stephanie Boyd was not telling him the whole story. Her expression gave her away.

"Well?" Stover prompted him again.

John heaved a sigh and laid the pen down. "She says not. But they're divorced."

"Do you think she was involved?"

John had seen the way Stephanie's gaze darted from his several times, especially when he'd questioned her about her ex-husband, Gene, and Sheriff Morse's involvement in the crime. "My gut says no. Did you send men out to the campsite?"

"Yeah." Ben pulled his shirt sleeve back and glanced at his Timex. "They should report back soon."

"Then we'll know if she is telling the truth."

"A campsite doesn't mean she's clean." Ben pulled his cigar from his shirt pocket and stuffed it between his lips. "You know she knocks off the ex and the kids get his survivor benefits, life insurance policies, etc., etc. They're too young. As their guardian, she gets control of their finances. She could be sitting damn sweet."

"You saw the way she protects those kids," John said. "I'd doubt she put her kids in danger for any amount of money. Besides she came here."

"Crime gone bad. Maybe she wanted to cover her ass. With Morse and her ex out of the picture, who is going to give her up? The other guys? I don't think so."

Ben trapped the waggling cigar between his fingers and pointed at him. "In fact, we don't know *they* exist. Do we? Maybe Morse and Boyd were behind the heists. This heist went bad and tempers flared. Bang, bang and they're both dead. It's her word against whose? Maybe she shot them herself."

Ben was already role playing as the devil's advocate to his train of thought. Luke and he had worked out many cases doing the same thing. It felt good.

"No. Morse and Boyd were hick cops. I questioned Zohara about them. They didn't have the capabilities or connections to pull off the heists. They were pawns, not master planners."

A smile tugged at John's lips as he ripped three pages from the borrowed notepad. Only the top sheet contained his notes, but he wasn't going to take any chances and make it easy for anyone to do tracings.

He stood and folded the pages in half and then into a quarter before he stuffed them into his back pocket. "I have to make arrangements to get Ms. Boyd and her children to a safe house."

"You think they'll come after her and the kids?"

"Wouldn't you?"

Ben pulled the cigar from his mouth. "If my life depended on it."

"Theirs does."

"Sweet."

"Yeah. Let's see if you still feel the same way when you come face to face with them."

"Then I'm on your team?"

"Is there a way I can stop you?"

"Hell no."

"Let's get busy. While I make arrangements to get her and the kids out of here, can you run some names?"

"What you got?" Ben pulled a notebook from his coat pocket and snatched up the pen from the table.

"Let's start with the ring leader. She said his name was Victor."

"Last name?"

"Steph didn't catch one. All she got was Victor, Bean Counter, Mac and Dog."

Ben's brow arched. "Steph?"

An irritating grin flashed around Ben's cigar.

"Ms. Boyd. Whatever. Can you run the names?"

"Sure. I'll run them all, but do you know how many hits we'll get with just first names?"

"Narrow the search on Victor; white, male, approximately six-foot-five-inches, blonde hair, dark eyes. And, I figure, the bean counter has to be someone with an accounting background. Maybe—" A familiar voice from the hall turned John's head before he could continue.

A moment later, she stood in the threshold. Alexandra Mosley, the agent who had killed his partner.

A mixture of hatred and sympathy assaulted John. It had been five months since he'd last seen the tall redhead. He knew the internal affair's investigation had determined Luke's shooting to be an accident on the rookie's part, but he couldn't find it in himself to forgive her. "What are you doing here? I thought you were pulled from the case."

John saw her stiffen as their gaze met.

She notched her chin up. "I was sent for."

Her blue eyes quickly shifted to Ben.

Realizing Ben apparently had a part in Alex being here, John turned on him. "What is she doing here?"

Ben lifted his hand in the air in a stop-cop fashion, his cigar still trapped between two fingers. "I got the word while you were talking to Ms. Boyd. The Treasury Agency has a right to interrogate the witness. She—"

"Ms. Boyd told me all she could remember for now," John lied. He intended to find out what Steph was hiding before anyone else did. Especially Alex.

"Are you willing to share your notes?" Ben pointed to his back pocket.

John's jaw clenched and his thumb worked the band on his finger while tension electrified the small space.

Ben had him. He wasn't going to discuss anything with anyone unless he was one hundred percent sure the information would be held in confidence and only passed on to trusted personnel. He didn't trust Alex. And someone in the Treasury Department had to be leaking information to the thieves.

He shook his head.

Ben shoved his chair back, scraping the floor, and rose.

"Agent Mosley is on our side, John. Whether we like it or not, we have our orders. She'll need to ask Ms. Boyd some questions."

Ben popped his cigar between his lips. The action stated loud and clear that the conversation was over.

"Sometimes a woman tells another woman something more," Alex interjected.

Her mellow tone made John's stomach roll. He wasn't going to waste time arguing. Alex was a Treasury agent.

Ben was right. Whether he liked it or not, she had every right to question the witness.

He had to stay focused on what was important. His first concern was the safety of his witness and her two children. Keeping his gaze fixed on Alex, he crossed the short distance toward her. "You have until I make the transport arrangements to the safe house."

Alex remained standing on the threshold, blocking his quick exit. She stared up at him. "I'm looking forward to working with you again, John." She turned, allowing him only enough room to squeeze by her.

"I work alone," he said coldly as he brushed by.

Feeling her glare on his back, John walked down the hall as if he was completely in control, even though every nerve inside of him wanted to get far away from Alex and the onslaught of adverse memories she forced on him.

Maybe Alex was right and Steph would open up to her, woman to woman. That would piss him off. He couldn't have shown more compassion.

Forget about Alex. Forget about the past. Concentrate on the now. He pulled his notes from his pocket. Steph had said the old sheriff was part of this. He could see how locals on the take could help with the tracking and hijacking of tractor-trailers.

Had Steph's ex been involved? Is that what she was hiding?

Maybe his witness wasn't a witness, but actually part of the puzzle like Ben suggested. How likely was it she and the kids happened to be camping right off the highway where the takedown occurred?

Zohara had sent men out to check the area and verify her story. If Steph and her kids hightailed it out of there as fast as she said they did, their camping equipment, tents, something would still be there.

Either way, he was going to keep Steph Boyd close to him until he found out the truth.

He needed to check out everything about Stephanie Boyd—make inquires on her character. And also, check the courthouse for the filed divorce papers for Gene and Steph Boyd and financial records and employment history. The list was growing and time was getting short. If he was going to chase the leads this woman had given him, he was going to make damn sure her background story checked out and she was clean.

John stopped for a moment by Zohara's office and peered through the window. The female officer on guard immediately spotted him and nodded.

Sitting once again between her children, Stephanie rested her head on the back of the couch. The oversized sweater she wore hung off her shoulder again, a seemingly innocent act which had turned John's eye and stirred his desire. A feeling he hadn't allowed in ages. Why now? Why her?

Stephanie's lashes rested against her tanned cheeks. She was pretty even with her wheat-colored hair disheveled and pink lips slightly gaped.

The woman wore no make-up. She was as earthy as they came. She smelled only of the faintest mixture of soap and charred wood.

Why would any man let someone like her go? Or had it been the other way around?

John shoved his notes back into his pocket and checked his watch. He wanted them moved before dawn cracked.

"John, wait." Both Alex's voice and the click of her heels scratched his nerves as she approached. "I want to talk to you."

Reluctantly, he turned. "What?"

"I know you don't want me here—"

"Oh, you've got that fuckin' right."

His cutting remark shoved Alex back on her heels. Her face turned red as she trapped her top lip.

"I know you still blame me for what happened to your partner. I don't know how many times I can say I'm sorry."

"You haven't even begun."

He was being rough on Alex, but he couldn't help it. He found it hard to forgive anything anymore. Luke had been more than a partner. Luke had been his best friend.

She stuffed her hands into the pockets of her blue blazer and jutted her chin forward. "Okay. Fine. I'm sorry. Add it to your list, but you better get used to the idea that I'm here now. And will be until this case is solved."

Heat rose through his veins. He'd like to tell her to go to hell, but it wouldn't do a bit of good. "I've been working this case for six fuckin' months. Now that the thieves screwed up and we have a witness, everyone suddenly wants to command the damn front line."

"I've been working the same case on our end." Alex stepped closer to him, holding his hot gaze. "Don't look so surprised. You think the department was going to sit back and twiddle its thumbs waiting for the FBI to solve the case? These guys are good. I'm beginning to get heat, just like you. I think it's time we pool our knowledge and get these jokers."

John's chuckle reflected his cynicism. "We're going to work together? Right."

He started to turn but she grabbed his hand. Her fingers felt cold against his skin, much like his patience for her.

"John, please. Don't let one little rookie mistake get in the way of this investigation."

"Little! Luke would be alive and we'd have these sons of bitches now if it wasn't for your *little* mistake," he hissed. "I don't know if I can trust you, Alex." The veins in his neck strained. He inhaled through his nose and nodded toward the door. "You have about ten minutes with Ms. Boyd. After that, they're leaving with me."

John wrenched his wrist from her grasp and stalked toward the front desk. He had to find Zohara and a secure land line.

Time was running out.

~~~~

Chapter Six

Outside, in the hall, someone yelled, "Watch out!"

Stephanie nearly jumped off the hard-backed chair. She searched past the Treasury agent seated knee-to-knee across from her.

A second later, two officers jokingly passed each other in the hall.

Stephanie sighed with relief. Every bump, every car pulling in and out of the parking lot, every door opening or closing caused her heart to clench as if in a vise while she waited for the man with the cold glare, the one who'd ordered them dead, to show up and blow her and the kids away.

She pinched the sandy grit from her eyes. Above her, she heard the air conditioning kick on and she felt cool air flow across her. She shivered and pulled the sweater closer to her body.

The sky outside turned a mossy gray. Soon it would be dawn and most residents of Laurel Dam would rise and go about their daily routines as if the world hadn't gone crazy last night.

But it had.

Their lives, Bobby's, Em's and hers had changed forever.

Curled on the couch under a blanket, the kids snored softly.

She envied them.

If God had mercy, their slumber would erase the vision of the trucker's murder from their minds, but for her, there would be no reprieve from the nightmare. She wouldn't forget. And the last moment she and Gene had spent together would haunt her forever.

She stretched her neck and arched her lower back away from the hard chair, releasing a bit of her tension. She was tired. She wanted to go home and at least try to eradicate last night from her memory for a few hours. Her mind was quickly turning to mush and the surly agent in front of her wasn't helping.

"Now, Ms. Boyd, you stated the driver was alive when you arrived at the scene. Is that correct?"

Alexandra's *I'm-in-charge* tone, along with her superior attitude, poked at Stephanie's raw nerves. The redhead had thrown questions at her for twenty minutes. The same damn questions she'd answered before, to Agent Dolton. Didn't they compare notes?

Were the agents trying to trip her up?

Stephanie's spine stiffened against the plane of the chair and she eyed the poised woman facing her. Did they suspect she'd lied about Gene's involvement?

Why else would they ask her the same questions over and over?

She dropped her hands to her lap, planted her feet on the vinyl floor and deliberately stared at Alexandra. "That is what I said."

"Who shot the driver?" The agent crossed her legs. Her pinstripe pant leg pulled up, exposing the sparkle of a gold chain around her lean ankle.

Stephanie knew she had to be careful for the sake of Bobby and Em's future. "Sheriff Morse."

"Why do you think Sheriff Morse would shoot him?" The agent's head remained bent while she jotted notes, seemingly not at all surprised by her answer. If Agent Dolton had told her about Morse, why ask the question again?

"That was my question too, when it happened. But, it became apparent real fast that Morse was involved with the theft."

Both Alexandra Mosley's head and brow shot up. "Did anyone mention robbery?"

"No. Let me make it very clear. I had no clue what was going on."

"Then why do you think it was a robbery and not a kidnapping or hijacking?"

"Agent Dolton told me. He said the truck carried money."

"He did?"

Had Agent Dolton breached some kind of code telling her what had been in the trailer?

Alexandra's eyes narrowed, making her shift on her seat. Stephanie focused on the woman's pointed chin, keeping her eyes and expression unconcerned and waited for the next question.

"You said there were four other men. Can you describe the man in charge?"

She trapped her bottom lip between her teeth and nodded.

"He was tall, built. His hair was cut short and light-colored. An odd shade of blonde, I think."

Alexandra's chin dropped to her chest and she quickly jotted notes.

It seemed every word she said was important to the agent. "I couldn't really see the color of his eyes. If I had to take a guess, I'd say brown. They were dark."

"Anything else?" Alexandra peeked up from her notebook.

Stephanie tried to remember if the guy had a scar or a mole like the tiny one perched on the Alexandra's cheek bone right below her eye. Or even an impairment. But he didn't. She shook her head.

Alexandra sighed.

Remembering something new, Stephanie sat straighter in the chair. "He had an accent."

"Okay. What kind?"

"I don't know. European."

"Italian?"

"No. Baltic States."

"Good." The agent made a note on her pad. "You said his name was Victor?"

"Yes. Victor." His name caused a chill to run through her. "He was completely cool. When Morse shot the driver, he got angry but I could see him, Victor calculating the next move, which was to kill us." She shivered again, hearing his order echoing in her mind. "He was cold. You know what I mean?"

For the first time, a smile appeared on Alexandra's lips. "Yes. I know exactly what you mean."

The office door swung open.

"It's time," John Dolton stated, letting go of the door's handle.

Again Stephanie jumped, but this time for a different reason. Her heart skipped a beat at the sight of the handsome agent. Quickly, she rationalized her reaction to him. She felt safer with him close by.

"Where are we going?" She glanced between Agent Mosley and John.

"I'm taking you to a safe house." His gaze feathered over her legs.

She conceded he was checking her out because of the cuts. "A safe house. Why?"

Yet. Was that a flash of approval in John's eyes?

He cleared his throat and quickly crossed the room.

Agent Mosley shot up from her chair, stepping into John's path. At the sight of the cold metal tucked into the female agent's belt, Stephanie slid back on her chair, her pulse kicking up a notch. She hadn't noticed it before since Mosely had removed her jacket while sitting.

The woman was a federal agent, for God's sake, Stephanie thought. She stared with apprehension and interest as the agents squared off, inches apart. Their chests swelled with determination.

"Could I speak to you outside for a moment, Agent Dolton?" Mosely asked.

"There's no time."

"I'm not through asking Ms. Boyd questions."

Stephanie saw John's jaw clench.

"I told you ten minutes. You had more."

She felt like the grand prize and neither agent was about to give her up. She swallowed, waiting for the outcome.

"Come on, John. It took me ten minutes to walk in this room and wake her." Mosely emphasized her challenge by raising her chin.

"Not my problem."

"I'm going with you. I'll finish asking my questions en route. Are you taking them to Bushkyll or Thorpe?" Their debate didn't mask the animosity or the familiarity between them.

"Neither."

"Then where?"

Ignoring her question, John sidestepped the tall woman.

"We need to go, now." His heated glare cooled, while staring at Bobby and Em lying on the couch.

Mosley's blue eyes, like lasers, burned into the back of John's head for a moment before she whipped around and grabbed her jacket. She stuffed her notebook into a pocket and yanked on her coat. Then she stood between them and the door, waiting.

The tension was so thick in the room it would be obvious to a blind man. The two agents hated each other. Why?

Stephanie gripped the chairs edge. "Where are you taking us?"

"I can't tell you that," he said, looking down at her.

"Can't we go home?"

"I'm sorry. No. Can you wake the kids?"

She shot off the chair, causing him to take a step back. Stephanie glanced over her shoulder. She didn't want to wake Em and Bobby. Facing him, she forced her voice to stay level. "Not yet. For the past six hours I've been told what to do. First by Zohara. Now by you. Now, I'm being fought over by different agencies of the government. I need some answers before we go anywhere."

John folded his arms across his broad chest and his eyes locked with hers, "Okay. What do you want to know?"

"Why can't we go home, with police protection? The kids would feel much safer in their own home."

"Trust me, it won't be safe."

Something in his tone told her he knew what he was talking about. The same chill she felt whenever she thought about Victor's evil stare flashed through her. "How long do you think we'll need to stay at the safe house?"

"Until we break the case."

"That could be years."

The tight set of John's jaw told her two things. One, she was right. Two, he didn't like that she was.

Fear grabbed her by the throat. She swallowed a lump and asked, "Who do you think is involved, the mob?"

He glanced at Mosely, then the floor at his feet and back at her. "We're not sure. But we haven't ruled out known crime rings. You're my first break in the case, Ms. Boyd."

"You think they'll come after us, don't you?" Her pulse quickened, recalling the dark barrels of the guns aimed at her kids.

He nodded. "I would."

His frank reply made her back up. She wanted to grab the kids and run, but she fought off the urge. She turned and looked at Bobby and Em. Her first responsibility was to keep them from harm. She couldn't do it on her own.

John was right. Their home would be the first place Victor and his men would search.

How would she defend herself?

Her hands curled into fists.

How would she keep Bobby and Em safe? She didn't own a gun. She hated guns. They brought violence into a home. She'd seen the damage and pain they'd caused while doing her rotation in an emergency room.

She had no choice. For now, they had to go wherever he took them. She faced John. "Can I at least call my parents? They'll worry about us."

"No," Mosely interjected.

John's fiery glare shot toward the Treasury agent for a brief moment before returning to her and mellowing. "I'll have Zohara contact them. He'll let them know you're safe. They can't know where you are. No one can. It would only put them in danger too."

Her parents. Stephanie crossed to the window and stared at her murky reflection. She balled her fingers in her hair, pulling the tension from her temples and stretched. How had this happened? A few hours ago her biggest worry was paying the overdue electric bill. Now keeping the kids and herself alive was at the top of her list. Her mundane life had morphed into a world filled with desperation, pain and death.

She really had no choice. Stephanie turned and faced the man patiently waiting for her decision. "Okay, Agent Dolton. I'm going to trust you on this one. But, before we go to this safe house you need to know I'll need some special foods brought to us. Em is allergic to wheat, peanut and dairy products. I'll also need an Epipen."

Without hesitation, he walked to Zohara's desk and retrieved a pen and pad. "You make a list of what she can have before you wake her. I'll make sure it's there." He handed them to her.

"Okay."

"The lieutenant will drive us in his car. You'll have to stay low for a few blocks. Until we're sure we're not followed."

Stephanie's scribble stopped in mid-stroke. Her brief feeling of safety flew out the window and uneasiness dropped into its place. "Why not use a squad car? With cops around us."

"We want everything to appear as normal as possible. In case we're being watched."

"You think they know we're here?" Her pulse quickened. It was one thing for her to think they might be watched, but it was another for Agent Dolton to have the thought.

"I'm not taking any chances. I've posted guards just inside the doors, so it appears you're still in the building. Once we're away from here and we're sure we haven't been spotted, we'll switch cars."

She arched her brow dramatically. "You're great at your job, right?"

A smile tugged at his lips. "Don't worry. I'll be with you every minute."

"And me," Agent Mosely threw in.

John's smile disappeared.

"There's no room," he clipped over his shoulder.

"You mean there's no room for a screw up." Mosely's harsh words shot at his back and revealed a little of the pair's history.

John's jaw tightened and anger sparked in his dark eyes. He whirled around to face off with the redhead.

"What I mean is there is no room. Once they're safe, I'll send for you. Until then, your questions are going to have to wait," he said with noticeable strained control.

"My superiors are not—"

"I don't give a rat's ass what your superiors want. Or you. Stephanie and her children are witnesses to the biggest heist ring in decades. I am not going to jeopardize their lives. This is my case. If you have a problem with that, go talk to Stover. He spoke to your commander."

The tension in the room amplified while both agents glared at each other and refused to back down.

Stephanie felt like a pawn in a game. Her stomach rolled thinking about the next move.

~~~~

Chapter Seven

No picking this car out in traffic, John thought sarcastically. He wished he'd thought to ask Zohara what kind of car he drove before they'd agreed to the plan. It was too late now. He was trapped in the backseat without easy access to a door.

"Mello Yellow," sung by Donovan, boomed from the stereo system of Zohara's classic, canary yellow, black striped Pontiac GTO.

He stared at the swaying peace logo dangling from love beads on the rearview mirror upfront. He hadn't taken the lieutenant for an aging hippie. Free spirited, free love, love the world and everyone in it. He'd thought Zohara was a hard-core military man like himself. Boy, was he wrong. The way Zohara sang along with the song caused John to roll his eyes.

John's leg cramped and he tried to stretch his calf by arching his toes up, but he got little relief. He couldn't move a fraction of an inch and not bump into someone. Steph and the kids were squashed together with him in the backseat.

He was too big to scrunch down in the front passenger seat and fear kept the kids from letting Steph sit up front on the floor. It wasn't a good situation.

Lying on the tie-dye tapestry covering Zohara's back seat, Steph's warm breath on John's neck sent incredible charges straight to his groin. He couldn't help the reaction. The woman appealed to him like no one had in a long time.

He just hoped her ten-year-old son, lying on the floor in front of him, didn't notice his rise. The boy was at an age where he would.

John repositioned his hand, just in case, and fought to redirect his thoughts away from her. But keeping his eyes closed intensified the feeling of her lower body pinned against his. Thank God they wore bullet proof vests, otherwise he'd have suffered the full effect of her body pressed against his.

The last woman he'd laid was his wife, Julie.

He opened his eyes to get away from the memory of the flames engulfing their home and was damned by the frightened stare of Em Boyd who crouched on the floor behind Zohara. Her bangs hanging in her wide eyes, her freckled nose and missing tooth tore at his heart, reminding him of his Katie.

He brushed his thumb over the band on his little finger and squeezed his eyes shut again, blocking out the reminder of his shame. But Em's fresh little girl scent wrapped around his throat like a noose, choking him like the smoke which had suffocated the life from his little girl and wife.

He needed air.

Zohara had the air conditioner cranked but the backseat was hot. And getting hotter.

Beaneath him, John's arm prickled with a thousand invisible needles. But he couldn't sit up. Not yet.

"How far, Zohara?" He kept his attention glued to the back of the lieutenant's head.

"Another ten minutes," Zohara mumbled.

"Have you noticed anyone following us?"

"No."

Relief washed through John. "Good."

"Just Mosely."

"Mosely?" John fought the urge to shoot up and peek out the rear window.

"Yes. She told me she was going to follow us for awhile before turning off. You know. Acting as a decoy. And she did for about six blocks. When she turned, I didn't see anyone follow her." The lieutenant bopped his head like he was singing along to the radio.

"What the fu—" John checked his language in time.

"I haven't seen anything else unusual so I think we're in the clear."

Zohara shifted the car down and stopped at a red light.

John heard the thumping of Zohara's hands on the steering wheel keeping time with the music.

"I know what you were going to say," Bobby piped in, grabbing John's attention.

"Bobby, quiet," Steph scolded from behind him.

"He was going to say f—"

"Don't you dare, young man!" She jumped up, using John as leverage, enough to peek over his shoulder. "I mean it. You will do the dishes all next week."

The boy's expression hardened. "I heard you talking. We're not going home."

"No, we're not. Not today, but soon. And I'm sure wherever, Jo—ah, Agent Dolton is taking us, there will be dishes to do. Right, Agent Dolton?" She nudged his vest covered ribs with her free hand.

"Ah. Yeah, right," he stammered.

"Lots of them," she added.

The car lurched forward and John came nose to nose with Em as she cried, "I'm hungry."

He blinked not knowing how to respond. He had one breath mint in his pocket. It was hardly something to quiet the child.

"I know, hon. We'll get something to eat soon." Steph's words feathered his ear, sending hot ripples through him.

"I have a candy bar in my console if she is allowed to have it," Zohara offered, again acting as if he was really into his music.

"Thank you, but no. Em's lactose intolerant."

"Can I have it? I'm hungry too." Bobby started to rise.

John crowned the boy's head with his hand and held him down.

"No." Steph ordered. "We'll all eat together when we get to the safe house.

She gazed down at him. Her emerald eyes reflected concern. "You gave the list to—"

"Yeah." He turned his head, fighting off the attraction he felt with her lips so close to his. "The stuff will be there."

"When will that be?" Bobby asked, twisting John's watchband.

Pain pinched John as hair plucked from his arm. He snapped his arm away.

Bobby's playful sneer turned into a profile of a mug shot.

If the kid wanted to see pissed off, he'd show him. But, it would have to be later when he didn't have bigger adversaries with guns to worry about.

He reached for the smooth handle of his weapon which now hung off his belt at his gut.

"My foot's asleep, mommy." Em reached over him and turned her mother's face.

John jumped at Em's soft touch.

"Sorry," Steph said over his shoulder.

Her smile caused his heartbeat to shift into a higher gear.

"Wiggle it, honey. We'll be there soon. Right, Agent Dolton?" She answered Bobby in the same breath.

Verbally, Steph was joining Bobby and Em in their quest to get under his skin. Physically, she already had his full attention. He cleared his throat of the desire building in him and mumbled, "I hope so."

Em plopped her teddy bear on the edge of the seat. The bear's tail tickled his nose. "Why do they call it the safe house, Mommy?"

John couldn't help his heavy sigh. He pushed the bear forward. He'd been through many interrogations, but none as nerve racking as this.

He raised his head slightly, trying to catch a glimpse of their location. "Are we there yet, Zohara?"

"Two minutes."

John dropped his head against the seat with a thump.

Em stared at him, stuck out her tongue and crossed her eyes.

John darted his eyes to the swinging peace logo and willed himself to relax. Two minutes. He could survive a lousy two minutes. One hundred and twenty seconds. One Mississippi. Two Mississippi. Three…

The car slowed as the lieutenant shifted gears. The blinker clicked a steady rhythm. Zohara made a sharp turn. John grabbed the seat as he and Steph edged forward toward Bobby and Em.

The car rolled to a stop and Zohara cut the engine. "Okay, we're here."

Anxious to get out, Bobby ignored John's earlier instructions and shot off the floorboard.

Afraid for the boy, John grabbed Bobby's arm and forced him back down. He needed to check the area himself. "Stay there until I tell you to move."

Bobby slumped to the floor; his mug face returned, accompanied by a protruding bottom lip.

"Listen to Agent Dolton. He's helping us," Steph said behind him.

"Do you see anything unusual?" John asked Zohara.

He could see the officer checking all angles. "No. Everything seems normal."

Zohara opened the door and stepped out.

"Don't move," John commanded Bobby, hosting a mug face of his own. He eased up from the seat, carefully swinging his legs over Bobby's head.

John scanned the mall parking lot before looking down at Steph. Her cheeks were flushed. As much as she could, she moved her body in a lazy stretch. It didn't matter that her brown hair was a mess; she still stole his breath away.

John quickly stopped the path of his thoughts. He had to focus. "I need Em to move so I can get out."

"Come here, hon." She reached for Em and the little girl scampered up onto the seat next to her.

"Where are we?" Steph asked.

"South Mall."

Zohara pulled the seat forward and he promptly exited the car, leaving her and the kids in the backseat alone.

John's musky scent still clung to her. Confined for more than thirty minutes against his hard body had Stephanie's heart racing.

She stared out the open door. John bent over and stretched. She couldn't help but note the tight fit of his jeans. His hips were lean. His legs muscular. Not weight-lifter-brawny but more defined, like a runner.

"Do you like wearing this, mommy?" Em tapped her index finger against the bullet proof vest, interrupting her thoughts.

"Shhh." She shook her head while pressing her finger against her lips. She glanced at Bobby who remained crunched into the corner. His scowl told volumes about the thoughts running through his mind.

They'd been through hell in the past twelve hours and he was not taking it well.

She extended her hand toward him and Bobby quickly intertwined his fingers with hers. "It'll be only a few more minutes before we can get out of here," she whispered.

Looking out the door again, she saw John had disappeared from her view but the State Police lieutenant remained by the car. She listened as John's footsteps faded.

Stephanie waited for what seemed like hours, listening for his return, but all she heard were the normal, every day sounds of early morning life at the mall; delivery trucks beeped as they backed up and rush hour traffic increased as the minutes ticked off.

All of a sudden, the approach of a vehicle caught her attention. It didn't whiz by like the others. Its engine whined down. Cautiously, she pushed up on her elbow and glanced out the rear side window. She saw the blue roof of another car, but she didn't see John.

Sliding back into place, her throat dried as she noticed the officer had moved out of her sight also. Instinctively, she folded Em into her arms. Her mind and every sense and muscle went on alert while she waited.

She heard voices. A door lurched open and footsteps slapped the pavement, coming toward them.

John leaned into the car from the rear and she jumped.

"Okay. Let's go." His expression was all business and she knew they had no time to waste. John pulled the driver's seat forward.

Bobby shot from his nook and out of the car before she could caution him to stay close to John. Seeing her brother's reprieve from the backseat, Em immediately wiggled out of her embrace and, as always, followed him. Stephanie swung her feet to the floor and sat upright, and instantly felt the assault of a thousand pin needles as blood rushed back into her left arm. Stepping from the car, she wobbled.

John's warm hand grabbed her elbow and steadied her. "Are you okay?" His brow lined with concern.

"Yes. My legs are asleep. I'll be fine. Thanks." She smiled.

He released her elbow only after she took two steps.

Zohara remained on guard near the front fender of his prize baby. Bobby, standing with legs spread apart and between the two vehicles, tried to touch both cars at once by stretching his arms wide. Em did the same, while Mr. Blakeslee dangled from her right hand.

The fresh morning air filled Stephanie's lungs and the bright sun warmed her face as she raised her arms above her head and stretched the kinks out of her back. "Oh, God. It feels so good to be able to move."

John slammed the GTO's door behind her and she turned. He opened the sedan's rear door. "We need to keep moving."

After a summer of freedom, sitting still for so long was a real chore for Bobby and Em, but John knew what they needed to do. "Come on, kids. We've got to go."

"I don't want'a go with him." Bobby dropped his arms to his sides. His small hands curled into fists.

Stephanie mentally saw his feet anchor to the parking lot.

Following his lead, Em did the same, except she folded her arms across her chest big chief style, hugging her teddy bear in the embrace.

"Ms. Boyd." John prompted her to take action. Tension worked his jaw as he nodded toward the open car door.

"I'm not kidding. Get in the car, now." She stalked toward Bobby and Em, but before she could grab Bobby's hand, he wheeled past her. She spun on her heel in time to see him dart under John's extended arm, escaping his clasp. Bobby raced around the front of the car and into the parking lot.

"Bobby, get back here. I have no idea why he's acting like this," she apologized to John. She pushed past him and, with Em close on her heel, followed Bobby.

"We need to go," John called after her.

She turned. "I know." She threw him a visual plea for understanding before she turned again and raced after her son. "Bobby, we have no time to play games. This is serious. Get in the car."

Bobby skidded to a stop between two cars and wheeled on her. "No! I want my dad."

Stephanie studied the fury in Bobby's expression. How much did he overhear last night? If he didn't know about Gene's death, she couldn't tell him the truth now. That discussion had to wait until they were safe and she had time to answer all their questions. She needed to reassure them she would always be there for them and she couldn't do that standing in the middle of a mall parking lot while they were running for their lives. "I know, but right now we can't go to your dad."

"Why not? He's a cop. He'll help us."

Stephanie's heart cracked, listening to Bobby's request, knowing he probably wouldn't even get a chance to say a final goodbye to his father. "Your dad won't be happy with the way you're acting. You know that."

After several seconds, she saw his anger dispel. Bobby bowed his head. He kicked a stone a few feet in front of him and scampered to pick it up before crossing the remaining distance to her.

"It won't be much longer. I promise. Then we'll get something to eat and wash up. We'll feel much better after we do that." She brushed her hand through his soft hair and hugged him next to her hip, sighing heavily. Afterwards, when they were alone and safe, she would destroy their worlds by telling them their father was dead.

A blast hit the air and a micro second later the windshield of the car beside them splintered. Grabbing Bobby and Em, Stephanie dropped to the tarmac, the skin tearing from her knee.

"Stephanie, get down," John yelled came too late.

She was already flat faced on the blacktop. Her heart thundered, barely covering the voice inside her screaming, "Not again." She strained, stretching her arm, her fingers, grasping to protect her children.

"Son of a bitch," Zohara hollered while pounding footsteps followed more blasts.

Tires screamed to halt. Deep male voices exchanged words. "Shit, bastard, die mother fucker." Glass shattered above her and covered them with shards.

"Keep your eyes closed," she ordered Bobby and Em during a brief lull.

Rapid gunfire discharged and casings pinged against the tarmac.

Then a *pop pop* followed.

Stephanie trembled. It sounded like their assassins had come prepared, having more firepower than John and Zohara. They all were going to die.

As if reading her thoughts, Em started to bawl. And Bobby trembled with fear. She had to get them out of here even if it meant she died in the attempt.

Ignoring the pain, she hunched low on her scraped knees. Glass fell from her back to the pavement. Quickly she scanned the kids. Most of glass had landed on her. None had fallen on their heads or cut them.

John crouched behind the door of the blue car, firing his gun.

"Close your eyes Bobby and stay right here."

"No, mom. Don't go." Bobby clung to the hem of her sweater. He desperately pulled her to him. "Dad—"

Bobby's tears told her he knew his father was dead. A lump formed in her throat. She cupped his face in her hand and swiped the tears from his pale cheeks. "I'm not going anywhere, babe. Just taking a peek. Then we're getting out of here. It'll be okay, I promise. Okay."

She saw he wanted to say more but he bit back his protest. She placed his arm over Em and told them to stay down and to keep their eyes closed.

Her knees trembled as she edged forward, keeping her back plastered to the van. Slowly, she rose and peeked over the edge of the fender. She gasped. The van she'd seen last night blocked the lane behind Zohara's car, its doors fanned out like wings. Using the doors for protection, on either side stood, Mac and Dog.

She blinked. Mac and Dog were alive.

Zohara and John returned fire from behind the opened door of their getaway car.

How did they find them? The lieutenant had said he hadn't seen anyone following them. He couldn't have missed that van.

Where was Victor? She searched the area to the left and right and then spun around and scampered to the back of the minivan. Nothing. Not even a car to block the view of their escape in the mall's direction.

Moving toward Dog and Mac was out of the question. And toward the west was no good. The McDonalds restaurant, with only a few early morning patron cars parked in front, was more than a hundred yards away. If she was alone, she might chance it. But, with Bobby and Em, they'd be running targets. She was pretty sure either Dog or Mac could pick them off with one shot in broad daylight without blinking.

No. She had no choice.

She crawled forward to the front fender again and eased up. Their only chance was to belly crawl across the lot, using the cars as shields. They needed to get behind John and Zohara.

Mac yelled at Dog.

She heard the word "move" during a short lull followed by metal against metal. They were reloading.

She couldn't wait. It would be only a matter of minutes before either Mac or Dog would circle around them and they'd die.

Before she lost her nerve, Stephanie ducked down and motioned for Bobby and Em to follow her. Three abreast, elbow to elbow, they crawled from the protection of the minivan toward Zohara's car. Pain radiated from her knee every time she pushed off but she kept moving.

Stephanie's pulse raced as she peered under the car's chasse and between the wheelbase.

Good. The vehicle was angled just enough. They could make it to the passenger door. Then if—

No. There was no *if* about it. They would make it to the door. They would make it inside the car. She would get the kids the hell out of there.

She motioned to Bobby to follow her. Em shadowed her just shy of her knees and Bobby right behind Em. At the car's door, she crouched and yanked it open. Good. Zohara had left the keys in the ignition.

Reaching under the door, she helped Em and Bobby up and into the backseat. "Stay on the floor."

Bullets hammered the car next to them while she crawled inside. She caught John's eye while sliding over the console and for a brief moment their gazes locked.

John nodded toward the exit.

He was telling her to get the hell out of there. John and the lieutenant were picking their shots and their time was running out. It was now. There wasn't a later.

Even though her hammering heart made it hard to breath, Stephanie collected her courage and slammed the clutch pedal to the floor, turned the key and gunned the engine. The car lurched forward. She gripped the steering wheel so hard she feared it might crack under the pressure and concentrated on shifting gears instead of on the havoc around her. It had been ten or more years since she drove a stick shift and stalling the engine now would be a very bad thing.

Stephanie stomped on the accelerator. The tires squealed. She popped the clutch and the car fish-tailed. Whipping the vehicle right, she steered toward the parking lot exit.

Out of nowhere sparks flew as metal screeched along the passenger side of the car.

Em and Bobby screamed simultaneously, "Mom."

"Stay down," she ordered. Glancing in the rearview mirror she saw she'd clipped the front end of a delivery truck. A good portion of its front fender spun on the blacktop.

Zohara was going to be pissed.

If he lived.

Guilt ripped at her gut as they sped away from the nightmarish scene, leaving the men who were trying to help them to die.

~~~~

Chapter Eight

Standing in the middle of the bullet-scarred parking lot with his fingers still wrapped around his gun, John trembled with the realization that somehow, he had cheated death, again.

Sirens wailed in the distance, getting louder with each passing second. He hoped the paramedics arrived soon— not for the man who lay at his feet, they couldn't help him—for Zohara's sake.

The blue sedan, riddled with bullet holes, its windows shattered, tires flat, leaned like an old horse. Stuffing puffed out of the head rests. Shards of red taillight glass peppered the chewed up tarmac.

Zohara rested against the car's front fender. Dried blood caked his arm below the make-shift tourniquet he held with shaky fingers. He tilted his face toward the sun. Pain tightened the lieutenant's ever increasingly pale features while he waited for help to arrive.

John's trepidation escalated into anger. He wasn't a damn rookie. He'd known the attack would come. The fact he'd been hiding in the backseat, appreciating Stephanie's warm body lying next to his was nothing short of pathetic. "Son of a bitch."

"You or him?"

Startled John spun on his heel. Alex was no more than eight feet away from him. Another slip, John chastised himself. He hadn't heard her approach.

She reached behind her back and holstered her Colt 45.

By his side, she stared down at the silent body sprawled on the parking lot. "Nice shot, between the eyes, but don't you think it would've been better to have him alive? He could've told us who is behind all this."

"It was him or me. I had one shot left. When you showed up, his buddy turned coward. He jammed the van into reverse and knocked him down. He came up blasting." John stared at the semi-automatic laying next to the guy. No one had to tell him how lucky his final shot had been. A thick crimson stream drifted through a furrow in the assassin's forehead and into his long dark hair. "I wonder who he is."

Alex stepped to his other side and nodded over her shoulder. "We'll know soon enough. Ben's on his way. How's Zohara?"

John pulled his gaze from their attacker and inhaled deeply. "He got hit in the upper arm. He lost a lot of blood."

"And you?" Alex pointed to the blood-stained handkerchief tied around his left forearm.

"Just a cut."

Alex scanned the surrounding area. Her lips perched in thought for a moment. "Where's our Ms. Boyd and her kids hiding?"

"They're gone."

Alex rounded on him. Her eyes gleamed with fury. "What do you mean, *gone*?"

"She took off in Zohara's car."

"You didn't try to stop her?"

John's laugh was strained. "I was a bit busy."

Alex waved her arm in the air toward the mall's exit. "I can't fuckin' believe it. We finally get a damn break and she flies the proverbial coop. And she drove off in the middle of this, leaving both of you?"

"Steph did the right thing. She's an elementary school nurse for Christ's sake. There was nothing she could do. If she'd stayed, she and the kids could be looking like this guy." The thought made him turn away from the lifeless glare staring up at him.

"Are you sure you're okay?" Alex grabbed his right arm. Her warm fingers were pressed against his pulse.

Surprised by Alex's show of compassion, his eyes widened. She quickly released her grip.

"This is my fault. More than anyone, I knew what we were up against. I should've had more ammunition and another weapon. I should've had a whole damn squad surrounding us." John's tone exposed every bit of the anger burning inside him.

"You never would've gotten a whole squad. You know that. Maybe another car to escort you, but I doubt two more men would have helped much with the firepower these guys had. Look at the damage." She pointed to the dozen or so cars parked in the corner of the lot. Their windows were blown out, tires flat and bodies punched through by flying bullets. "You did the right thing. An escort would've been a red flag waving, 'Here I am.'"

John ran his hand through his hair. "How the hell did they find out where we were switching cars? They didn't follow us. Zohara would've sighted that van."

"You were followed by a black sedan."

The hairs on the back of his neck prickled. "How do you know that?"

"I followed you for a distance," she confessed. "Ben and I thought it would a good idea."

John's gut clenched. "Ben knew you were following us?"

"Yeah. I had my orders to not to let Ms. Boyd out of my sight."

"He didn't tell me."

"You were loading the Boyds into Zohara's car. Anyway the guy, he was behind me. I spotted him right away. After a few blocks I turned off, hoping he'd turned with me. But he didn't. I did a U-y and picked him up again. He turned off on Lexington Street. I trailed him thinking he was still tailing you. I didn't know where you were headed. You never told me. He drove west ten blocks and then circled."

"You didn't hear about this over the radio?"

"No. I drove right into it."

John's stomach twisted as he watched the traffic driving by. "He knew. He came to watch."

"How could he?"

John faced her. "Someone had to tell him. Any ideas?"

Mosely's spine stiffened. Her teal eyes widened with anger. "How should I know? If you think, I had—I didn't know where you were going."

She was right. Only four people knew; him, Zohara, Ben and the person who had parked their getaway car nearby. His gut told him Zohara was okay. He trusted Ben with his life. He didn't know who parked the car here. He'd get that info from Zohara.

"Why didn't you take him out?" he asked.

"Because I wasn't positive he was our man until I got here and I had to make a decision, take him or help you. The decision was easy. I needed to help you." She stuffed her hands into her jacket's pockets and held his stare.

The vulnerable way she looked at him brought back a flood of memories. Three months ago, she'd wanted to help and, in the end, had killed his partner.

He blamed her.

He knew Luke's death wasn't deliberate, but regardless, he never gave her a chance to explain. He never listened to her apologies. The bitterness which ate at him stopped now. "Thank you, Alex. You saved our lives."

"You're welcome." A smile played on her lips for a moment before her serious façade returned. "Now, how do we find Ms. Boyd?"

~~~~

Chapter Nine

"Stay down, kids." Stephanie literally shook from the inside out. She weaved dangerously in and out of the morning rush hour traffic. Her blood raced through her veins as fast as she drove the car. She had to get as far away from the killers as possible.

No one would try to stop her. Every cop in the county had probably responded to the call for help at South Mall.

But what if they were followed? There would be no one to help her.

She glanced at the rearview mirror, relieved the kids were still on the floor, and checked the highway behind them. Em's muffled cry edged her nerves. "We're okay, baby. The bad men are far away."

She whizzed past another car. Her nerves zinged as she glanced at the driver, waiting for a gun to appear and blow her away. None did. The driver was just a guy in a suit, drinking his coffee, reading his paper stretched across the steering wheel, probably on his way to work.

Stephanie inhaled deeply. She had to get a grip on herself or she'd make a mistake which could cost them their lives.

She eased up on the accelerator, hoping the effort would make the kids feel safer. "Bobby, help Em up on the seat. Hold her. But stay low." She glimpsed in the mirror again, and watched them slide up and onto the rear seat. They looked so small against the black leather, and terrified.

Her stomach twisted into a knot. All they had was each other. John had said she couldn't contact any family or close friends. She might put them in danger too.

Stephanie pulled her gaze away from Bobby's and Em's image and focused on the vehicles in front of her. She slowed her speed even more, blending in with the traffic.

Warm blood seeped from the cut on her knee. "Bobby, hand me my purse off the floor."

He plopped the leather bag onto the console. She grabbed it and dug inside. Finding a tissue, she tossed the purse on the passenger seat, wiped the blood from her leg and compressed the tissue against the cut, wincing.

She prayed John and Zohara were alive. If they weren't, their deaths were on her head. If only she'd listened to Gene and got the hell away from the accident scene when he had told her, she wouldn't be in this mess.

Her fingers worked the steering wheel. What if someone in the state police barracks was also in on the heists? What would she do without John to help her? Where would she go?

She glanced at the gas gauge. The dial on Zohara's classic car virtually dropped toward empty as the blocks sped by. She wouldn't make it far driving the gas guzzler. She had to ditch the car anyway. Heads turned as she cruised by in the neon yellow car.

She'd have to find another way to get out of town. But how? She had twenty dollars in her purse. Her credit card and ATM card were at home. She didn't dare go there.

Stephanie bit her lip while thinking about her options. Anything. Something. She needed time to sit still in one place and come up with a plan. Through the windshield, she stared ahead on the building to her right and spied a billboard sign advertising the Organic Warehouse. It was only four blocks away and opened at eight.

Yes. No one would look for her there. She could get Em and Bobby something to eat. They gave out free samples. Even bathroom-sized paper cups of herbal tea. She could sit and gather her thoughts.

Checking the rear mirrors one more time, she veered off the highway and into the parking lot of a medical association. She drove to the back of the building and parked with the scraped side out of view, taking up two spots, just like an owner of a classic car would do.

"Come on, guys." Stephanie yanked the keys from the ignition and tossed them under the seat. She opened the door, stepped out and hesitated, checking over her shoulders before shrugging out of the heavy bullet-proof vest. Stephanie immediately felt freer with the weight off of her. She tossed the vest onto the front floor of the car where it landed with definite thud.

Em crawled out first.

Stephanie's heart nearly broke looking at her little girl's tear streaked face. Em's arms were scratched and her jeans torn.

"Bobby, grab my purse." Stephanie took her bag from Bobby, turned and knelt on the tarmac in front of Em.

Bobby jumped from the car. He looked like he was dragged through a war zone. His hair stood up in spots, his clothes were dirty and his elbow caked with blood.

Her children couldn't walk down the street looking like they did. People would stop and stare, wondering if she abused them.

To be safe, they had to blend in. They couldn't turn any heads.

"Where are we going, mom?" Bobby asked.

"We're going to go shopping and get something to eat." She dug in her purse for the wet wipes she always carried. She couldn't do anything about the dirty torn cloths but she could clean Bobby and Em up.

The children's happy chatter for what they wanted to eat filled Stephanie with hope. With any luck, in a few days, their lives would return to normal.

Almost normal.

Gene would no longer be a presence in their lives.

She quickly pushed the memories of last night from her mind. She had to focus on now and the danger they faced.

"Let's clean up a bit, first." She forced a smile to her lips, handed a wet wipe to Bobby and quickly wiped Em's face free of tears.

Stephanie pulled a brush quickly through Em's hair and fixed her pony tail. She wanted to hold Em tight until all her fears were gone, but she couldn't. They had to get moving.

"You look great." She twirled Em on her sneakered heel.

Her daughter giggled and her eyes danced.

God, Stephanie hoped she could think of something to get them out of this mess. Standing, she grabbed Bobby's and Em's hands and headed in the direction of the Organic Warehouse. "Let's go eat."

By nine o'clock they'd strolled around the Organic Warehouse, had gathered free samples of dried fruits, pumpkin and banana toast, and rice cakes. They found a table in the café area and took a seat.

Stephanie counted the money she had left after spending eight dollars on a small container of powdered rice milk for Em and a dollar on a bottle of juice for Bobby.

With the loose change she found in the bottom of her purse, she now had exactly eleven dollars and forty-nine cents.

Her mouth watered smelling the fresh baked breads, and her stomach rumbled, the dinner of hotdogs she'd had the night before long gone. Stephanie sank back on the plastic chair and watched as her kids nibbled on the food and sipped their drinks.

"Aren't you hungry, mommy?" Em bit off a piece of fig with her eye tooth.

"No. I had two hot dogs last night. You only had one and no roll, remember." She tapped Em's nose. Em's giggle warmed her heart.

Nodding, Em hungrily bit off another chuck of fig.

What was she going to do? They needed everything. Stephanie glanced at the television tucked into the corner over the counter. Its volume was turned too low to hear, but according to the screen and the forecast, the weather was to turn much cooler. She and the kids were dressed for warm weather. She had to get them warmer clothing.

And Em could only eat certain foods. One bite of wheat or any form of peanuts and she'd have an allergic reaction. She only had one EpiPen in her purse.

Stephanie sipped her herbal tea. They couldn't stay here, living off free samples. Where could they go? The police would be the most obvious answer to anyone. But how many of Sheriff Morse's men were in on the heist? Was there only Gene or were there more?

There could be someone waiting for her to call for help, and Victor would order Mac and Dog to pounce on them, again.

She could try to make it to the state police barracks, but what if the building was watched? And who had told Mac and Dog where they were going?

Her gaze rose to the TV screen. The camera scanned the parking lot of the South Side Mall. Stephanie immediately shot forward on her seat. Windows were blown out of cars. Debris littered the parking lot. The driver stood next to his delivery truck, the one she'd hit, pointing at the truck's mangled fender.

The area looked like a war zone.

"What's wrong, mom?" Bobby looked at her warily.

Stephanie stood and stretched. She didn't want Bobby to see what they had run away from. "Nothing. I just have a kink in my back."

She waited until his interest turned back to his pile of raisins before she sat down and, from the corner of her eye, watched the TV again.

The camera shifted. Her eyes narrowed, seeing the minivan she and the kids had stood beside when the first shot blasted the air. Where was the van Mac and Dog drove?

The picture panned out.

It was gone! The van was gone. Mac and Dog were alive.

Her pulse kicked up a hundred times over. She laced her trembling fingers together and trapped them between her thighs. She had to remain calm. She had to know the facts. Her stomach rolled watching the report. Their planned getaway car had been inundated with bullets. An ambulance sat off to the side. A covered form lay on the blacktop.

A lump formed in her throat. Was it John? Zohara?

She saw Agent Mosely walk by.

Hope burst through Stephanie. Follow the redhead she willed the cameraman. Her fingers clenched tighter, turning her knuckles a ghastly white. She edged front on her seat again. God, she prayed John and Zohara had survived.

Her optimism faded as the cameraman panned in on the blue sedan, its shattered windows, bullet besieged door, flat tire and the pool of blood next to it. The scene cut off and went back to the newsroom.

Damn. Stephanie nearly jumped off her seat wanting to know more. Whose blood? It had to be either Zohara's or John's. The way the car was shot up it would be short of a miracle for them to be alive.

Beside her, Bobby and Em continued to play a game. They now built towers with Bobby's bread cubes.

Closing her eyes, she raked her fingers through her hair and stretched instead of screaming angrily at the top of her lungs. They had to disappear. But she needed money to do that.

Her mind raced. She watched the counter person give a customer change and, for the first time in her life, wondered how to steal from someone. The man behind the counter picked up the remote and suddenly she heard John's voice.

He was alive. Stephanie watched John walk alongside a gurney. Zohara lay on it. Alive.

"Thank you, God," she whispered.

She studied the lines of John's face. He looked tired, but he was alive. A mixture of relief and joy washed through Stephanie. Somehow she had to get in contact with him. But how?

Watching John smile down at Zohara, she decided to buy a cup of coffee to celebrate the one bright spot so far this morning. She reached in her shorts' pocket and pulled out the change she'd received earlier from the cashier. A folded piece of cardboard lay among the coins.

Her eyes widened. She'd forgotten all about John's card. She flipped it over. On the back he'd written his cell number.

~~~~

Chapter Ten

John swore under his breath as the EMT swabbed his cuts with alcohol. The man in him wouldn't show the young blonde his weakness by wincing. Instead he focused ahead, staring at the exit to the mall and relived the last moment he'd seen his witnesses. He had to find them before they were found—

By who?

The question stung him more than the antiseptic seeping into his wounds.

"Where do you think Stephanie and the kids went?" Alex asked straightforward after rounding the rear of the ambulance.

His gaze shifted to the EMT. Alex knew better. He wouldn't discuss anything in front of the young woman. He shook his head.

Understanding his gesture, Alex offered him a McDonald's Styrofoam cup. "Here. It's strong and black. Just the way you like it. Right?"

Steam and a rich aroma spiraled from the container. He accepted the cup with his free hand. "Thanks." Caffeine surged into his system the moment the hot liquid hit his tongue, making him feel almost as alive as he had during the attack.

"I really think you should have stitches, sir." The young blonde smiled up at him as she padded the butterfly bandages she'd placed on his left forearm.

John pushed from the tailgate. He had no time for hospitals. "This is fine. Thank you."

"So you have no idea where Stephanie went?" Alex questioned him again, when they'd walked several yards away from the ambulance.

He hoped Stephanie heeded his warning and didn't go home or to her parents. John downed the rest of his coffee and tossed the cup onto the backseat of what was left of their getaway car. "No. None."

"Well, she shouldn't be too hard to find in Zohara's bumble bee car. I'll put an BOLO out on the car right away."

"Stephanie's smart. She probably ditched the car already."

Alex's brow arched. "You think so?"

"I know so."

Alex stared at him as if trying to read his thoughts.

He turned his back to her.

Stephanie was a spitfire. Hell had unfolded around her and she had kept her head. She'd picked up on his signal and had the guts to do the right thing. Run.

With the amount of firepower that had exploded around them, most rookies would've frozen—maybe even ended up on a gurney like the guy the ETMs were finally loading into the silent ambulance.

"If found, it'll at least give us the direction she headed." Alex pulled his thoughts away from Stephanie. "Towing two kids, she can't be too far from it."

Alex was right. He had a feeling the city was already being scoured.

A tow truck, contracted by the police, backed up to the car and dropped its deck plate. Its driver jumped from the cab and started releasing the winch.

"Put the APB out right away, starting with her house," John said.

"I thought you said she was smart."

"She is. But she's a parent and the kids wanted to go home. She might try to get in and get some personal items, clothes, toys, money, whatever and get out before being found."

"True." Alex nodded. "I'll notify Zohara's men right away."

John's cell phone vibrated against his hip. He snapped it from his belt and glanced at the strange number before flipping it open. "Dolton, here."

"John."

He stopped in step while his adrenaline kicked up.

"Yeah." He noted Alex's immediate interest. He nodded once, letting Alex know Stephanie was on the line. "How did you know? Oh. No. I'm okay. He'll be fine."

Stephanie's voice was filled with anxiety.

He searched the area around him as he pushed the button on the phone's side, lowering the volume. He pressed the cell closer to his ear and walked away from Alex. "Are you and the kids okay?"

"Good." John glanced over his shoulder. Alex waited close by. Her arms folded across her chest as if she stood guard for him. "Where are you? Good. I knew you would."

After devising a plan to meet Stephanie, John snapped his phone shut and clipped it to his belt. The hair on the back of his neck prickled. He scanned the crowd across the street held back by wooden barriers and yellow tape. Every eye watched the clean-up taking place behind him.

He turned, knowing one particular set of eyes watched his every move. He had to be careful.

"Was that her?" Alex asked as he'd crossed the parking lot.

"Yup," he clipped, careful not to give away his eagerness to meet Stephanie. He passed Alex and walked toward the tow vehicle. She followed close behind him.

The noise of the car scraping onto the roll-back would cover their conversation, if anyone was honing in on them. Turning, he stepped around Alex, shielding her from the crowd's line of sight. John dragged his hand across his face. "We're being watched."

Alex's expression lit up and a smile hinted on her lips. "Really? Where do you think he is?"

Alex loved the game. A good agent did.

"He has to be across the street. My gut tells me he's close by." He stuffed his hands into his pockets and rocked back on his heels, smiling like he didn't have a care in the world.

She openly smiled at him. "Okay. How do you want to play this?"

"I need to get out of here without him seeing me."

"Are you meeting Stephanie?" She pointed toward a CSI member as if she were talking about the crime scene. With a sidestep, she aimed her finger toward the crowd across the street as if trailing the assassin's path. John saw her quickly scan the crowd, taking note of anyone suspicious.

"Yeah. In thirty minutes. Did you pick anyone out?"

"No. Where are they?"

"Now, Alex, you know me better."

She exhaled loudly and pinned him with her glare. "Look, John, Stephanie is as much my witness as yours. You can't save her without help. You need someone to watch your back. You know that."

"That would be Ben."

Disgust gleamed in her eyes. "Ben's not here, yet. He didn't cover your ass or rescue you today."

John hated to admit she was right, but she was.

He wondered what was holding Ben up.

He checked the area, feeling the seconds tick away. He had to move now. Stephanie would wait at the pickup location no more than three minutes. If he wasn't there, she was to wait thirty minutes and call him again. Every minute she and the kids were on the street unprotected, their chances of being spotted by a snitch increased.

"Well?" Alex urged him to make a decision.

A uniformed cop blew a whistle behind him. He turned and the cop looked at him with a brazen stare.

Again, John's skin crawled. Did Sheriff Morse have other men involved?

At this point, he couldn't be sure. This was a small town, maybe twenty-seven thousand residents. The local mayor and a few chamber members would be the internal affairs department. He'd get little help in uncovering a mole.

Alex was right. If it were just Stephanie, he could disappear with her, but towing two kids, especially one with food allergies, made the act near impossible. He needed to get to them fast and take them to the safe house.

John conceded, "Okay."

A smile pulled at Alex's lips. She nodded in the direction of her government issued vehicle. "My car is over there."

John fought off the urge to look at his watch while he worked out his options. "No. He knows your car. Can you create some kind of diversion?"

"I thought—"

"We can't leave together. Meet me at the corner of Hamilton and Fifth in an hour. We'll be waiting."

She nodded and spun on her heel.

He grabbed her arm and she stared over her shoulder at him. "Make sure your car is clean, Alex. No GPS. No cell phone. Understand?"

"You got it." Immediately she turned, and with cause, yelled at the local cop picking up the mirror that had been blown off the van, "Hey, you."

Alex took off toward him, reaming the officer for touching a crime scene. All eyes turned toward the young officer and, while his face turned a bright shade of red, John disappeared.

~~~~

Chapter Eleven

The loud static scratched his nerves. Victor punched the off button on his cell phone. The bean counter actually had the nerve to hang up on him. He would make Randall pay.

Slamming his Porsche into fourth gear, Victor passed a tractor-trailer on its right side, the blind side. A second later, he yanked the steering wheel and swerved his car into the left lane within inches of the rig's front bumper causing the truck driver to veer to the next lane. The truck's air horn blast mingled with the eerie sound of sheering metal as the eighteen wheeler collided with several cars.

Victor glanced via his rearview mirror at the havoc which unfolded behind him. No flames. No explosions— just a multi-fender bender. Traffic would be tied up for hours.

The cell phone buzzed in its holder. The signal meant Papa needed him. Victor hit the speaker button. "I am here."

"Are we set for tonight?" Papa asked.

Victor's jaw locked. He knew the penalty for lying to Papa would be harsh if he were found out, but what choice did he have? It didn't matter that Morse had caused the screw up. As far as Papa was concerned, he was the one to screw up.

He was not going to tell Papa about the bean counter. He would handle the Treasury agent. "Ya. I will have Tankson's load to him before morning."

"Good. We've had enough bad news today. I think after tonight you will leave for Mountain Pine. Go undercover for a while."

"Why?"

"I want you away from here, just in case."

His papa sounded uneasy. Victor shifted on his seat, tugging his belt buckle from pinching his gut. "What is wrong?"

"We were unable to get to Mrs. Boyd."

Victor grinned. His cousin had intercepted Mrs. Boyd and her children and had failed to eliminate them. Papa was not happy.

"I fear for you."

Papa's show of concern for Victor made him happy. He squeezed between two cars for the hell of it. Horns blared.

"What was that?" Papa's voice shouted over the car's speaker.

"Traffic," Victor answered flat-toned, knowing his Papa would not approve of his lack of concern for the lives of the innocent. "Do not worry about me, Papa. Randall will not give me up. He would die first."

"I'm not so sure."

"I am." Victor knew he had to make it very clear to Randall his family's lives were at stake. "Do we know where Mrs. Boyd is now?"

"Nah. There was trouble. She ran like a scared rabbit. Dug herself a hole. I wait to hear something from Pasha."

"She will surface soon enough." Victor hoped when Stephanie Boyd did make the mistake, he'd be available to help with her capture. The woman was pretty, like the bean counter's daughter, but more of a woman. And she had fire in her eyes. It would be a shame to kill her.

Maybe Papa would allow him to sell her and her children, after he had her a few times himself of course. The clean-cut All-American family would bring a nice price on the black market. He would make that suggestion at the correct time though, if opportunity allowed.

"Where is the take-down tonight?" Papa broke into his thoughts.

Victor glanced at the digital clock on his dash. He should have the bean counter's daughter within the hour. It wouldn't take long for Randall to get the message. "I'm expecting Randall's call with the truck's dispatch information within the next two hours."

"Good. I'll have Shermin tell Denis and Rurik to wait for your call."

His cousin's men watching his back. That was not good. "My men are Mac and Dog."

"I've pulled Mac for awhile. And I'm sorry to tell you this way, but I have no choice. Dog is dead. He was killed while trying to get to Mrs. Boyd."

Victor let off the gas, steered to the slower lane and exited the interstate. Mac and Dog had gone with Pasha because they knew what Mrs. Boyd looked like. It was to be an easy drive-by. What had gone wrong?

He pulled up to the stop sign and sat ignoring the world surrounding him. Dog had been a loyal man to him and deserved a moment of remembrance. "He will be missed by his wife and children. Send them my condolences along with a hundred thousand dollars."

"I'm sure his widow will be most appreciative of your generosity."

"She will take the money for the sake of his children, but his Anna will want revenge."

"Yah. And she will have it," Papa assured him, and Victor knew the order had already been given to end the life of the man who had caused grief to Anna and her family.

"Maybe we should send Mrs. Boyd a message? Her parents live in town," Victor suggested.

"Not just yet, my son. We do not want the authorities to look in our direction. Everything about this operation must not have our signature. It is too sweet a deal. Your cousin has the ear of the man in charge. We will know where Mrs. Boyd has run to soon enough."

Victor had no choice but to wait.

He dangled his hand over the top of the steering wheel and cruised on toward the local high school. Rachael Randall's cheerleading practice should be over soon.

~~~~

Chapter Twelve

Alantown was big enough to get lost in.

If one tried.

Yet the city was small enough to be sighted in, if one wasn't alert every second. How careful could Steph be with two kids?

Driving down Main Street, John noted the newly planted Maple saplings and the emulated cobblestone sidewalks—apparently part of the city council's restoration of the downtown business district. If he wasn't working a case, he might enjoy being here. Right now he didn't.

John whisked his hand through his hair and winced with pain in his shoulder. He had banged it good when he'd dropped to the tarmac and rolled before taking his last shot at the assailant.

Had Alex told him the truth? Had Ben told her to follow him? He thought he was doing the right thing, sneaking Steph and the kids out of the station undercover.

Was it possible Alex had something to with the attack? Had she lead the assailants to them? If she did, why save him and Zohara? Why not finish them off?

Why would Ben step on his toes?

Noting the street sign ahead, John veered into an open parking spot in front Koch's appliance store, cut the sedan's engine and checked the rearview mirror for any vehicles darting into parking spots behind him. He didn't want to get too close to where he was to meet Stephanie in case he was followed.

John jumped from the car he'd commandeered at the mall parking lot and scanned the area. He turned on his cell again and punched in Ben's number as he headed downtown. The digital sign on the bank across the street didn't give him much time. He had to move fast.

"Where the hell are you, John?" Ben said without a greeting. "I get here and you're gone."

"Didn't Alex tell you?"

"Alex? No. She's not here either. I thought she was with you. Where are the Boyds?"

"Gone."

"What the hell is going on?"

"You tell me. Alex said you told her to follow us." John didn't hide the anger boiling inside of him. If he and Ben were going to work together, they had to be on the same page. Luke had read his mind and he knew Luke's next thought before he had it. That was the way partners worked.

"I had no choice. Her superior made it very clear to your boss she was to stick with you. The call came last minute. Zohara was pulling out of the parking lot already when I hung up. There wasn't time to argue with you."

"Well, that decision almost got all of us killed."

"We don't know that," Ben said coldly.

Feeling as frustrated as Ben sounded, John admitted, "You're right. We don't."

He jumped from the curb and crossed the street between cars. The driver of the pickup coming toward him slammed on his brakes and laid on his horn. John ignored the guy's less-than-couth salutation and mingled in with the shoppers. Picking up his pace, he strode faster than the UPS guy. He pressed the phone against his cheek and lowered his voice. "Did you find anything out about the guy who dropped the car?"

"Not much," Ben said. "The officer is cleaner than a nun's cell. He didn't even know what was up. No one clued him in on anything as far as I can tell. He thought he was doing a buddy a favor by dropping off his girlfriend's car at the Donut Hut. He lives only two blocks from the mall."

A chill ran up John's spine. "The only one who knew where we were headed was Zohara, you and me."

"I know I sure as hell didn't say a word. And I don't think Zohara did. I have my doubts about you, however."

John knew Ben's chuckle was meant to break the tension.

Ben cleared his throat. "The only other explanation is someone overheard Zohara tell the rookie where to park the car."

"It's a possibility, but I don't think Zohara would be that careless. There is one other option."

"What's that?"

"Alex. Someone followed her. It wouldn't be the first mistake she's made."

John heard Ben's sigh.

"I wish you'd get off her case, John."

"I'm not saying she had anything to do with the attack. I'm just supposing maybe someone followed her. She's messed up before."

"Yes, and she learned from that experience. She's a sharp cookie. Her superior has nothing but praise for her. Take my advice, John let the past go.

That was easy for Ben to say. He hadn't lost his best friend because of the woman.

"Now where are you?" Ben broke into his thoughts. "Are the Boyds with you?"

"No."

"Where are they?" Ben sounded surprised. Alex hadn't told him anything. Why didn't Alex stick around to tell Ben the plan? Maybe she was scared too. There was a leak somewhere. As part of the team, she was a target too.

"I don't know," John said.

"You're not going to tell me, are you?"

"I'll have them at the safe house this afternoon. We'll talk later." John cut the power to his phone and backtracked through an alley toward Hamilton Avenue.

~~~~

Chapter Thirteen

Each step forward was a battle—one Stephanie had to win. She hated the trepidation in Em's eyes when she'd left her and Bobby with Susan Merkel, the local librarian.

Pride swelled in Stephanie as she thought of Bobby's reaction to his sister's anxiety. He had gripped his little sister's hand, acting like the man of the family, and led her back into the children's section of the library.

They knew Susan well enough. A double dose of story hour at ten would take them away from life for a couple of hours and they'd be safe.

Stephanie repeated the thought over and over with each step she took toward Baker Street and Fourth. She straightened the strap of her tank top. The borrowed sweater tied around her waist flapped against the back of her thighs as she hurried. She had five minutes to travel six blocks.

John wouldn't be happy she'd left the kids somewhere, but she wasn't taking any chances. Until she knew John could pick them up with a whole squad of armed cops, no one would know where they were. She couldn't put Bobby and Em through anguish a third time.

Suddenly, a hand slapped across her mouth and a strong arm circled her waist, lifting her off her feet. Her nostrils flared against the ridge of skin as she fought to suck in air and the scent of the man dragging her away.

A car whizzed by but didn't stop. The street ahead was deserted except for two elderly women waiting for a bus and a couple standing on the corner. They had their backs to her. They didn't see her.

She searched wildly for anyone who would come to her rescue. There was no one.

The street disappeared and red brick imprisoned her and her attacker on both sides as the man carried her deeper into the deserted alley. Foul smelling dumpsters, broken crates and cardboard boxes limp from the downpour on Saturday night filled the alley.

While her toes fought to touch the ground, her fingernails dug into tan skin. She struggled helplessly to free herself.

"Owww. Will you stop clawing me?" The deep tone heated her ear.

"John," she mumbled against his hand. She twisted and strained to look back. Relief washed through her.

"Quiet." He deposited her into a deep doorway.

Her purse slipped from her shoulder and dropped to the ground as she spun on her heel. Without thought, she flung her arms around his neck. His hard chest crushed her breasts. "I was so scared. I didn't want to leave you and Zohara. I'm so glad you're alive."

"Me too," he whispered into her ear.

She pulled back. His smile was faint, but it was there. Her hands trailed down his arms and found the bandage. "Your arm."

"It's nothing. A cut."

"I shouldn't have left you and—"

"You did the right thing, Steph. Where are the kids?"

"They're safe."

He looked at her warily, probably wondering where she could hide them and feel safe about doing so.

She squared her shoulders. "No one saw us. I wasn't going to bring them until I knew it was safe. Whoever is looking for us could spot us faster if we were together, so I left them at the library with Susan. No one will look for them there. And if something happens to me…" Stephanie swallowed hard, fear rippling through her. "Well, Susan knows my mother. She'd call her."

At the sound of a door opening, John glanced around the doorway's edge. He pushed her into the corner, shielding her with his body.

With her nose pressed against his chest, she drew in a mixture of his musk scent and blood.

The sound of someone throwing trash into the dumpster mingled with the throb of her heart. Protected by John, she closed her eyes and waited.

"Damn," he said.

Stephanie's head snapped up. "What do you mean, damn?"

"Shh." John's hands found her hips and pulled her even closer—hip to hip. The butt of his gun poked her ribs. No protective vests shielded her from the feel of him.

His burning gaze told her of his plan only a moment before his lips, full and hot, crushed hers.

His hands trailed down her backside, lifting her against his hard body. She ran her hands up his strong arms. The world reeled away, leaving her and John alone, enjoying the warm comfort of each other as their bodies molded together.

"Hey! Hey, buddy. What are you doing there?" A man called from a short distance.

John pulled back. Instantly the air between them cooled and Stephanie shivered, wanting more of him.

"Calm down, Mac. The lady and I are on a coffee break. Right, babe?"

Dazed, her gaze locked with his. She knew what he wanted from her.

"Miss?" The stocky man wearing a bloody butcher's apron glanced at her purse before his hard glare landed on John. The man's burly arms hosted clamped fists and his stance changed. He was ready to pounce on John at her word.

"Leave us alone. We've only got ten minutes." Stephanie slowly laced her arms around John's neck and flashed a wicked smile at the man. She went up on her toes and buried her face in John's neck and nibbled away, enjoying the salty taste of him.

She felt John's reaction to her assault when he pinned her against the doorway. She wrapped her bare leg around his jean-clad leg and willed him closer. His erection pressed against her mound. Her skin tingled hot as his fingers skimmed up her leg and inched under her shorts.

Stephanie's thoughts spiraled into another world—one of passion. She forgot about the butcher until he said, "Geez. Why don't you save it for later and get a room."

His footsteps pound the tarmac, and moment later a door moaned and then banged closed.

John stepped back and gazed down at her with hooded, dark eyes. His lips were swollen and moist from her kiss.

Had he enjoyed the kiss as much as she had?

"I hope that was all right." Her husky voice gave away her desire. Her face heated under his stare. She noted his fiery red neck and quickly looked to the ground.

He tipped her chin up, forcing her to look at him. "You were great."

His gaze fell to her mouth and instinctively she moistened her lips.

John's breath caught.

Taking pleasure in his reaction, Stephanie smiled.

As if something inside him clinked, John stepped out of the doorway, scooped her purse from the ground and handed it to her. "We better get going. Alex is probably waiting for us."

"Agent Mosley?" She looked at him quizzically while slinging her purse over her shoulder. John had wanted nothing to do with the Treasury agent before. Why was he accepting Mosley's help now?

"Yeah." He headed toward the back of the alley.

"And who else?" She jogged after him.

"No one."

She grabbed his arm and dug her heels into the soft gravel. "Look. My gut tells me you know what you're doing but I really think we should get a lot more cops involved here. I mean, we've tried getting away undercover and what happened? Bobby and Em were almost killed. And me. And you and Zohara." She shook her head. "No. I think we need a lot more good guys with guns. I'm not putting my kids in danger again." She stuck her finger in his face. "I won't. I can't." She began to tremble. Quickly, she folded her arms across her chest and refused to budge another inch.

John's jaw tightened as he held back his rebuttal. He wanted to grab her and make her run but that wouldn't work. He saw her determination, but he also saw her slight tremor. He understood her concern. He knew the anxiety of being a parent and wanting to protect your child. He also knew the heartbreak of not being able to save his child.

John pushed the memory of his Katie away before it interfered with the job at hand.

Steph had to trust him. He couldn't keep her safe unless she did. "Steph, I know you think an army of cops is the way to go, but believe me, it's not. The only way to keep you and the kids safe is to disappear. If Victor doesn't know where you are, he can't hurt you. But if he does, he'll come at you with everything he's got. You've seen that."

He saw her willpower wane. Before she could change her mind, he grabbed her hand and quickly led her the few blocks to the rendezvous point he'd established with Alex.

Ten minutes later, as they jumped into the backseat of the agent's sedan, Alex asked, "Where are the kids?"

"Drive." John slammed the car door and pulled his weapon from his belt. "Did you do what I told you?"

Alex nodded. "Yeah, we're clean."

Stephanie's gaze latched onto John's gun for a moment before moving to his face. He reassured her with his eyes.

The car lurched forward and Alex steered it around a corner.

Steph slid back into the corner of the seat while he twisted around and positioned himself to peer out the back window, checking for any cars following them. This time he would make sure himself.

"Where are the kids?" Alex demanded.

"Safe for now." John winked at Steph. He had to admit she probably had been smart to leave them behind. They had moved faster. "We're going to drive around a while, make sure no one is following us before we pick them up."

"How long is a while?" Steph asked anxiously.

"An hour."

Alex glanced over her shoulder. "We're going to drive around town for an hour. This town isn't that big, John. In an hour, they'll find us."

"Just drive, Alex. Get your car washed. Go through a drive-through and pick up some coffee. We'll give it forty-five minutes. I'll tell you where to drop me. I'll get the kids and meet you and Steph at another point."

Steph sat forward and turned to him. "What do you mean you'll get the kids? Susan wouldn't let them leave with you."

"Susan? Who is Susan?" Alex's gaze jumped to the rearview mirror.

"She will, if you tell her to." John ignored Alex. "I won't let anything happen to them." He placed his hand over Steph's and gave her a few seconds to think before he asked, "Do you know the number?"

"Yes."

"Susan who?" Stopping at red light, Alex turned in her seat and stared at Stephanie. John held the blonde's hand.

The driver behind them honked his car's horn.

"The light is green again," John said. "Keep moving. We don't want to draw attention."

Noticing John's red neck, resentment fumed in Alex. She whipped around and pushed on the gas pedal, speeding forward through the intersection.

Like a man, John had thought with his dick. He'd worked fast, earning Ms. Boyd's trust. Now they sat in the backseat holding hands like a pair of lovesick school kids while she played chauffeur. Well, as the Treasury agent in charge, she had every right to interrogate Stephanie Boyd fully, just as Dolton had.

Alex studied Stephanie in the rearview mirror. What did John see in her anyway? She bit back the smile welling up inside her. She wasn't going to let John's actions bother her. His relationship with Ms. Boyd would be the shortest one in history. The moment John got out of the car to round up her two brats, she and Stephanie Boyd, her witness, would disappear.

~~~~

Chapter Fourteen

Before they returned to the library, they stopped at the truck stop off of Route 611 to fuel Alex's car and use the restroom. John bought antiseptic and bandages for Stephanie, and she tended to her scraped knee and other cuts.

It was near noon and the smell of bacon and eggs mixed with fried burgers and onions drifted from the restaurant area. Stephanie's stomach grumbled in response. She'd love to grab a burger but she had little money and there was no time.

She moved further down the aisle away from the convenience store's cashier. With her cell phone to her right ear, she trapped a finger in her left ear. The voice over the loud speaker called an Emil Sidle to the repair shop and she couldn't hear what Susan was saying.

"Tell Em and Bobby I'm coming. No. I can't tell you what is going on, Susan. Please don't ask any questions."

"Em told you what?" She listened as her worse fear verbalized. She hadn't meant to get Susan involved. She didn't want to see her hurt. Closing her eyes Stephanie sighed. "Did anyone else hear her? Good."

Stephanie glanced around, checking prying ears. John stood at the exit, next to Alex, waiting. He checked his watch, said something to the woman and glanced in Steph's direction.

"Listen. Forget what she told you. You never heard it. Don't repeat it to any one. Not even Don. Promise me. I'll explain later," Stephanie pleaded. "Just take Bobby and Em to the back door in ten minutes, wait for a knock and let them out. I'll be there. One more thing, Susan. It's very important. You can't tell anyone you've seen us. No, not even the police. Okay. Thanks."

After Susan hung up, Stephanie continued to hold her cell phone to her ear, listening to dead silence. She studied the way Alex stood elbow to elbow with John. Together, they looked like a normal couple, not federal agents. It was only because she knew who they were that she noticed their guns poking at their jackets.

Nervous irritability showed on John's face as he watched the activity in the truck stop parking lot. She knew he was working on a plan to pick up the kids and get them all out of town without being seen by the local police.

She was about to throw a wrench into his scheme.

Alex, however, seemed almost ecstatic. Why?

As if sensing she was being watched, Alex turned. Her curved lips might've been perceived as warm but the coldness in her icy stare caused a chill to run up Stephanie's spine.

She didn't trust Alex. Why John had done a turnaround in his attitude toward the woman baffled her.

She snapped her phone closed, dropped it into her purse and again ignored her stomach's grumble. She ran her fingers through her hair while she crossed the tiled floor.

Alex nudged John and he turned. "Is everything set?"

"She'll be waiting for me at the back entrance," Stephanie mumbled as she passed him.

"You!" John grabbed her elbow and swung her around. "No way. You're staying with Alex."

She shrugged her arm free. "Em is crying. She might not come with you. It's better if I go."

Stephanie felt Alex's glare on her but continued to disregard the agent.

"If anyone sees you—"

"No one will." Determined to convince John to let her do this, she kept her voice firm. "The post office's parking lot is adjacent to the back of library. At this time of day the carriers are all out on their routes. It'll be empty."

John's gaze lifted over her shoulder and latched onto whoever approached her from behind.

Stephanie's heart leaped into her throat. She turned and her heart dropped back into place. Two truckers stood near the cashier and showed open interest in both her and Alex. She wished she had something else to wear besides cargo shorts and a sweater that kept slipping, exposing her shoulder. But her attire was the least of her worries.

Ignoring the men, she turned and noted John's noticeable irritation with the drivers. "John."

"I can't let you take the chance." He stared down at her.

"Em and Bobby might fight coming with you. Think about it. You represent danger to them. You're a stranger to them and for the few minutes they've been with you, they've been terrorized."

She saw in his brown eyes he knew she was right.

John exhaled, grabbed her elbow and led her through the doors. Alex followed. Outside he stopped on the sidewalk and waited for a tractor-trailer to roll by. "Is there an alley or road running along the parking lot?"

"No. The gate to the post office is at the front just to the side of the building, past the blue drop off boxes. There are businesses on both sides."

"You can't let her do this." Alex stepped into the circle of conversation. "It's too dangerous."

With Stephanie's jaw set and gaze on fire, she threw Alex's glare back at her. "I faced hell last night and this morning. Nothing could compare to that."

"You think so?"

Alex's glare sharpened on her, making her want to step back, but she refused. With determination, she said, "I know so."

Alex raised her pointed chin. "If one of your children is killed, you'll feel differently."

Alex's frank words set Stephanie back on her heels. She stared at the tarmac. Her stomach knotted thinking about Bobby or Em lying dead, their lifeless eyes staring up at her like the truck driver's last night, blaming her.

The imaged ripped at her soul. She wouldn't be able to go on living without either of them, which was why she had to do this. They couldn't cause a scene leaving the library. With John they would.

She faced Alex, feeling the heat in the redhead's stare. "That's not going to happen."

"No. It's not," John agreed. He grabbed her arm, pulled her from the sidewalk and around the tail end of the moving trailer. Quickly, they crossed the lot toward Alex's car.

"John." Alex's pumps clattered on the tarmac as she chased after them.

"Discussion is closed, Alex. This is my decision. Not yours," he said over his shoulder. Reaching for the door handle, he stopped and looked down at Stephanie. "You didn't tell Susan what was going on?"

"No. She's knows nothing." Stephanie shook her head, knowing she'd only told a half-truth.

"Good." John checked his watch. "We have ten minutes. I'll drive. Alex you sit in the back with Steph."

The next ten minutes seemed like an hour to Stephanie. John maneuvered the roads, flowing with traffic. If it wasn't for Alex, she'd be calm. The Treasury agent rattled her nerves.

Alex fiddled with her gun, lying in her lap. Almost as if she expected an ambush.

Stephanie pushed the thought away. No one had followed them. No one could possibly know where they were or where Bobby and Em were. Everything would be fine.

~~~~

Chapter Fifteen

Mid-day customers crammed the King of Prussia Mall, trying to escape the heat outside. Victor mingled with the shoppers while he kept the girl in his sight. She was a ripe eighteen. Her full pink lips tilted in a pouty seductive way as she window shopped.

Blue-eyed and blonde, Rachael Randall would bring big bucks on the black market if her father didn't get his head out of his ass.

She stopped at a cosmetic counter and sniffed several perfumes.

Victor pulled back the pressed sleeve of his dress shirt and looked at his watch. Time was getting short.

If Randall thought he could stop feeding information because two hired yahoos with tin badges got killed, the bean counter was sadly mistaken. The Treasury agent had made his deal with the devil. The routes and truck information for twenty loads were required to clear the Treasury agent's gambling debts owed to the Zosimoskys, his family. Randall had only supplied seven. He had a number to go.

Finally, Ms. Randall hooked her purse over her shoulder, picked up her bags and headed toward the exit.

Her magnificent blonde mane swung freely about her hips and covered the area of her tan back he'd seen earlier, exposed by her skimpy top. Her car keys were clipped on her purse and jangled against her hip with each sway.

Victor followed Rachael out into the sunshine and across the parking lot. American teenage girls dressed like cheap whores. Randall's daughter dressed like a harlot headed for the beach in a halter top and a short skirt that barely covered her ass.

Her flip-flops flipped and flopped, smacking the tarmac as she walked. Anticipating the chase, Victor's heart beat jumped. Grabbing Ms. Randall was going to be so easy. The girl had no clue he followed her, or did she?

She swung her hips like a woman hoping to attract attention. Foolish girl. Her father should take a strap to her for acting like a whore. He would have to tell Randall about her actions. Discipline was important.

Victor knew where Ms. Rachael had parked. He had followed her from her cheerleading camp. To throw his target off, he quickened his strides, like a busy self-centered American businessman, and passed her, throwing her a casual once-over as he did so.

He scanned the parking lot. It was unusually quiet. Except for two other mall shoppers, he and Ms. Randall were alone. The pair of shoppers was not a concern. The afternoon's heat and humidity drove them toward the mall's air conditioning at a racer's pace.

Victor hurried to a gray Lexus parked two spaces beyond Rachael's car. His black Porsche was parked in another section. He made a show of removing his coat and tie, tossing them on the roof of the car and unbuttoning his collar.

She glanced his way.

He smiled.

In her glimpse, he saw her apprehension and his muscles tightened. His friendly grin had said too much.

With the speed of a startled rabbit, Ms. Randall popped the trunk of her car, stowed her packages and rushed to her car door, but she was too slow.

She never saw or heard him close in. He grabbed her forearm and spun her around. Her purse and keys flew to the asphalt with a clatter and her flip-flop strap tore from its sole. Rachael lost her balance and grabbed his arm.

"Let me go. Hel—" Her cry was cut short as Victor cupped her mouth with his hand.

"You must not scream." Victor pinched her jaw hard for emphasize. "I can snap your neck before you can take a breath. Do you understand?"

Her shimmering stormy eyes stared up at him and she blinked her surrender.

"Good." He held his hand a fiction of away from her mouth, waiting for a stupid move.

A gasp escaped her pink lips as she righted herself. Her jaw and cheeks were red from the imprint of his fingers. Rachael would have black and blue marks perhaps. A shame. Such a pretty face.

Her father would be livid. Victor chuckled inside imaging the bean counter's pathetic fit of outrage.

He stepped closer, hip to hip, and wrapped his hand in her soft hair. He pulled down on the silky strands, titling her face up, until his gaze locked with hers. "I do not intend to hurt you, little one."

"Who are you? What do you want?"

She trembled in his grasp. The bean counter's daughter's young body was toned yet soft. Her breasts were the size of sweet ripe peaches, just large enough to fill a hungry man's appetite. "I have a message for your father."

"My dad? What do you want with my dad?"

"It is business. Nothing to worry your pretty self about."

Voices drifting from the mall's entrance drew Victor's attention. Three women and one man exited the building and headed in their direction. Clerks. Shift change.

He had to get his message to Randall.

Victor looked back at Ms. Randall with his coldest glare. "I'm going to let you go. But before I do, I want to tell you I know where you live. I know your little brother is staying with his friend Jimmy today, and I know your mother prefers long baths. I know your family. I do not want to hurt any of you. Understand?"

Her pink tongue darted across her lips before she nodded.

"Good." He kicked her keys and purse under her car. Grabbing her hand, he placed it on his crotch. By the way her eyes widened, he knew she could feel the hard bulk of his gun he had stuffed into his pants pocket. Her fingers shook against his penis, causing his member to stir to life. She felt his reaction too. She pulled her hand away but he forced it back into place. "Keep it there and put your other arm over my shoulder."

"But you said you were going—"

Victor saw the clerks getting closer. "Do it now."

Rachael was a good girl. She did as she was told.

He wrapped his arm around her tiny waist and buried his face in the crook of her neck. The young thing even smelled like a sweet peach. Victor thought *why not sample the wares while in this predicament.* He licked her neck.

She winced and strained against his hold. Her efforts were fruitless, however. His strong grip crushed her to him. "Move your hand as if you are pleasuring me."

"I can't," she cried against his shoulder.

"Do it or die here." He nuzzled against the pulsing vein of her neck. "And don't do anything foolish. I can kill five as quickly as one. Do as I say and you will live to see your papa and mama."

Slowly her hand moved up and down along the length of him. He grinned and nipped at her ear. The girl had some experience. Maybe he would send all of his messages to Randall through his daughter.

"Hotel down the street is only fifty-bucks," one of the lady workers called out to them as the foursome passed by.

Victor felt Ms. Rachael stiffen in his arms. She was going to cry out. He crushed his mouth against hers, cutting off her plea.

When they were once again alone, Victor pulled back from her, keeping his hand wrapped in her hair. She slumped against her car. Her cheeks were tear and mascara streaked.

"Now, little one, I want you to call your papa." He reached into his shirt pocket and pulled out his cell phone with his free hand. He hit the speed dial for Randall's personal cell number and put the phone to her ear.

Victor knew the second Randall answered. The submissive glaze disappeared from Rachael's eyes and was replaced with panic. "Daddy, this man, he grabbed me—"

Victor yanked the phone away from her and smiled. "Enough, little one." He heard Randall calling his daughter's name and slowly lifted the phone to his ear. "Randall, time is running out for me. I need the dispatch information for tonight."

"You son of a bitch," Randall screamed at him.

Victor grinned. The man's fury amused him. "Many people have referred to my mama as a bitch, but she was simply a strong woman."

"I'm not kidding, Victor. I will kill you if you hurt Rachael."

"Do not make promises you know you cannot keep. Now, will you fulfill your contract or does your daughter disappear? You will not know if she is fish food or lives as some pervert's sex slave."

He twisted her hair and pulled. Rachael cried, "Daddy."

"Think before you answer, Randall. Because your son will be next."

~~~~

Chapter Sixteen

Outside, long shadows crossed the backyard of the safe house and the mercury light on the streetlamp flickered in an attempt to remain lit. Twenty-one hours had passed by since their world had turned upside down. Twenty-one hours and forty-seven minutes, approximately, since Gene died.

Exhausted, Stephanie wiped off the safe house's kitchen counter top with what seemed to be her last ounce of energy and turned toward the sink. She had to keep busy.

John entered the kitchen and her pulse quickened. He'd left their simple dinner of burgers and fried potatoes more than a half hour ago to take a call from Ben Stover, the other FBI agent who worked with John.

Searching John's taut expression, she knew he probably had more *great* news for her. News she didn't want to hear. She braced herself against the counter and waited for him to say something, but he remained silent.

From the corner of her eye, she saw him snatch the ketchup off the table, yank open the refrigerator door and stick the bottle inside before he crossed the room and poured himself a mug of coffee.

With everything going on in her life, she shouldn't notice the way his hair, wet from a shower, had a cowlick.

But she did.

Or, the way his forearms stretched the sleeves of the white T-shirt he now wore.

But she did.

Or, how his bare feet, peeking out from under his jeans, padding across the kitchen somehow made her feel secure.

But they did.

And the fact she was barefooted too, made their being alone together feel intimate. She didn't want to be attracted to the man.

But she was.

He turned and, over the cup's rim, caught her stare. She saw the cool mask he wore slide into place. His expression now said *I'm in control.*

"I see you took your turn in the shower." She grabbed another plate. Her face warmed thinking of him naked.

"Yeah." His attention remained on her as he drank his coffee.

Ill at ease under his scrutiny, she glanced around the country style kitchen, hoping to turn his attention away from her. "This is a nice house. Are they all like this?"

"What do you mean?" His gaze remained trained on her as he walked toward her.

She swallowed. Hoping to hide the jumpiness she felt, she continued the line of conversation. "The safe houses. Are they all this nice?"

"No. I've been in a few that are low-income, one room dumps not much bigger than a closet. They wouldn't be bad if you didn't have to share the space with rats and cockroaches."

Stephanie's nose cringed. "Rats?"

"You're not particular when you're hiding from someone who vows to kill you."

"I guess you're right."

John swallowed a gulp of coffee. "Hmm. It just happens this house was the closest to us and open."

She washed a glass and placed it on the drain board. "How does the government account for a house sitting vacant and all of sudden people plop in? I mean, that has to look suspicious to the neighbors."

"This one is listed as a time share. A management agency cares for it when not occupied. At times the owner, our front, an elderly lady who can be a bit forgetful, calls and within a few hours vacationers will arrive."

She arched her brow and smiled. "So we're vacationers?"

"Yeah." He smiled and looked out the window where another agent, posing as a landscaping service, mowed the lawn in the coolness of the early evening. "It'll be dark soon."

The thin forest surrounding the home already loomed in darkness.

John hadn't let his guard down once. At least not in the hours she'd been with him. The fiasco at the mall had been her fault, and Bobby's. If only they'd exchanged cars faster, perhaps they would've disappeared before they'd been found, and Zohara wouldn't be in a hospital. "Are there more agents out there?"

"Yes. Two. They're posted around the perimeter."

"A well oiled machine."

"Huh?" He looked at her quizzically.

Her cheeks warmed. "That's something my grandfather used to say when things were organized and ran smoothly."

"Oh. Right." He continued to survey the neighborhood.

She wondered what kind of background John came from as she rinsed and placed a bowl on the drain board. What urged a boy to grow up and become a FBI agent? The action? The guns?

John looked tired. Did the boy in him regret his career choice after the reality of the job set in?

"Are you going to tell me what Agent Stover had to say?" She dreaded hearing the news he'd learned. It couldn't be good. He would've told her good news immediately.

"They lifted the prints from the guy at the mall and ran them through the system. Ben had a hit. A small time thief named Doug Antonelli, a.k.a. Dog. So you were right about his name. But, we haven't had any luck searching the data banks for a Victor, yet."

She held onto a glimmer of hope. "You think you will though?"

He nodded. "This guy didn't just fall to earth with a plan to rob the U.S. Treasury of millions. He has to have come from somewhere—have some kind of record. We'll find him. It's just going to take some time."

"I won't be stupid and ask how much?"

"I appreciate that." He smiled. As if realizing for the first time that she was washing dishes, he said, "I told you I'd do those, Steph."

She'd noted before he'd shortened her name. She kind of liked the nickname.

"That's okay. This is therapy." Stephanie shrugged and smiled at him as she rinsed another plate. "After the last twenty-four hours, I really needed to do something normal."

"I understand. I do the same thing when I'm done with a case."

Her hands stilled under the warm water. "You do?"

"You look surprised." He set his mug down, snatched the tea-towel from the counter and started to dry the dishes from the rack.

Gene had never helped her with the dishes.

She washed and John dried. It was kind of nice standing side by side, talking, even though some of their conversation dealt with their lives being at stake. But there was something about a man wearing a gun, drying dishes that struck her as funny. Especially a barefooted one.

Shaking her head slightly, she laughed.

John's eyes narrowed and his brow pulled together. "What?

I'm sorry. It's just you're FBI." Her cheeks warmed, again, the moment the idiotic words spilled from her mouth.

"We have lives too," John said with a chuckle. "We don't wait in sterile closets for the next case."

She liked his laugh and the way his eyes sparkled.

"Well, actually, I sort of had this picture of you in a smoke filled room, playing cards, waiting for the call. Then going to the sterile room to be briefed on the high-tech gadgets you'll use on your mission."

"You've got it all wrong. I haven't played cards in years."

"Oh, I see. That's the only part wrong?"

"Well, yeah."

"Hmm." Stephanie's heart pounded so hard against her ribs she thought for sure John would hear its beat over the steady stream of tap water.

She'd noticed he wore no ring and longed to ask him if there was a Mrs. Dolton, but she didn't have the nerve.

Waiting for another dish, he leaned against the counter and watched her hands at work. "Do you mind if I ask you a question? About your divorce."

Her hands stilled for a moment, wondering exactly what he wanted to know, and why? "Summary. I grew up.

Gene didn't. There were parties. Lots. Which I didn't attend."

John nodded, seemingly reading the truth beyond her Cliff Notes version. Stephanie licked her lips and changed the subject. "Where are Bobby and Em?"

"They're still watching T.V."

"They've lived without the thing for a few days, so they'll probably be glued to the screen until I chase them to bed." Stephanie frowned at the thought of their home and the things they'd left behind. "Bed. That sounds funny."

"Why is that?"

"Well, this isn't home." She heard her voice crack and fought the turmoil of emotions threatening to bring her to tears.

"Think of it as a hotel," he said with gentleness.

She simply nodded, keeping her eyes downcast while she let the water out of the sink. He was right. She had to believe their situation was only temporary. Ben would find out who Victor was and capture him and his men. Afterward they could go home. She had to have faith.

"I know. You're right." She shut off the water and grabbed a paper towel to dry her hands. When she turned, he blocked her exit. His clean male scent surrounded her, causing her knees to weaken.

"I promise, Steph. I won't let anything happen to you or your children."

She stared into the depths of his soul, where she saw the truth. John would die, trying to protect her and the kids. She didn't want him to die.

Reliving the deaths she'd seen, a chill swirled down Stephanie's spine.

"Are you okay?" His hands clasped her upper arms.

More than his touch, his concern pulled at her heart. "Yes. I'm just tired. I'm not used to pulling these thirty-six hour shifts anymore. I think I'll take Bobby and Em upstairs with me now. They can watch T.V. there."

"Well, this makes for a homey picture." Mosely had entered the kitchen and stood with her arms folded across her chest. Alex's stare cut through her. "Should I take the kids out for ice cream?"

"No." Stephanie stepped away from John's grasp. John might not have recognized the resentment in Alex's voice but Stephanie did. Again she wondered if there was a relationship, or a past one, between the two. It didn't matter. She wasn't going to get involved. Regardless of how attracted she was to John. She had always feared for Gene's life and she'd been right doing so. "That won't be necessary. The kids and I are going upstairs. Good night."

"Steph," John called after her.

She turned in the door's archway, her skin still burning where he'd touched her.

"Don't worry. Get some sleep. We're here."

John's smile made her feel safe.

Alex's look, on the other hand, made her want to run.
****

Alex whirled on him the moment Stephanie and the kids climbed the stairs and the door above closed.

"What the hell are you thinking, John?"

"What are you talking about?" Knowing exactly what Alex referred to, he picked up his cup, swallowed his guilt and crossed the kitchen. The desire to hold Steph in his arms still trembled inside him.

"Don't give me that innocent *I don't know what the hell you're talking about* crap. You know exactly what I'm referring to. If I hadn't walked in here when I did, you'd probably be suckin' face with her." Alex jabbed the air toward the ceiling with her finger.

His chuckle sounded strained to his own ears. "Now, I know you're off base. You want a cup of coffee?"

Alex's hard features expressed her anger as she stomped across the linoleum floor. "No. I don't want coffee. I saw the way you were looking at her."

He shrugged. "I'm concerned. Stephanie's exhausted, physically and mentally. She's been through hell. And she has no idea of the long road ahead of her."

"You don't get close enough to offer your shoulder, John. It's dangerous."

Alex was right and the fact she pointed out his mistake irritated the hell out of him. He did find Stephanie Boyd attractive but he wasn't going to do anything about it. He wasn't looking for a relationship. Nothing long term at least. Long term meant devoting your heart. He wasn't ever going to set himself up again to face the agony that had consumed him when he'd lost Julie and Katie. And Stephanie Boyd had long term written all over her.

He frowned and shook his head. "It wasn't like that. Steph looked a little shaky. I grabbed her to keep her upright. Okay?" He set the coffee pot down hard. Who was Alex to judge him anyway? "Besides *I* don't let my guard down, ever."

He saw hurt flicker in Alex's eyes and immediately wanted to kick himself in the ass. He had to let the events of Luke's death go. Alex had apologized for the mistake a hundred times. "I'm sorry. I didn't mean—"

"Yes, you did." She folded her arms across her chest as if shielding herself against further attacks. "I guess it's going to take a long time for me to earn your trust. I understand that. But, you've got to give me a chance."

Alex's bottom lip trapped between her teeth for a moment while she seemed to fight an internal battle. She shifted her weight from one heeled foot to the other.

John gave her time.

"Luke was a good man, from what I'd heard. My mistake cost him his life. I am truly sorry for that." She held his gaze. "I have to live with that fact. I'm determined not to make another mistake and put someone else's life at jeopardy."

Standing in front of him, holding his stare and admitting her part in Luke's death, John had to admit the woman had balls.

Her spirit made him feel like a heel. Alex had saved his ass today. If it wasn't for her quick thinking he'd be laying on his back, refrigerated, wearing a toe tag.

And now, she was only watching his back. Getting too close to a victim could cloud his judgment—put the case at jeopardy, not to mention place all of their lives at risk. Without Stephanie, they'd be back at square one and millions more of U.S. dollars could disappear, and more lives could be lost.

John reached up into the cupboard and pulled down another mug. He poured coffee and offered her the filled cup. "You saved my life today. I think you've earned my trust."

After a cool second, Alex's taut expression relaxed. A reserved smile played on her lips as she accepted the coffee. "What do you say we discuss our game plan to keep our witnesses safe?"

~~~~

Chapter Seventeen

Something needled at John. Again, he felt as if he was being watched. But everything was secure. All posts were in place. There was no indication that their position had been compromised. He should be able to relax, but his instincts told him differently.

At four a.m., only the whir of air conditioning covered his footsteps as he edged toward the bedroom door. Silently, he turned the handle and stared into the room. Moonlight fell across the bed. Stephanie lay flat on her back with her arms spread out like wings while Bobby and Em snuggled against her. A small snore escaped her parted lips.

She slept soundly. They all did.

Thank God. It hadn't been easy for Steph to tell them about their father or for them to learn the truth. The kids cried for hours.

Steph's breasts swelled in a rhythmic motion against the thin nightgown bought by a shopper for the bureau. If he closed his eyes, he could still feel her warmth and the curve of her hips and legs as she'd spooned against him in Zohara's car.

Feeling his desire for her, guilt hammered him. He pushed away from the door frame. For two years he'd been loyal to the memory of Julie. An eternity spent in hell.

Then, twenty-four hours ago…Only twenty-four hours. It seemed like days ago. Steph had looked at him with her cat-like eyes and parted the thick fog of isolation surrounding him. From that moment on, he'd wanted to hold her, make her feel safe and allow her warmth to push away the cold pangs of loneliness.

He was torturing himself, looking at her, yearning for something that could never happen.

She was his witness.

Even when she stopped being his witness, there wasn't a possibility of a relationship between them. It wasn't because he was FBI and she was a small town girl. Julie had been small town born and raised too. They had worked out the details of his secret life. It was Katie's memory and her resemblance to Em that stopped him cold.

Em stirred under his watch. She was so like his little girl; freckles, smiling eyes, twirling on her toes the carefree way little girls do when they're happy. Even Em's dressed up scruffy teddy bear, Mr. Blakeslee, lying near Steph's knee, reminded him of what he'd lost.

What he had failed to protect. He had been Katie's daddy.

John's gaze drifted over Steph again. He didn't have the right to feel, no matter how much he wanted too. He clamped his lips tight, fighting the pain which filled his heart and stepped back. They felt safe enough to sleep. Leaving the door ajar, he ran his hand over his face. He was damn tired, but he needed to stay alert.

He crossed the hall and hesitated at the door to the room where Alex slept. He really didn't need to check on her but he cracked her door anyway and peered inside. Tucked under a blanket, the agent's rigid lines were barely a silhouette against the wall in the dark room.

She slept.

He should too.

At least try.

Two agents were on guard outside.

He closed the door. Passing the room where Steph and the kids lay without a second look, John silently descended the steps. He stretched out on the couch with his forearm over his eyes and forced his mind to relax as he'd been trained to do.

Hours felt like minutes when suddenly John felt a tug on his belt. His eyes snapped open and he grabbed the hand on his Sig's butt.

~~~~

Chapter Eighteen

"Strip." Victor pointed his Browning pistol at the driver. The man's government had him drive through this section of Philadelphia unescorted, thinking thieves would never wait for him within the city limits.

Victor's lips curved. They were wrong.

His cold glare locked with the driver's. The rig's bronco was scared shitless. Tonight, Victor wasn't worried about him or his men being recognized. They all wore black clothing and masks—just like in the American cat thief movies. "You have ten seconds to get buck naked, cowboy."

"Are you fucking nuts? This is the Goddamn hood. It ain't no place to be without a weapon, much less nude!"

The toothpick of a man was right. Victor chuckled inside. The factories and warehouses surrounding them were crumbling, brick by brick. The only living creatures stirring at this time of the night were the sewer rats scurrying from garbage pile to garbage pile and, the more dangerous, the desperate homeless who probably watched from their dens.

"It is too warm for you to catch a cold, my friend. What you don't realize is that making you naked will save your ass. These homeless thieves, laying in wait, can't steal from you if you don't have anything. You will be able to walk from here safely." The man's body was more valuable than anything on his back—as a whole or in pieces. Victor kept that bit of information to himself.

The man's gaze bounced from building to building while he ripped open the snaps of his cowboy shirt, peeled it from his back and dropped it to the pavement. When the brakes of the truck released, Buckaroo lost his balance stepping out of his boots and fell to the sidewalk.

"That tractor is all I've got," he cried as Victor's men drove the rig away from the curb.

"Your government can reimburse you for your rig, but it cannot give you back your life. I have another appointment. You are making me wait too long." Victor cocked his gun.

Papa would be so proud of him. Two loads in one night.

~~~~

Chapter Nineteen

"Ouch," a tenor voice crackled.

"What the hell do you think you're doing?" John swung his feet to the floor and stared crossly at Bobby, who stood next to the couch, tugging furiously, trying to escape his grip. Why did the kid want his Sig?

The child's pulse pumped frantically against his fingers. John relaxed his hold slightly. What did Bobby have on his mind?

Sunrise gleamed off the oak coffee table and John wondered how long he'd been out. "What time is it?"

"I'm going to tell mom you said a bad word."

John rolled his eyes. Not again. "Hell isn't a bad word."

"It's one of the words I can't say."

"That's you. Are you going to tell me why you were trying to get my gun?"

Bobby looked as scared as a cornered mouse. The boy wore only his boxer shorts and John could actually see his small heart pound inside his bare chest.

John suppressed the smile fighting to curve his lips as he looked at the kid's knobby knees. "Bobby?"

The light in Bobby's eyes paled. Something was going on inside his head besides curiosity over the gun. The lump the kid forced down before he spoke foretold the huge burden he carried.

"My dad," Bobby's voice cracked. "He never wore his gun when he went to sleep. Are you that scared?"

John could only stare while his mind whirled, wondering, could he tell the child yes, he was? He was shaking at that very moment, realizing he'd slept too soundly. Victor could have made his next move while he had snored.

"Bobby, take a seat." He let go of the boy's arm.

Bobby slouched onto the coffee table.

John scrubbed his hand over his face and back through his hair. His nerves danced under Bobby's scrutiny. After the horror the boy had seen in the last two days, he deserved the truth. "I'd be lying if I told you I wasn't."

Bobby's chin jugged forward. "My dad was never scared."

His words were smeared with pride for his father. Boyd had to have been a good man. With that thought, for a split second, John wondered what had caused the divorce between Steph and Boyd? Yeah, he had Steph's short version, but there was always two sides to a dispute. "He was just better at hiding it from you than I am."

Bobby shook his head briskly. "No. He never was. He told me. Only sissies are afraid. Only babies cry."

John was sure the boy was making the conversation up. It was Bobby's way of dealing with his father's death. But Boyd's bravery really wasn't the issue here. Why Bobby tried to get his weapon was. "Bobby, what were going to do with the gun?"

The boy's gaze dropped to the floor where his toes curled into the pile carpet. "I thought, maybe—I, I wanted it in case those men came after us again."

"The bad guys aren't going to come after you here. Trust me."

The morning light caught the shimmer of tears in his eyes, making them look larger. "I don't want my mom to go away like Dad."

John had suspected as much. His heart nearly broke, watching the boy's bottom lip quiver. The kid was brave. Maybe he did take after his dad. "I understand about wanting to protect those you love, Bobby. You'd do anything to keep bad things from happening to them. Even things you'd never done before or ever thought you'd do. Things maybe you shouldn't."

"Like what?"

"Like trying to take my gun when you know you shouldn't. Guns are very dangerous. Handling them in the wrong way could kill you. Who would help your mom, if that happened?"

Bobby hung his head and swiped a backhand across his eyes.

"Do you understand what I'm trying to tell you?"

Bobby simply shrugged.

John exhaled. Then he scooted forward on the cushion, reached to his side and pulled his Sig from its scabbard. Why? He didn't know, but he felt a connection with Bobby. "Did your dad ever show you his gun?"

Bobby's attention followed the gun to John's lap before darting up to meet his gaze. His smile brightened his blue eyes like the morning sky outside.

"No," the boy said eagerly, nearly dancing on his toes.

"Okay. I'll show you something, if you call me John. Deal?"

"Deal."

"Okay. This is important. Along the side, right here, is a switch called the safety. When it's pushed up, the gun is locked and won't fire, but if it's down, the weapon is armed. You *never* pick up an armed gun. It can fire accidentally and someone, including you, could be seriously injured." He ducked his head, staring directly into Bobby's eyes. "Do you understand?"

Bobby nodded quickly.

John continued showing him the different parts of the Sig and explained the mechanics of how the weapon fired a bullet. Bobby ate up every word and surprisingly asked very intelligent questions.

"Can I hold it?" The kid asked when John finished.

John leaned back on the couch. "I don't think that is a good idea."

"Please. Just for a second," Bobby pleaded, looking to the Sig. The kid's fingers inched forward on his legs.

For the first time, since they'd met, Bobby wasn't giving him attitude. John knew it was wrong to let Bobby to hold the gun, but the kid was nearly jumping in place and he was right here. The safety was on. What harm in allowing him to hold it for one second cause?

~~~~

Chapter Twenty

John rested the weapon in his palm, weighing it and his decision. "No. I can't."

"Bobby, get away from that gun."

Both of them jumped at the sound of Steph's cry. She stood on the stair sub-landing. She probably woke, noticed Bobby missing, threw that oversized sweater of hers over the top of whatever she wore underneath, which he could see was very little, and dashed downstairs.

As she gripped the rail, her knuckles turned white and her sweater did that slide-down-over-her-shoulder thing. Her hair was bed-tangled and stuck out in different directions. Steph looked sexy as hell and John's lower body told the story. Heat of desire pumped into his blood.

But he wouldn't go there. She was his witness.

He leaned away, as far as the couch cushion allowed, but remained fixed on her.

In a flash, she descended the last three steps and rounded the railing.

John couldn't help but take in the great view of her long, bare legs as she crossed the living room barefooted. Another pump of longing and he caught his tongue dancing across his lips. He trapped it, fighting the want he felt for Steph.

She stood next to them. Her leg barely touched his jean-covered knee but the closeness was enough to shoot a direct hit of need to his center.

She grabbed Bobby's arm and tugged him off the coffee table. "Go upstairs."

"Mom, we weren't doing anything," Bobby protested. "John was—"

"I saw what you two were doing. Go upstairs, now. I want to have a few words with Agent Dolton."

Her livid glare shot at him. He was back to Agent Dolton. He was in trouble. He slipped the Sig into its holster.

"John was showing me—"

Steph let go of her son and folded her arms across her chest. She seemed to grow taller, towering over them both. "Go."

Bobby's joy vanished as he realized 'Go' was the final word.

Again, John felt for the kid. Bobby's dilemma was his fault. He should've given Bobby hell for touching his gun and kicked him back upstairs instead of giving the kid firearm lessons. He'd take full responsibility and the wrath from Steph.

"Go ahead, Bobby." He flashed him a smile and nodded toward the stairs. "We'll talk later, buddy."

Her brow rose at the familiarity.

The moment Bobby was up the stairs, Steph hit John with a glare that had push. Without a word, she promptly turned on her heel and stomped toward the kitchen.

The quick move gave John a nice view of the pink panties she wore. He gripped the sofa's cushion for a moment while he steadied the wildfire rushing through him.

What was he, some kind of hormone-driven kid?

No. He was a man who hadn't had a woman in a long time. And, Steph prancing around here in nothing much didn't help his sanity. Didn't she realize what she did to him?

Apparently not or she'd have followed Bobby up the stairs.

He pushed off the couch, knowing he was in more trouble than he could probably handle in his delicate situation. Maybe he should follow Bobby up the stairs and head for a cold shower.

John cautiously entered the kitchen, half expecting Steph to hit him with something. But with her jaw set, she grabbed the coffee pot, rinsed it out and filled it with fresh water.

When the Pyrex pot clunked onto the burner, he crossed over and leaned against the counter. "Are you going to talk to me?"

"I need my coffee." Her hands shook as she spooned coffee grounds into a filter.

"Can I at least explain what happened in there? Bobby—"

In one swift motion, she slammed the drip tray shut and turned to face him. Her glare seared his lips closed. "What gives you the right to show my son how to use a gun?"

He cautiously reached over and hit the start button on the coffee maker. "I wasn't."

"That's what it looked like to me."

"I was showing him the mechanics of a gun. A lesson in mechanical engineering."

"That's not showing him how to use that, that…?" She snarled her lip while pointing toward his holster.

"There is a difference."

"Right."

John leaned against the counter. "Do you even wonder what started all this, with Bobby?"

"What?"

"I woke up when he tried to get my Sig. My gun."

"Why would he want your gun?"

"He had a good reason. He wanted it to protect you and Em. He thought he'd stand guard while I slept."

A long, silent moment hung in the air before she spoke again, "Regardless of why he wanted the gun, his own father never showed—"

"I know."

"What do you mean, you know?"

He'd captured her interest. John pushed away from the countertop and reached up into the cupboard for two cups. "He told me. Bobby and I talked."

"He talked to you about Gene?"

"Yes. And without attitude." John smiled, seeing the hope shimmer in her emerald eyes. "He's a good kid."

"He hasn't mention Gene since—since I told him Gene was gone. I tried to talk to him last night, but he shut me out."

"He heard every word you said and made the decision to keep you safe."

He could see the realization hit her. She trapped her quivering bottom lip between her teeth and he crossed to her and said quietly, "You have every right to be proud of him."

She blinked back the tears that threatened to spill and turned her eyes to the floor. Unable to speak, she simply nodded.

John ran his hand up and down her forearm, feeling her warmth through the soft sweater. Alex's words from last night horned in on his thoughts. *You don't get close enough to offer your shoulder, John. It's dangerous.* Alex was right. John stepped back and fought off the overwhelming urge to pull Steph into his arms and offer her comfort.

Her palms smoothed away the tears that had escaped to her cheeks before trailing over her sweater to its hem. Suddenly, her cheeks brightened while she brushed by him. "Oh, God. I was so worried about Bobby I forgot—I'll go get dressed until the coffee is ready."

"Good idea," John said, thinking it would be the best move for both of them. Her movements had lifted and lowered the sweater, teasing him with glimpses of her bottom. "Don't be too hard on Bobby, Steph. He thought he was doing right."

She stopped and turned on her bare heel. Holding the door frame, she smiled. "I won't. Thanks, John."

Warmth encased her heart as he watched her pad across the dining room hardwood floor toward the living room. He was John and not Agent Dolton again.

His phone, clipped to his belt, beeped, breaking his muse. He snapped it up and held it to his ear. "Dolton here. Yes, Ben."

Steph's brown hair swirled around her shoulders. From across the wide area, her anxious gaze landed on him.

As she moved toward him, John focused on the pattern of the vinyl floor. He couldn't concentrate on what Ben was telling him while appraising Steph's long legs.

"The mothers didn't wait too long. They hit again last night," Ben said. "Twice."

"Son of a bitch." An icy shiver ran up John's spine as his grip tightened on the phone. He wanted to head out the door, go to the scene of the hijackings and search for clues but he couldn't. He had to guard Steph and the kids.

"What happened?" Steph stepped into his line of vision. "Did they capture Victor?"

John shook his head. She was still his best bet to get these guys.

"Where?" John closed his eyes and concentrated on every detail Ben told him.

"The first driver never made it out of the city," Ben said. "They hijacked the truck right in Philly. Twenty minutes out of the dock and they had him. They left the driver standing on the corner in his birthday suit. At four in the morning, the guy is damn lucky he didn't get knocked off by some junky and sold to medical research."

"Maybe that was their plan. Let someone else off him and take the blame. Not that it matters. They've already killed two cops." John looked at Steph and immediately he regretted speaking of her ex's death so unsympathetically. The pain he saw in her eyes made his chest clench.

"They're going to go down hard," he said and pledged the promise to Steph with his eyes. "Where did they take the second?"

"An hour later," Ben replied, "they grabbed the other driver on the Pennsylvania Turnpike. He was running with another driver, not Treasury, just someone he hooked up with on the CB after a car had cut the guy off. About ten miles out, the guy started having engine trouble. Our driver pulled over with him at an emergency spot to help and, bam, a black Porsche pulled up behind them, and so it went down."

"Victor," John suggested.

Steph backed up. Her hands curled into fists. She shivered and he wanted to reassure her she was safe, but he couldn't. Instead he pointed to the chair, suggesting she sit.

She didn't move.

"Don't know," Ben's voice pulled John back into the conversation. "There were two men. He couldn't describe either of them or the driver. They all wore ski masks. But if I had to guess, I'd bet my next year's salary it was him. The guy was—"

"Cocky."

"Yeah, exactly the word the Treasury's driver used. Very cocky. They left the guy handcuffed, buck-naked, to the guardrail, a foot away from the emergency call phone. The morning traffic backed up big time. These guys have balls the size of grapefruits. Don't they?"

"Yeah, but the thing about that type, sooner or later they fu—" He cut his thought remembering Steph. "They make a mistake. They did the other night and they will again."

"Yeah, you're right. How are things there?"

"It was a quiet night. I haven't been out this morning to check the perimeters."

"You slept in, huh?"

"Right." John rolled his eyes. "Any other news? How about the bean counter or Mac?"

He listened as Stover filled him in on his attempts to identify them. All the while he was fully aware of Steph's closeness.

He wanted good news for her but Stover wasn't telling him any. His stomach knotted with frustration. "Damn. I was hoping at least one of them would show up in the system. Give us some direction."

He shook his head at Steph, signaling he had no further news.

She sighed her disappointment. Steph had hoped Victor and his men would be identified and their asses hauled in quickly. But it didn't work that way a good percentage of the time, especially when the crime was grand larceny, murder or treason. Unlike petty crime offenders, who were picked up fairly quickly, these lawbreakers were members of organized crime rings and had to be dug out. Sometimes it took years. And sometimes it never happened, but he wasn't going to give her that information.

"I think our next move is to start at the source," Ben said.

"What do you have in mind?" After listening to Ben's idea for their next move, John said, "Let's not wait. How soon do you think you can have the IDs ready? Good. Have the mailman deliver them. We'll get on it as soon as they're here."

John snapped his phone closed and pushed it into its case.

"Are you talking about the Federal Protection Program? You said IDs," Steph questioned him anxiously. "Are we leaving? Can I at least say goodbye to my parents?"

Tears glistened in her eyes, again. Standing barefooted in the middle of the kitchen, wearing nothing but a sweater that nearly swallowed her, she looked vulnerable. Again, John longed to hold her, reassure her, but he couldn't. Touching her was not an option for him. "No. We're not going anywhere, yet."

Behind them, heels clicked on the floor.

"I smell coffee."

Both he and Steph whirled toward the door. Dressed, and with every hair in place, Alex's official look reminded John he was a federal agent.

"Stover called," John said.

Her gaze flew from taking note of Steph's attire to meet his with unbridled interest. "And?"

"Victor and his men hijacked two more loads last night."

Alex's jaw tightened. "Son of a bitch. Victor? Where? Did they get them?"

"No—"

"Wait." Alex raised her hand. "Maybe Ms. Boyd will excuse us while we discuss the matter."

"I am the matter and I'm not going anywhere!" Steph crossed her arms, pulling her sweater up an inch and planted her feet. She kept her chin high and eyes trained on Alex.

"I would think you'd like to get dressed."

"My dress is not the priority here."

"Apparently." Alex looked to him for support.

"Steph's right." John shrugged. In his book she had every right to know everything. He liked her spunk. And the way she was dressed.

"This is a democracy," Alex stated flatly. "Go ahead. What did Stover say?"

John summed up the night as Ben had relayed it to him and quickly added. "The bureau hasn't found any information on any of them. The leads are drying up."

Alex grabbed a mug from the counter. "I overheard part of your conversation. What is Stover having delivered?"

"We're going to start at the source," John replied.

"What do you mean?" Steph asked.

"The Treasury Department. Ben has to ordered photographs from all the personnel files. They're compiling them for you to look at."

"Everyone at the Treasury Department has been thoroughly investigated." Alex looked up from pouring her coffee. "That's going to be nothing but a waste of time."

Steph looked from Alex to him.

He took the pot from Alex. While he filled his and Steph's cups he said, "I don't think so. My gut tells me there is an inside man. How else would they know when and where to hit?"

Steph thanked him, accepting the drink and slid onto a kitchen chair. John noted the way she lifted a thigh and repositioned her sweater and then lifted the other leg and did the same move, covering a portion of her bare legs. Lastly, she crossed her ankles and tucked her feet under the chair.

"I'm not saying there isn't an inside man," Alex replied.

"I thought you just said everyone has been investigated?" Steph sipped her coffee while watching Alex over the mug and waited for an answer.

John saw Alex's neck muscles tense and her spine stiffen. Steph was pushing Alex's buttons and he had to admit Steph's mockery amused him.

Alex ignored Steph's comment, however, and yanked the refrigerator door open and pulled out the container of milk. While she lightened her coffee, Alex continued as if she was in complete control. "I'm saying I don't think this Victor, who was at the accident scene and then had the balls to trail you when you left the barracks, would be an employee of the Treasury Department. He's a link but I doubt you'll find him there."

John took a seat next to Steph. "It's a chance. And if not, maybe whoever the traitor is will get nervous, thinking we're on to something."

"You're assuming he'll know you're looking." Alex offered him the milk.

He shook his head, wondering why when she knew he took it black.

She put the container back into the refrigerator and moved around the table. "I'm not assuming anything. I'm sure he has clout. If he knows when the loads are being transported, he'll know we're searching the personnel files. All Stover has to leak out is we've got a hot lead."

"How are they going to transmit the files?" Alex asked.

"They're not. Ben is sending them the old-fashioned way. We're not taking any chances on our location being zeroed in on."

"More time wasted." Alex frowned. "I think if we're going to nab this guy, we need bait."

"No." He knew what she had in mind and he wasn't going to go there, yet.

"It might be the only way, John. You know that."

"What do you mean?" Stephanie looked confused. Her gaze shifted from Alex to him. "What does she mean, bait?"

The thought of putting Steph in deliberate danger made his stomach roll into knots. John rose and positioned himself between Alex and Steph. "We're not going in that direction, Alex."

"It's the quickest way to nab this guy and to stop the thefts. This sitting around waiting for pictures is a waste of time."

Alex sidestepped him before he had a chance to stop her and stood over Steph. "What do you say, Ms. Boyd? Are you willing to put your life on the line for your country?"

~~~~

Chapter Twenty-one

Victor combed his hand through his dark hair—freshly dyed back to its natural color per his Papa's request—and followed Shermin through the dining room's oak doors.

The aroma of freshly baked bread and ham attacked his senses, causing his mouth to water. A day had passed since he last ate.

Ten members of the Zosimosky family, who lived in the compound, were seated in the dining room with Papa and Grandmama; three of Victor's female cousins, absent of their husbands who were away on family business, and seven children, ranging in age from three to twelve. With his back to the wall, Papa, wearing a smile, watched over them from the head of the massive table while his wife, at the other end, nurtured them.

Bright sunshine spilled through the huge pane windows and illuminated the polished hard-work floors and the rich mahogany furniture. The backdrop to the morning meal merriment was the courtyard where a hundred huge red blooms hung from Grandmama's rosebushes. The chatter, even those of the children, ceased the moment the double oak doors had swung wide.

"He is here." Shermin stepped aside and took up his post just inside the door.

"Ah, Victor." Grandmama reached out to him with arms that Victor remembered were as soft as cashmere cushions. "Come sit. Eat with us. You are growing too thin."

His cousins smiled at him. But their eyes didn't disguise their contempt for him. They knew one day he would sit in Papa's chair.

Who else? Not their husbands. None of them had married a man with balls large enough to touch him. Well, maybe Kiska's husband. He and Pasha were the only one who had any balls.

Even metaphorically.

Victor ran his palm over his silk shirt covering his flat stomach. A daily workout kept him trim. "Thank you, Grandmama. I am starving this morning."

Victor adjusted his belt buckle before he bent to receive Mama's warmth. She cupped his face with velvet fingers and kissed both of his cheeks with gusto. "It is good to see you. Your papa keeps you away too long."

"I am happy to help Papa," Victor replied against her cheek loud enough for Papa to hear.

"You are such a good boy. Sit."

"I need to talk to Papa." Victor was anxious to share his good news with his mentor.

"First you eat. Like your grandmama has told you, Victor. Then we will talk business." Papa pointed his knife at him and to the only vacant chair at the table.

"Yes, Papa." He did not like to sit with his back to the window, but Victor did as he was told and rounded the table.

Catching Kiska's glare, he hesitated only a fraction of a second before pulling the chair out and taking a seat. Her husband had been away for several months, setting up another money laundering project for the family.

Papa nodded his pleasure at his obedience and continued with his meal.

Immediately, Hilda, Grandmama's trusted housekeeper, entered the room. She carried a tray hosting a mug of steaming coffee, chilled orange juice, a plate filled with fried potatoes, scrambled eggs and a slab of ham. Quietly she placed the food and drinks in front of him and then twitched his ear.

Victor could not fight off his smile of affection for Hilda.

As Victor watched the old woman hobble back to the kitchen, he wondered if Hilda always had her ear to the door, listening. It seemed every wish of the family was thought of beforehand by the woman who had served them for more than twenty years.

Victor's stomach growled in response to the smell of the food. His niece, sitting next to him, giggled. Her action triggered laughter among the children and Grandmama.

He drew a breath. Papa was right. Family first. Then business.

Twenty minutes later, Papa laid his knife and fork across the lip of his plate and wiped the morsel of fried egg from the corner of his mouth with a linen napkin. He glanced around the table. "It is time we work."

Silence covered the room like a drop cloth.

Grandmama and Victor's cousins took the cue. While the four women made quick work of wiping mouths and hands and ushering the children from the room, Hilda filled his and Papa's mugs. When the door clicked closed behind Grandmama and her brood and Hilda disappeared into the kitchen, Papa asked, "Did you get Tankson his load?"

"Yes, Papa." Victor arched his brow and his lips curled upward in anticipation of Papa's pride. "In fact, Tankson received two loads last night."

Papa's sunken eyes widened. A sparkle danced in them. "He did?"

"Ya. I felt we needed to make amends with him for not delivering the night before. He is quite happy and sends his regards." Victor grinned, happy with Papa's reaction to his news.

"That is good." Papa chuckled. "That is very good."

Victor could feel his position in rank solidify.

Papa's expression tensed. "Do you think we can complete our obligation to Tankson within the week?"

"I do not believe there are loads scheduled. I will need to ask Randall."

"Ask."

Victor sat up straighter. "Why rush? What is wrong, Papa?"

With a grunt that told Victor his papa's rheumatism was acting up, Papa pushed back and rose from his chair. He shuffled to the window. His cable sweater hung from his shoulder blades as if on a hanger. Deep in thought, Papa worked his tongue along his teeth for a moment and pushed his thin hands into his pockets.

"Pasha got word to me. The news is not good. The FBI has decided to pull photographs of every Treasury employee, including the janitors. They're making copies to show to Mrs. Boyd. They are searching for you."

The FBI wasted their time looking for him, but they'd find Randall. And Papa knew this.

"They will find him," Papa said, as if reading his thoughts.

"He will not talk. He fears for his family." Victor's blood rushed under Papa's stern stare.

"The U.S. government will protect them just as they do Mrs. Boyd."

"Why do we not just kill her? Why wait?"

Papa sighed. "I was hoping not to blow your cousin's cover but what choice do we have?"

Victor leaned forward, with his elbows on the table, held his head, fighting to keep his expression taut. Everyone had told him taking Randall along on the job the other night was a mistake. But doing so might turn out to be good news.

At least for him.

With his cousin out of the way, who else would challenge him in replacing Papa as head of the family?

Kiska's husband. Victor chuckled inside. He would deal with him when the time was right.

Victor looked up at Papa and said reverently, "We have no choice. Pasha should kill Mrs. Boyd now. And the agent that has hounded us."

~~~~

Chapter Twenty-two

Even though the sun's brilliant rays toasted her legs and arms, an icy shiver ran up Stephanie's spine. Perched on a patio chair, she watched Bobby and Em play a game of bean bags in the backyard. Their continued argument, along with the birds soaring in the blue sky and the sun-laden breeze, reminded her life went on. No matter what, life went on.

Alex's words, spoken two days ago, still haunted her.

Could she put her life on the line for her country?

She could for her children. She had for her children.

But did she have the courage to act as bait and help John capture Victor and his cohorts, stopping the Treasury's heists?

A direct hit with the bean bag had Em squealing and doing a happy dance with her bear. Bobby's set jaw told of his annoyance with his little sister.

Stephanie rubbed the chill from her arms. Why was she worried? John would figure out the perfect plan. He wouldn't let anything happen to her. She'd be well guarded. Once they captured Victor and everyone involved, she and the kids could go back to their normal life.

But what if things didn't go as planned?

A frosty orb encircled Stephanie's heart. What would happen to Bobby and Em without her? Would they be able to live with her parents?

Probably not, if they were to be kept safe. Bobby and Em would become wards of the government—given new identities and forced to live with total strangers as a family. They'd never see their grandparents again. Mom and Dad wouldn't know where they'd been sent.

She couldn't do it. She slid forward on the lounge chair and dropped her feet to the patio. She had to tell John she was a coward.

A hand grabbed her shoulder, holding her in place.

Fear speared Stephanie. She slumped and twisted free of the grip. Breathless, she turned.

John stood behind her, holding two bottled soft drinks hooked between his fingers. "Are you okay?"

"Oh, my God." She curled the neck of her T-shirt into her fist. "Why did you grab me like that without saying something? You scared the crap out of me!"

"I asked you if you wanted a drink, but you were so deep in thought, apparently you didn't hear me." He rounded her chair and pulled the other lounge closer to her. He studied her as he sat. "Are you sure you're okay?"

Stephanie slid back on the chair and took the ginger ale he offered. She rubbed the cold bottle against the throbbing pain in her forehead. "Yeah, as okay as I can freakin' be."

"That good, huh?"

She snatched her purse from beneath her chair. She dug inside, searching for the bottle of aspirin. "How do you do it, John?"

"Do what?"

"Live the way you do? With constant danger. I mean, it doesn't seem to bother you." She struggled with the cap.

John took the bottle of pills from her, twisted the lid off easily and offered her two tablets.

"Thanks." She swallowed the tablets with a gulp of soda. Relaxing back against the lounge, she studied him as he watched Bobby and Em playing, arguing like all kids did. A smile tugged at the corner of his lips. She wished she was as composed as him, but she had the kids to worry over. "Really. How do you do it? You always seem so cool, even when you're being shot at."

He shifted on the seat, seemingly contemplating how much he should reveal. "If I'd worry, I wouldn't focus. If I didn't focus, I wouldn't have to worry about worrying."

She raised her brows, amused. "Okay, that makes sense—I think."

He chuckled. "Sure it does."

She relaxed back on the chair and tilted her face to the sun's warmth. "Don't you ever feel like just running, forgetting all of it?"

"Sure."

"Where would you run to?" She shielded her vision from the sun.

"I have a little place up in Potter County. It's isolated. No neighbors for miles. I go there sometimes, to think. Ben hunted there with me once. Outside my family, he is the only one who knows about it."

"And now me."

John returned her smile. "And now you."

She wanted to help him capture Victor but…she was a pessimist or at least she'd become one over the last few years.

She had to tell him before she lost her nerve. "I can't be bait, John. I thought about it. Thought I could. If I was more like you, maybe, but I'm not. I have to think about them." She nodded toward her children.

"You don't have to do it. What happens next is my call. I told Alex, using you wasn't an option."

Relief surged through her and immediately her headache eased. "How did Alex take it? I mean she really seems to want to get these guys."

"We both do." The carbonated gas escaped from the bottle as he twisted the cap. He took a gulp of his soda before saying, "Alex still hasn't learned patience."

"You worked with her before. I thought so."

"You did? How?"

Stephanie nodded. "I could tell there was something going on between the two of you back in Zohara's office. How long did you work with her?"

"Only for a short time." John quickly swallowed another gulp of soda, washing the bile down his throat.

"You don't like her do you?" Stephanie's gaze dropped to his left hand.

He immediately stopped rubbing Katie's hair band on his little finger and swiped his moist palm along his jeans. He shifted his attention to the kids. It wasn't he didn't like Alex. There was just a part of him that couldn't let go of Luke's memory and the details of his death. "She needs experience."

He wouldn't tell Steph the story. If they came under ambush again, Steph needed to listen to Alex—not second guess her. Their lives would depend on trusting the Treasury agent.

"When do you think the mail will be here?"

John looked at his watch. "Soon. The first package should be here today, about two o'clock."

"You really have the regular mailman delivering the package?"

He nodded. "The neighborhood's normal routine doesn't change."

"Normal. I don't think I can remember what normal feels like anymore. It seems my life has been in turmoil for years. What am I saying? It has." She closed her eyes and chuckled sarcastically.

He had a feeling Stephanie didn't tell him everything about the heist. If he pressed her, maybe he'd find out what she had held back. "You're just feeling the pressure, Steph. It won't last."

She peeked at him. "How can you be so sure?"

"Experience."

"Experience, huh. Have you ever woke and found your whole life is a lie? The person you were married to wasn't the person you thought?"

"No. I woke one morning and learned the two people I love more than life itself were gone." The words had slipped from him before he'd thought. John shoved his hand through his hair. Why had he told her that? He was supposed to be questioning her and in a single moment she had him talking about something he'd kept locked away inside.

"What happened?" she asked softly.

He heard sincere concern in her voice and saw it in her eyes. He'd never spoken to anyone about Julie and Katie's death. "It's a part of my past I really don't want to talk about. I think I'll go check—"

Her tender touch on his arm kept him from rising.

"For months after I left Gene, I went to counseling, searching for the reason of why I couldn't make things right. During those sessions, I learned you can't blame yourself. You can't control other people," she said.

She was right about blaming himself. He did. Every waking moment.

But, Steph thought Julie had left him. He'd give his life to turn back time and have Julie and Katie alive. It wasn't going to happen. He tried bargaining with his soul to both the devil and God for their return, but neither had listened.

Steph let go of his arm, giving him room, and waited for his story. For some unexplainable reason he wanted to bare his soul to her.

He ran his tongue across his suddenly dry lips. "My wife and daughter were killed in a house fire while I was away on assignment."

"Oh, my God. I'm so sorry, John. How long ago?" Steph paled with remorse.

John peeled the label off the bottle he held. The little bits of paper drifted to the cement like the years gone. He sighed, relieving some of his penned up pain. "Two years ago."

He curled his lips into a seal, fighting the desire to vocalize his anguish and lowered his head so Steph wouldn't see his pain. It was his alone to bear.

"John, you can't possibly blame yourself for what happened to them." She reached out to him again. Her gentle fingers traced comforting circles on the back of his hand.

"I was the target." Ashamed, he turned away and met the vision of his daughter, in Em.

Em ran between him and Steph, breaking their link. "Mommy, Bobby won't play with me anymore. You come and play."

"John and I are talking." Steph tossed him an apologetic glance.

Em's soft innocent scent brought a rush of memories to the front of his mind. It was as if his Katie were there hugging him, singing to him, kissing him.

He had to get away.

"We're done, Steph. Play with her. I'm going to check on the delivery." He rose quickly, not giving Steph a chance to stop him with her caring touch or sympathetic ear. He stalked across the backyard.

He didn't deserve either.

~~~~

Chapter Twenty-three

Bean counter. Morse's words haunted Randall, along with the memory of the dead Sheriff's stare.

The phone he held rang relentlessly.

No answer. Randall hit the off button and slammed the phone down. Like a wild beast, he paced his office, waiting to be executed.

For fifteen spotless years, he'd been with the Treasury Department, working his ass off to rise to the top. And now, because of one drunken night, he was about to lose everything, including his life.

Had he been targeted?

His gut coiled around his spine. He bit back a spew of obscenities. His mama had raised a fool. Of course he had been set up. Somehow the Zosimosky family had found out about his gambling habit and had played him like a wet-neck boy from the black swamps of Georgia. The invitation to a free weekend at the Atlantic City casino resort had seemed innocent enough. Now, they owned him.

He had the Zosimoskys on one side and the U.S. government on the other, both breathing down his neck like hounds chasing a raccoon.

Death would be his only escape—unless he figured a way out of this mess, and soon.

His gaze darted to the picture on his desk and his heart wrenched. He didn't want to leave his wife and kids. He loved them.

What was he thinking? He couldn't leave them. Victor would make them pay for his weakness. Images of the Russian making his little girl do unspeakable acts filled his head, causing Randall's stomach to lurch. He had to stop this madness. He hit the redial button and rounded his desk for the hundredth time that morning. The top of his head was about to explode.

The blasted ringing stopped and a voice mumbled, "Yeah."

Finally!

He gripped his cell phone tighter. "Do you know what they're doing?"

"Where are you?" He could hardly hear the words and knew by making the call he was putting both of them in risk. He didn't care.

"In my office. Where the hell do you think I'd be?" He opened the door to his private washroom and flipped on the lights. He desperately needed an aspirin.

"I told you not to call me. It's dangerous."

He gulped down two pills and a palm full of water. "Dangerous. Ha! I'm sitting here like a freakin' goose waitin' to have my head chopped off and my ass deep fried. They're—"

"I know. They're scanning all the personnel files. Calm down before you blow your cool."

He heard a door open and close.

"How in the hell am I supposed to calm down? Mrs. Boyd is still alive, isn't she?"

"Yes."

"She saw me." He caught his image in the mirror. His wild eyes reflected his panic. He loosened the silk tie strangling his neck. He needed air.

"Is there anyway you can pull your file?"

He hit the light switch and stalked back to his desk. "No. Agents from the FBI have been ordered to monitor the scanning. If Ms. Boyd sees my picture, she'll identify me. I'm dead. The U.S. government will track me down. Label me a traitor. There won't be a log in the world for me to hide under."

A hardy laugh resounded in his ear. "I hate to tell you this Randall, but you are a traitor."

Accepting the statement as the truth, he turned numb. He sank onto his leather chair and bit back a cry. Through bleary vision, he stared at his family's portrait. His shaking finger traced the outline of his wife's jaw.

A traitor.

He loved his country.

But he loved his family more.

Would the U.S. government understand?

The four pairs of loving eyes staring back at him from within the picture turned cold, blaming him for their shame. Sickness welled up in him. He had to do something. "If that happens, I'm not going down alone."

"Are you threatening us?"

The hair on the back of his neck prickled. "I'm just stating facts. The whole Zosimosky Empire will crumple."

"We don't like being threatened, Randall. I'd hate for anything to happen to your family. You know Victor and how he prides himself in handling problems."

"Victor has already showed his muscle."

"What are you talking about?"

"He visited my daughter yesterday."

"Why would he do that?"

Did he sense a bit of surprise in his contact's tone? Was there a lack of communication between them? "You tell him to stay away from my family or I'll—"

"You'll what?"

The icy tone cut through him. He'd gone too far, making his point. He needed help to get out of this mess. Morse was right. He was nothing more than a bean counter. He didn't even own a gun.

He needed the Zosimoskys behind bars right now. And that wasn't going to happened quick enough. They would get to his family before the he said boo to the Feds.

He had no choice. He had to play along with the Zosimoskys until he found out if there was only one infiltrator in the Treasury. If there was, he'd spill his guts to the Feds in return for his family's safety.

Randall licked his lips and laced his tone with a quiver. "I…I'm not threatening you. I'm just on edge here, watching the Feds get closer." His nerves stretched while listening to the silence between them, wondering if the Russian sensed he had something up his sleeve. "Are you there?"

"Yes. Listen. Act normal. Go about your business. I'll take care of things here on my end."

"How?"

"They can't identify you without a witness. I think it's time for Ms. Boyd and her kids to go away for good."

He didn't want another killing, but what choice did he have? It was him and his family or the Boyds. "Do it now."

~~~~

Chapter Twenty-four

"I'm sorry, John. I'd hoped Victor would've been in the second stack of pictures. He wasn't."

Without asking, he'd known the moment Steph entered the room that the package they'd received from the Treasury had been a bust. The light had disappeared from her emerald eyes and John felt helpless to do anything about it.

Victor's true identity was still a mystery.

"Don't apologize. It's not your fault. My gut tells me we're on the right track. The remaining files will be here tomorrow. Until then, relax." He laced his fingers together and resisted the urge to pull her into his arms and comfort her.

"I don't know if I know how to relax anymore." She pulled the band from her hair and scratched the strands loose. The soft light from the lamp behind her danced among the highlights of her glossy tresses.

"Things will work out. Trust me," he said, mesmerized by her beauty.

A smile grew on her full lips and John's heart leapt. The magnetism between them grew stronger as the seconds ticked by. He was losing circulation in his fingers from the effort not to touch her. How he'd love to taste her again. But he couldn't. "I think I need some air."

She glanced at the glass doors leading out to the patio. "Oh, okay. I guess I should check on the kids again."

"Yeah. I think that's probably a good idea." John watched her climb the steps. Was it his imagination or was her exit a bit reluctant?

When her long legs finally disappeared from view, he quickly slid the glass door open and stepped outside, drawing in a long breath. He stared up at the black sky speckled with dazzling stars and allowed himself to relax against the patio's roof column.

He couldn't believe he'd told Steph about Julie and Katie today. Not once in the last two years had he spoken to anyone about that night and what it cost him. Or the fact that he blamed himself for their deaths. Not the shrink his superiors had sent him to. Not his family. Not Luke. No one. Until now.

He was getting too close to the family he swore to protect. The kids were getting to him, especially Bobby. The boy had sought him out and stuck by his side the entire day, asking him questions and at times acting like the man he'd eventually become. The kid had guts. He could handle having a son like Bobby, someday.

John pushed away from the post. He was in trouble. The first rule in witness protection was not to become emotionally involved with the trustees. Preoccupation with a witness could confuse an agent's judgment at a crucial moment, jeopardizing lives. The manual was right. Alex was right. With each passing moment he spent with Stephanie Boyd and her kids, they occupied his every thought. He was beginning to think of them as family.

John stalked further into the backyard, the darkness swallowing him up like life had. During the day, watching her play and laugh with Bobby and Em, Steph made him smile and yearn for something he couldn't have. He had to fight not to touch her.

At night, he clutched his pillow, dreaming of her wearing nothing but that big sweater, reaching for him, wanting him as much as he wanted her. He could almost feel the silkiness of her thighs as he ran his hands up over them, cupping her bare bottom and—

John felt his rise and glanced over his shoulder past the lightening bugs flickering in the darkness. Lights illuminated the mini-blinds on the windows upstairs. It was quiet except for the tree toads call.

Would Steph come back down?

He wanted her to.

Frustration wrapped around his heart. His time with Stephanie was limited. The arrangements had been made. In a few days, whether Steph identified Victor or not, she and the kids were scheduled to be whisked away. They would be starting a new life somewhere.

He knew that wasn't what Steph wanted. She hated the idea of leaving her parents behind, but for the sake of Bobby and Em, she'd have no choice. In a few months perhaps, after this part of her life, including him, faded into a bad memory, she'd meet someone and marry the lucky guy.

His hands curled into fists. He should feel relief for her, happiness even, but he didn't. He didn't want anyone else holding Steph, looking into her soul, making love to her. But what choice did he have?

None.

Laying in the yard at his feet was the blanket the kids had used for their picnic lunch earlier this afternoon.

A pine cone crunched behind him.

John spun on his heel, dropping to his knee. Instinctively, he drew his Sig and aimed in the direction of the sound. He squinted, zeroing in on his target.

"John, it's me. Stephanie," she cried out, her outline frozen in step.

John's heart pounded while a trickle of cold sweat traveled down his spine. He'd almost shot her. "Damn. What are you doing out here? I thought you went up to check on the kids."

"I did. They're still sound asleep. I didn't want to be alone. Are you okay?" Her tone reflected her uneasiness.

He was as okay as a nut case could be studying the outline of legs that he wished were wrapped around his waist.

The weight of the world kept him on his knees.

Barefooted, she approached him cautiously. "John, answer me. Are you okay?"

"Yeah. Why wouldn't I be?" He slid the gun into its holster, trembling as she drew closer. "Where's Alex?"

"She said she was going to take a shower."

A soft summer breeze swirled Steph's sweet scent around him like a seductive cloud, tantalizing him, igniting desire low in his gut.

"I wanted to ask you something."

"Okay," he said. That was all he could utter without disclosing his want for her.

She stepped closer coming into his circle of darkness. Her toes curled into the grass. "You were really quiet during dinner. Is there something you're not telling me?"

As his gaze traveled up her legs, the warm night became hot. He couldn't stand. His knees, his legs, his whole being, felt weak. He was a slave at her feet. Another bead of sweat rolled down John's spine and he ran his tongue across his dry lips. He longed to taste Steph's sweetness and drink from her very center.

Looking up over the swells of her breasts, he gripped his jeans at the side of his legs. He needed to keep from reaching out—touching her would be wrong. "No. I, ah, just needed some time alone."

"Has something happened?"

He heard her anxiety. He'd tell her about the Federal Protection Program tomorrow when she had the light of day to help her work things out. "No, nothing new."

Silence.

"Okay. Then I'll let you alone." She stepped back.

"Don't go." He wanted her all to himself, if only for a few minutes. He reached out, touching the smooth skin above her knee and immediately his desire intensified.

Steph froze under his touch and for a moment he thought he'd made the biggest mistake of his life, until she took a tiny step toward him. His fingers inched around her shapely legs. He closed his eyes and relished the feel of her soft skin against his rough hands.

Stephanie's legs trembled as she willingly inched toward John. For a full minute, he simply held her, breathing in her scent. Her hands combed through his thick hair before trailing down his neck. She massaged his strong shoulders, feeling the strength in them and his upper arms. Power she no longer feared.

As John's hot breath caressed her thighs, Stephanie's knees weakened. He supported her legs against his broad chest while his warm fingers moved, tracing tiny, delectable circles on the back of her thighs. She longed to have him touch her higher.

As if reading her mind, his fingers brushed under the hem of her shorts, sending a shiver of hot desire to her core. The ache between her thighs urged her to move her legs apart.

John's left hand held her in place, while his right slowly searched higher, seeking her already wet center.

What was happening was insane, but she didn't care. Every part of her body cried to feel his touch. She clamped her lips closed, keeping the moan rising in her throat from escaping. She trembled as his finger slid along the silken material of her panties and moved them to the side.

He lifted his head and watched her excitement build while he teased her nub.

She rocked against his hand, needing more. She had to have him inside of her.

"You're so wet," John said, his voice hoarse with need.

When he slipped a finger between her slick folds and entered her, she shuddered with pleasure and clung to John's shoulders while his finger moved in and out, working her into a delicious bliss.

Fuck it. She wanted all of John. If only once. She pulled back and his hand slipped from her, trailing warm juices onto her inner thigh.

His hot gaze snapped up to met hers, questioning.

Tomorrow he might be gone from her life forever. Tonight however, for a few brief moments, she wanted him.

Silently, she lowered to her knees. She heard his quick intake of air as her body moved against his. His broad hand hugged her hips, pulling her closer. His erection pushed against her mound, sending urgent signals to her brain.

"Steph—"

With her fingertips, she trapped his words. She didn't want to think logically. She sealed his lips with her own. Their kisses deepened, and they changed positions, desperately tasting, nipping, wanting more, while their hands sought satisfaction.

John's warm mouth trailed along her neck, nibbling and sucking, sending quivers down her spine. He yanked her top from the waistband of her shorts and his hand burned an impatient path over her ribs. Expertly, he unclasped her bra. She moaned against his lips as his hand cupped her breast. His thumb flicked over its tight peak, again and again, stoking the fire burning inside her.

Stephanie wanted John naked and next to her. She slid her hand to his chest and, with ease, the buttons of his shirt gave way. His coarse curls entwined with her fingers. His hard muscles flexed beneath her palm as he continued his own exploration of her breasts.

The ache between her legs intensified and she reached for his belt.

His breaths came in gasps as he grabbed her hand.

Nose to nose, she stared into his questioning eyes. She was not going to turn back. "I need you, now," she whispered.

"I want you too, but I don't have protection."

"I've only been with one man, ever. I'm clean."

"I haven't been with anyone since Julie." He planted kisses along her neck. "But what about pregnancy?"

"I'm at the end of my cycle. John, there might not be a tomorrow for us." She cut him off, pressing her lips to his. "We have now. Not even tonight. Just right now."

John grasped her head and held her place while crushing her lips.

His zipper rasped in the silent night.

He moaned with pleasure as she slid her hand along the length of him, feeling his heat. His reaction thrilled her.

"I want you to make love to me," she said between hot kisses.

Quickly, he pulled her T-shirt over her head and tossed it and her lace bra to the side.

She pushed his shirt from his shoulders. His coarse chest hairs brushed her taut peaks, shooting charges down her spine. Her breasts ached to be squeezed and licked again and again, but she also needed more.

His hand trembled against her back.

She clung to him, nibbling the saltiness of his neck and enjoyed the musky smell that was John.

His vein pulsed rapidly against her lips and knowing the rush was because of her, she sucked harder.

Breathless, John pulled back only for a second before he dipped his head and pulled her sensitive nipple into his warm mouth.

Her eyes fluttered closed. She let herself relax and enjoy the sensations his tongue triggered as he played with her tight peak, bringing her desire to a fever. Damn. She needed him inside her, now.

"John, please," she pleaded.

He released her breast and slowly laid her on the blanket. His hands burned a trail up her bare leg. The smoky desire in his eyes caused her heart to beat faster. She sealed herself off from the world and waited for the pleasure she knew would come.

Leaning down, he kissed her stomach before stripping off her shorts and panties. She felt his grin on her stomach as his hands splayed across her breasts. Deliciously, his warm lips traced a path to her mound. Stephanie moaned as he parted her and his tongue flicked her nub.

Her body pulsed under his mouth. Her blood raced hot through her veins and she dug her nails dug into his muscular shoulders. Between gritted teeth she ordered him, "John. Now!"

He leaned back on his knees and dropped his pants. Holding himself on his elbows above her, his penis teased her sensitive spot. "You're so beautiful."

"Shut up and do me." Stephanie wound her arms around his neck and pulled him down and jutted her hips forward. Pleasure replaced ache as he parted her.

John hissed a groan.

She smiled against his ear and closed her eyes, centering on her own pleasure.

He slid further inside of her, filling her.

With each thrust, her pleasure grew. She moved her hands down the ridge of his back to his buttocks and urged him to dive deeper into her depths.

Urgently, he pushed up, arching his back, straining into her.

Her body clenched around him, sending him over the edge before she followed.

John's mouth crushed hers and behind sealed lips, their bliss climaxed.

.

~~~~

Chapter Twenty-five

John was starved. He hadn't had much of an appetite the last few days, but in the afterglow of making love to Steph, he was famished. Any sane agent would consider what happened between them an erroneous mistake in judgment on his part. But well, he already knew he wasn't rational.

Being with Steph had felt so right. His groin tightened, thinking how her pulsing warmth had surrounded him. She had given herself freely. If she gave him the opportunity to make love to her again, he would before—

He wasn't going to think about what would happen in the next several days. Thinking about her disappearing forever made him sick.

He was happy. For the first time in years, he wore a smile. John grabbed a chicken leg from the paper bucket and bit into it.

"Where's mommy?" The child's voice startled him. It was well after midnight. John peered, chicken leg in mouth, over the refrigerator's door at Em. She stood, dressed in an oversized T-shirt, clutching her teddy bear in one hand while rubbing the little sleep she'd had from her eyes with the other.

Anxiety tightened his gut and he glanced over her head, searching and hoping for Stephanie to be right behind her daughter. But she wasn't. Water still cascaded through the pipes from the bathroom overhead. John groaned. He was on his own.

He swung the door shut, pulled the chicken leg from his mouth and swallowed the lump in his throat. He was acting foolish. If he'd learned anything in the last couple of hours, it was that Stephanie was not Julie and this child was not Katie. It was time he faced his fears.

"Your mommy…She's taking a shower."

Em's tiny lower lip puckered.

She wasn't happy with his statement. What would he do if she started to cry?

"It hurts," Em whined, pulling at her hair.

Okay. Something hurt. What in hell was he supposed to do about it? John glanced toward the ceiling. The shower upstairs still ran. Damn.

He focused on Em, again. She continued to tug at something. It would be heartless to tell the kid to go tell her mom without at least trying to find out what was wrong. Concerned, John dropped to his knee. "What hurts? Your belly?"

That was stupid. She was pulling at her hair. What did he know? Kids' bellies usually were the problem.

"No. It hurts my hair." She combed through her fine hair and pulled the strand forward. The tiny purple clip she wore was tangled in her mass of blonde curls.

John gulped. Helping her would involve touching. He didn't know if he could.

"Ouch." Em continued to whine while she tried to pull the butterfly clip out of her hair on her own.

John glanced at the ceiling again. The water ran nonstop.

He had no choice; he had to help her. "I'm not an expert but I think I can help, if you'd let me. Can I try?"

Em's head bopped up and down.

"Okay, turn around." John trapped the chicken leg in his mouth again, stood, grabbed a paper napkin off the table and wiped the grease from his hands. Em's shoulders felt like chicken wings as he pulled her toward him. "Let me see," he mumbled around the leg while he surveyed the mess and tried to decide the best way to remove the clip without pulling Em's hair.

Her baby-fine hair was as soft as any rabbit's fur he'd ever felt. Katie immediately popped into his head. John fingers stilled.

Em tugged her hair.

With his teeth biting into the chicken bone, he fumbled for a minute with the tiny plastic clip. He snapped it open and in half.

"I'm sorry, it broke," he muttered as she turned.

"It's okay. It was old." She scratched her head where the clip had been. Static electricity made the fine strands take flight. John couldn't help but chuckle while he placed the clip in her tiny hand.

Happiness danced in her green eyes. They were so like her mother's. Suddenly he realized the chicken leg was still clamped between his teeth. He grabbed the bone's end and released it. Em's stare followed the leg.

"Are you hungry?" He worked the tension from his jaw by moving it back and forth.

She smiled up at him, exposing the gap between her teeth. Her mass of hair fell forward and she swiped it back. "Yeah! And Mr. Blakeslee. We're starvin'."

John chuckled. He rose and opened the refrigerator. "Well, I think there is a big leg in here with your name on it. A special barbequed one. Why don't you and your bear climb up at the table, and I'll get some plates."

Without hesitation, Em scampered to the table and waited patiently as John returned with plates and napkins. Em anxiously leaned into her chicken leg and her hair fell into her eyes, again.

John could see a mess in the making. "Wait."

Em's questioning eyes turned up at him.

His right fingers hesitated on the band on his left hand's little finger. He wore a hair band like Katie had worn to remind himself of his shame. It was only a rubber band. Nothing would erase the memories of his last moments with his little girl. They would stay with him forever.

He drew a breath and quickly pulled the band from his little finger. "Let's get that hair tied back before there's barbeque sauce in it."

Twenty minutes later, in the midst of having a serious conversation with Em and Mr. Blakeslee, Em's bear, John glanced over and saw Steph standing in the doorway.

She wore an expression most women displayed when something touched their hearts. He guessed her small grin was because Mr. Blakeslee sat on his lap and not on Em's. He couldn't let Em hold the stuffed toy. Her mouth, from cheek to cheek and tiny fingers were smeared with barbeque sauce.

Stephanie's hair was piled on top of her head. The oversized white T-shirt she wore, similar to Em's, hid her legs above her knees, but not her nipples. John's reaction to the sight of her pressed against Mr. Blakeslee.

"What are you two doing?" Steph pushed away from the door's jam.

Surprised by her mother's voice, Em spun around on her chair. Smiling, she held her sticky fingers up for Stephanie to see. "We're eatin' chicken, Mom."

Stephanie's smile grew as she padded across the floor. "I see. Don't you think it's kind of late to be eating chicken?"

"No. Mr. Blakeslee and John and me were hungry." Em shook her head, whirled on her chair and grabbed her leg.

"We had a bit of a problem," John said.

"Oh."

He nodded toward Em. "Her hair clip was tangled in her hair."

"It hurt," Em mumbled while gnawing on what was left of a full leg. "John got it out. He broke it."

Stephanie's brow shot up. "He did?"

"Yeah, I'm sorry." He picked up the broken clip and showed it to her.

"No. I mean, you got it out?"

"Don't look so surprised."

Her cheeks warmed as her hands rested on Em's shoulders. "It's just you didn't seem to like—I mean you haven't—"

"I know what you're trying to say." John looked at Em. "I've had a hard time dealing with…"

It suddenly hit her. Em reminded John of his daughter. After he'd told her about his family's death, she should've realized.

The muscles in John's neck worked as he visibly swallowed the pain she knew he'd carried for years. She understood part of his torment. Even though Gene had been her ex-husband, she'd had at least a moment to say goodbye to him. A chill cut deep into her. But, she'd never lost a child.

Stephanie smoothed Em's silky hair. Her daughter's warmth cascaded up her arms, through her body and to her melancholy heart.

Honestly, if she lost Bobby or Em, she knew she'd die of heartbreak. How John had managed to carry on, to live a productive life, to remain sane was beyond her. His strength and courage put her in awe of him.

Her fingers touched a rubber band and her gaze darted to John's hand. The band was gone. It had meant something to him and now he'd given it up for Em.

Wanting to ease his anguish, Stephanie moved from behind her daughter and touched his shoulder. "Thank you, John."

His sad expression creased to confused lines. "For what?"

She smiled. "For being the man you are."

John's expression was a mixture of pain and hope. She wanted to pull him close, feel his strong body melt into hers again and make him forget everything which caused his sorrow. Forever. But she couldn't, not with Em watching. Besides there wouldn't be a forever for them.

"John," Em called, breaking the trace between them. "Can Mr. Blakeslee go with you to get my Italian ice tomorrow? He knows what kind I like."

"Sure, kid."

Stephanie's heart melted all over again as she watched John and her daughter decide on their favorite flavor of ice. When the time came, leaving John was going to be too damn hard.

~~~~

Chapter Twenty-six

Garlic was supposed to be good for a headache.
Stephanie thought she'd read that somewhere. Smelling the
aroma for the last half hour hadn't helped. The pounding
now echoed in her head. It was stress and no amount of
garlic, or anything, was going to help unless she relaxed.

She rolled her shoulders and willed the tension from
her neck muscles. While she checked the backyard via the
kitchen window, she closed yet another cupboard door. The
house stood back, maybe a quarter of a mile, from the main
street and was surrounded by a thin forest. John had walked
down the drive to check on the mail a half hour ago. Where
was he?

Stephanie quickly blocked the thought that something
might've happened to him. He was probably just checking
with the agents who stood guard around the house.

"You mean to tell me Em can't have spaghetti either?"
Alex's offer to make dinner was turning out to be a bit of a
nightmare. Frustration angled the agent's features. She
dropped the box of dry noodles to the counter. Everything
she pulled from the cupboards, Stephanie shot down.
Stephanie had to, for Em's sake. One bite of anything
containing wheat, milk, or peanuts and Em's throat would
swell closed.

"No. She's allergic to wheat. You can make spaghetti.
I'll find something to make her. There has to be something
here." Stephanie yanked open the next cupboard door and

stared inside. "More than half the items I had on the list weren't delivered."

"That's not fair to Em. She'll sit and watch us all enjoying pasta while she eats what lettuce? She can have my homemade sauce, right?" Alex pointed to the pot simmering on the stove.

The contrast between what seemed to be Alex's Treasury issued suit and the apron decorated with red and green hot chili peppers made Stephanie chuckle inside, regardless of her throbbing headache.

"Yes. She's fine with all the ingredients." Maybe she'd misread Alex, thinking the woman was a cold agent. Mosely actually seemed concerned about Em. Alex had a heart after all.

"Isn't there a type of pasta she can have?" Alex rooted in the kitchen's small desk tucked in its corner.

"Yes. But it has to be wheat free and milk free." From the corner of her eye, Stephanie saw John cross the lawn. Relief washed over her. A second later her breath caught. He carried another priority mail package—a larger one this time.

Bobby ran up to him, probably asking his hundredth question of the day. The attachment forming between the two worried Stephanie. If Victor's picture was in that box, they could be leaving here as early as tomorrow.

Pangs of loneliness gripped her heart. She shouldn't be feeling heartache over a man she'd only known for a few days, but she did. Something had happened between them last night. They had grown closer and not because they'd shared their bodies.

Something more.

They had helped each other forget their pasts and take a step towards life.

"I'll check the pantry and see if they left a box with Em's supplies in there," Alex said, already on her way out of the room.

Stephanie sighed. She wanted to forget about the box John carried, its contents and what would happen after they reviewed the pictures. She wanted to crawl into John's arms and feel his lips on hers. She ached for his touch again, even though she knew her desire was fruitless.

She turned as John pushed open the backdoor and stepped into the room. Her headache became a distance memory as his gaze met hers. Excitement of the hunt sparked in his raven eyes and she knew what he wanted from her. Victor's identity.

She had to tell him about Gene's involvement. Maybe the information would help uncover a lead. She didn't know how it could, after lying to him, but she had to tell him the truth. As soon as she found the right moment.

"Did the pictures come?" Alex entered the room and broke the trance between them.

John looked at Alex. "Yes." He pulled the box from the crook of his arm and placed it on the table. He turned back to Stephanie. "We can start anytime you're ready."

Stephanie inhaled and exhaled slowly. This was it. John was depending on her to help solve his case. Once she did, he'd be gone. She had to face reality. There was no future for them. She licked her suddenly dry lips and said, "Let's do it. I want to get this over with."

"Before you do, we have a problem." Alex flashed an assuring smile at Stephanie before she faced John.

"What's wrong?" His body immediately tensed.

"Supply didn't bring most of the items Stephanie asked for. There's barely anything in this house for Em to eat. They filled the cupboards with the usual stuff for kids.

Macaroni and cheese, pizza bagels, those packaged noodle soups, peanut butter crackers, all things she can't have."

Alex was over exaggerating. There were some items in the cupboards Em could have, just not pasta.

Alex shifted her weight and posted a fist on her hip. "Don't look at me like I just came from another world, John. We have basically nothing here for the kid to eat. I'm making pasta for dinner and she can't have it."

"We might not be here for dinner." John traced the box top with his fingers and Stephanie's heart fell.

"Of course we will. Even if Stephanie finds Victor's or the bean counter's picture in there, we won't move until tomorrow. You know that." Alex's jaw firmed.

John leaned toward Alex as if his hearing had gone. He looked confused and a bit amused by her.

Stephanie shrugged her shoulders when he glanced her way. She had no clue why the change in Alex. Maybe she had an encounter with Em. Em had gotten to John last night.

"Ok. I promised her Italian ice anyway," John said. "I'll run into town and get what we need for a few days."

"No!" Alex fumbled with the apron knotted at her waist. "You won't have a clue as to what I need for tonight and what Em can have. I'll at least take time to read labels. You stay here with Stephanie. You can help her go through the files. If we're lucky, tonight's dinner will be our celebration dinner.

"I'll pick up some fresh Italian bread too." Alex's brow ceased with an afterthought. "Oh, that's right. Maybe I shouldn't. Em can't have it."

"No. That's okay. Em will be fine with others eating bread." A few days ago, Stephanie would've agreed whole heartily with Alex about the celebration. But now, part of her wished Victor's picture wasn't in the box and that she and John and the kids could stay here a little longer, pretending to be a family.

Alex finally worked the tie of the apron free, ripped it off and tossed it on the desk. She grabbed a pad and pen and handed them to Steph. "Make a list of what you need for at least three days and I'll go get the stuff. The poor kid has got to eat. I'll be right back down. I just want to grab my purse."

"A purse?" John's brow's arched.

"Yes. Women carry purses. I am a woman and I need to look average."

As John opened his mouth, Alex stuck her index finger in his face. "Don't say it." She backed away. "Put a few of Bobby's favorite things on the list, too, Stephanie. These kids deserve something special." Alex headed for the stairs. "And stir my sauce for me."

"What has gotten into her?" John faced Stephanie. He still wore a baffled expression.

"I have no clue. Maybe she just feels the need to do something normal too. She seems to love to cook." Stephanie picked up the pot's lid. Steam carried the herb and garlic scent swirling in the air.

"I didn't think Alex had *any* domestic skills. I figured she was born with a Colt 45 in her hand."

"Apparently, you don't know her."

The amusement faded from John's face as he moved to stand beside her. Every nerve in her body went on alert. In a flash, the ache to be held by him overtook her sadness.

"I don't really know her. We only worked together once, a few months ago. When this all started. It wasn't a good experience."

Torment rung in his voice. Something had happened between them. She tapped the spoon on the edge of the pot and rested it on the spoon caddy. "What happened?"

"She killed my partner."

His frank statement forced Stephanie's hand to her chest. "She what?"

"It was an accident. We had Victor surrounded—or we thought we did. There was so much going on. Luke, my partner, shifted positions and came up behind Alex. She spun and fired—"

"Oh, my God. Now, I understand why you didn't want her with us."

"Internal affairs cleared her, but I had this feeling—I couldn't trust her."

"And you do now?"

"She's apologized more times than I can count. And, she saved Zohara and me the other day. If she hadn't shown up, we'd be dead. I guess I owe her a second chance." He pointed to the box. "When do you want to look at these?"

He was anxious to get Victor. Now, she understood another reason why. Victor hadn't pulled the trigger, killing his partner but it was because of him Alex had.

"I don't want the kids seeing us go through them. They'll ask questions. Let me put Em down for a nap. I'll ask Bobby to sit with her. Maybe he'll nap too. Then we can get started."

With her hand on the back door handle, she turned to John. "Don't worry. I have a feeling you'll get him soon."

****

An hour later, Stephanie opened the second of four files and continued to scan the faces of the personnel at the

Treasury Department in Philadelphia. Not one of the hundreds of faces in the first file had looked vaguely familiar.

John sat next to her, waiting. His muscles tensed, like a lion ready to pounce on its prey.

She had to tell him about Gene. She scooted her chair back.

"Where are you going?" John looked startled that she'd stopped scanning the pictures.

"I need a break." She rose and stretched her arms toward the ceiling.

His gaze immediately traced the outline of her chest. She lowered her arms. Her face warmed while she thought about John's hands cupping her breasts last night. She had to stop thinking about the past and concentrate on what was best for her and the kids in the future. John wasn't in it, so there was no point in thinking about him or his hands or his…

She checked the sauce on the stove and glanced at the clock. "Alex should be back soon."

"Probably another forty-five minutes. It's twenty into town." John thumbed through the files. "Why did they include females? I told Stover to get the male files only. Damn. No wonder it took so long to send these."

"And you're telling me to relax."

John leaned back on his chair and exhaled a cleansing breath. "You're right. I need to relax."

He grabbed his coffee cup and kept her pinned in place with his intense stare as he drank the last swallow and licked the last drop from his lips.

Stephanie's blood heated under his scrutiny. She didn't know which way to turn. She picked up a tea-towel, wiped the counter and tossed it back down. "I think I should check on the kids."

"Okay." His gaze followed her. "I'll grab us a couple of sodas and the files. We'll finish looking at these in the living room."

"Sounds good." She scooted by him before he could rise and block her exit.

She ran up the stairs and stayed a little longer than it took for her to see both kids were fine and asleep. She needed…or rather, she and John both needed, a moment to cool the attraction building between them.

When she came down the steps, she hesitated on the landing. He had their drinks and the files on the coffee table positioned in a way so she'd have to sit next to him on the sofa.

Maybe sitting in the living room wasn't such a good idea.

She smoothed her hands along her sides. Okay. Cool. Calm. He wanted to find the bad guy. She wanted to find the bad guy. They both wanted to get out of this house and go on with their lives.

Part of her screamed, *No, not without John*. But that wasn't a possibility. What had happened between them had been sex. Hot sex. But that was all. As soon as she pointed out Victor or the bean counter, John would be gone. She knew that. He owed her nothing. She owed him everything.

Noticing her, John stood. "Are they sleeping?"

"Yes. Bobby fell asleep at the bottom of the bed. He had a bat in his hand. Looks as if he fell asleep while on duty."

"I'll have to talk to him about that."

"You look tired. Why don't you stretch out and nap while I look at these." She walked to the seat across from him, but John grabbed her hand as she reached for the files.

"We'll do this together." Still holding her by the hand, he directed her around the table. "I've been watching you."

She looked up at him. "I know."

"This isn't easy for you. You're doing great."

She felt as if she had no backbone at all, standing so close John. She wanted to lean into him. Become one with him again.

But she couldn't. Not here. And time and circumstances wouldn't allow for them to ever again know each. She'd had her moment with John. It was time to move on. He was anxious for her to sit down and get to work. "Thanks. I'm trying hard."

His lips lifted into an assuring smile. He released her hand and she sat. She felt the heat of his body as he took a seat next to her and flipped opened the next manila folder. "Take your time. We want you to be positive in identifying the guy. No mistakes."

We. He always said we, reminding her of who he was. John Dolton, Federal Agent, sitting next to her, doing his duty, nothing more. She drew a breath and pushed her disappointment aside. Biting her lip, she flipped through the file papers and scrutinized each picture carefully. Doing so was important to John. He wouldn't give up until he found the mastermind behind the heists.

She turned page after page and nothing. Frustration flared as she slapped the file closed. "I was so sure we'd find him."

"We have one more packet to go." John picked up the file and patted it. "He's here and we're getting closer. I know it."

"What will happen after I point him out?" The words had erupted from her. She needed to know if the next few minutes here were the last ones she'd have with John.

"What do you mean?"

"I know how much you want this guy. I'm sure you want to be there when he goes down, for Luke's sake. Will you leave as soon as Alex gets back? Will I ever see you again?"

He remained silent.

"I need to know, John. I feel something—"

His gaze lowered to her mouth, stopping her in mid-thought. Her pulse quickened as his tongue moistened his lips. He settled his arm around her back. His leg brushed against hers, sending a shiver up her spine.

John's hand visibly trembled as he traced the outline of her jaw. "Steph, I want you to know I never meant to—"

"You don't have to say it. I know what happened between us shouldn't have. We both knew last night was all there was ever going to be."

His expression turned sympathetic as he cupped her face in his hand. "I have to go after him, for Luke's sake."

"I know, you have no choice." He couldn't put his past to rest unless he saw this thing through. She loved that about him.

The thought caused her heartbeat to catch. She was falling for him.

Damn, maybe it was best if John did ride off on his white horse to save the world and leave her behind. She had no place in his world. And hers—well, she had no idea where she and the kids would be tomorrow. She turned her head and kissed his palm.

An explosion resounded through the house. Glass splintered the air. Pain ripped through Stephanie as the blast threw them to the floor.

With her ears ringing, Stephanie moaned and rolled off of John.

"Steph, are you okay?"

She heard his muffled cry. She struggled to open her eyes. Through a fog she saw John kneeing next to the couch, looking around the room as if he was searching for her.

She was right there. Why was he calling for her when she was right beside him? He looked frantic. Why?

She wanted him to hold her and make her feel safe.

He sat on the floor next to her. "Can you hear me, Steph?" Deep furrows lined his forehead. Blood trickled from a cut on his cheek.

She reached for him and winced. "My arm."

"Don't move," he ordered.

His fingers applied pressure as he checked her arm. She licked her dry lips. "I think it's broken." She fought the pain. Through the fog she heard a faint cry. Or were her ears ringing?

She drew a breath and coughed. Her eyes flew open. Her kids. Smoke crawled along the ceiling. She searched past John. A jagged hole fractured the wall between the kitchen and dining room. The wallpaper was covered with soot. The windows were blown out. The curtains were shredded into rags and on fire. Flames licked at what was left of the cabinets and they climbed upward.

"The kids. I've got to get Bobby and Em. They're crying. I can hear them." She slapped John's hand away and pushed herself up off the floor.

He grabbed her good arm.

She stumbled against him. Her thoughts blurred. Nausea rolled her stomach. "Help me. Please. I've got to get to the kids."

John flipped the debris covered cushion of the chair to the floor and pushed her onto the chair. "Stay here. Guard the door. I'll get them. We'll all go out together."

He pulled his weapon out of its holster and placed it in her hand. It felt cold and heavy. "If anyone—I mean anyone—comes in here. Kill them."

She stared up at him. "John, I can't—"

"Yes. You can. Now focus. Don't trust anyone." He took the steps two at a time. He had no choice but to leave Steph there. He couldn't take her outside. Whoever had set the explosion would be waiting for them.

He had to get to the kids. He could hear their screams. Adrenaline pumped through his veins. The bathroom door, blasted off its hinges, blocked the landing. With a hard thrust, he threw it aside. Flames ate through the bathroom floor. It would only be a matter of minutes before the whole house was engulfed.

Smoke burned a path into John's lungs. Coughing, he covered his mouth with his shirt, veered around the banister and forged through the debris in the hallway toward the bedroom where Em and Bobby were.

The door was jammed.

"Bobby, can you hear me," he screamed over the crackle behind him.

"We can't out," Bobby cried. "Should we go to the window?"

"No," John shouted. They would be sitting ducks to a sniper. "Stand back."

"I want Mommy," Em wailed.

"Mommy is waiting downstairs. Go with Bobby."

Flames curled its tendrils around the bathroom's door frame. Soon the floor to the stairs would give away.

Concentrating on the door in front of him, he drew a quick breath under his shirt and hurled himself toward the door with all his weight and strength. The jam splintered on impact and the door crashed against the wall with such force, the handle went through the drywall. John collapsed to the floor.

"Cool," Bobby exclaimed.

They stood in the far corner. They were unharmed, so far. Em looked as scared as she had the day of the mall shootout, but Bobby...excitement beamed in his eyes.

Relief washed through John. He extended his hand to them. "Let's get out of here."

Both children ran to him and he scooped Em up in his arms. She wrapped her arms around his neck tight as noose. He grabbed Bobby's hand. "Stay right by me, Bobby. Don't let go."

Flames now danced along the walls. Dense smoke hung like a thick, dirty veil of cotton from the ceiling. He hoped the floor joists were still able to hold their weight. If not, they'd go crashing through the floor.

"Cover your mouths. Em, close your eyes."

"Mr. Blakeslee," she screamed and threw herself back, jarring John off balance.

John stumbled but regained his footing immediately. He scooped the stuffed animal off the bed and handed it to Em. She slipped her toy between them and tucked her face into its fake fur.

Out of the corner of his eye, he saw Stephanie's purse. She kept Em's Epipen in there. Snatching the bag off the dresser, he slung it over his other shoulder and grabbed Bobby's hand. While he hunched down, with Em hanging on him like a bear cub herself, the foursome edged out into the hallway.

"Remember, Em, you and Mr. Blakeslee keep your eyes shut and your mouth and nose covered," he whispered into her ear.

The fire roared. Smoke bellowed around them. Bobby hesitated.

"Stay with me, kid. We're going to be okay."

Overwhelming heat fanned toward them. It was now or never. He hurried along the banister, pulling Bobby with him. They rounded the railing and raced down the steps.

"Mommy," Em called.

Seeing Stephanie slumped over in the winged-chair, John's racing heart stalled. His Sig lay in her limp hand. Was she dazed or had someone got to her?

The heat above them was becoming unbearable. He scanned the area for any movement before he dropped Em to her feet. He draped Steph's bag over Bobby's neck. "Get down on your knees. Go next to the door. Not out."

Bobby captured Em's hand and pulled her to the floor with him.

John snatched up his gun, stuffed it into his belt and carefully grabbed Steph by her good arm hoisting her over his shoulder.

She moaned in protest.

"That-a-girl, you tell me," John said, happy to hear her reaction. "Relax. I'm gonna' get you out of here."

With Steph firmly planted on his shoulder, he drew his weapon. The assassin could still be waiting outside. "Let's get out of here," he said to the kids.

A moment after they'd stepped through the threshold, the floor joist above them gave way, sending the second floor crashing to the first. The kids scurried around him. Sparks and ash spiraled around them.

Em's cry mixed with the sirens that wailed in the distance. They huddled against his legs. Em held her mother's dangling hand. Her bottom lip quivered with terror as she stared up at Steph.

"Shh. You've got to be quiet, babe." John's eyes watered. Where the hell were the agents guarding the perimeter? They should've responded the moment the blast ignited.

His insides turned cold. Unless they couldn't.

How in the hell did Victor find them?

The sirens grew louder. The emergency vehicles were getting closer. The onset of police and fire personal would force the assassin to run. He had to get Steph and the kids out of there. They couldn't be seen by anyone. The longer they were assumed dead, the better. It would give them a chance to get away and time for him to think.

They didn't have a car. Mosely had taken hers. He had to find one.

"This way." He led the kids toward the wood line, watching for any movement. The first emergency vehicles arrived as they hurried into the shadows. Em and Bobby stayed close to his heels. The cover gave him both a sense of security and apprehension.

They circled the property all the while listening to the firemen shouting. Fire and water battled over the remains of the house. The scent of charred wood permeated the air.

A few minutes later, they came upon the area where one of the agents had parked his vehicle. John could see its blue roof beyond the brush. He slid his gun into its holster, lowered Steph to the ground and leaned her up against an oak tree.

She was still dazed. She'd taken the blunt of the force from the blast and probably had a concussion.

"Steph, can you hear me?" He cupped her face in his hands. "Steph."

"Mmm. Yes." Her eyes fluttered opened. She winced and cradled her arm.

He didn't think it was broken, just badly bruised.

"Bobby. Em," she mumbled.

"Steph, the kids need you to stay awake. Understand," he said while he unbuckled his belt and tugged it from his pants. He buckled it again and looped it over Steph's head, creating a sling. Carefully he helped her slip her arm through the loop.

She looked up at him and joy washed through John.

She started to rise. "John, we've got to get to them."

He held her in place with his hand on her leg. "Stay still. They're here. Bobby, come here. Em, you sit over here." John placed the kids on either side of Steph. "Talk to your mom about anything."

Seeing her children, Steph sighed with relief. Em curled under her good arm while she laid her head against Bobby's. They were safe, but for how long?

"I'll be right back." John pushed back on his heels.

"Where are you going?" Fear widened Steph's drowsy eyes.

"We need a ride to get us out of here. I'm going to find one." He placed his hand on hers. "I promise. I'll be right back."

She turned his hand up and kissed his palm. The simple act of affection grabbed at his heart. He wasn't going to fail her. Determined, he pushed off and ran toward the agent's pickup truck. It was parked in a shallow clearing just off the highway. The agent's cover, a couple of fishing rods, hung on the rack in the back window.

John eased his Sig out of its scabbard as he approached the truck from the rear. No one was in the vehicle as far as he could see. Slowly, he crept forward on the passenger side and eased up, peering through the window. The back seat was empty except for a small cooler and a jacket. He moved forward and his stomach knotted. The agent sat slumped forward at an odd angle. A knife protruded from his neck.

~~~~

Chapter Twenty-seven

Warm air blew into the cab through their open windows. The air flow helped to rid the pickup's cab of the smoke smell which clung to each of them like a heavy cloak.

Bobby's dog-tired stare reflected back at John in the rearview mirror. A quick glance over his shoulder told him Em slept cuddled against Mr. Blakeslee on the other side of the cab.

Trauma had a way of making one tired. He was.

John glanced at Steph. At least she seemed better. She sat straight and diligently watched the road ahead. Maybe she was getting used to the action. Her face was smudged with soot and dried blood. Her hair was a mess, made wilder by the breeze. She still made his heart race.

Her arm, thank God, wasn't broken. He forced his attention to the winding stretch of I-80 while he gripped the steering wheel tighter. He sped by a tractor-trailer heading west toward Potter county.

He'd done what he vowed he'd never do again. He screwed up royally. He let his desire for Steph get in the way of doing his duty to guard her and the kids. If he'd been concentrating on protecting them, instead of thinking about kissing and holding Steph in his arms one more time while the kids were napping and Alex was gone, he'd have heard someone planting a bomb next to the house.

He knew once Steph identified Victor or the bean counter, he'd have to leave her. He had no choice. He needed to be in on the son of a bitch's capture, for Luke's sake. Afterwards, chances of seeing Steph again would be slim. He'd never have the opportunity to be alone with her again. His gut twisted knowing, beyond this case, they had no future.

When had she and the kids become more than a job to him?

Thinking about the last few days, he couldn't pin-point the moment when they'd captured his heart. All he knew was they had.

"Where was the agent?" Steph asked tearing him away from his thoughts.

"What agent?" He knew damn well who she referred to.

"The one who had this truck."

He saw her gaze dart toward the floor board in front of the console where he'd purposely rolled and stuffed the dead agent's coat to cover up the blood stain. "Don't ask."

Her face paled as she inhaled a shallow breath. The scent of blood and death tinted the cab's interior. He was sure she had a pretty good idea of what had happened to the man.

Steph propped her elbow on the cab's door and held her head. A full three minutes went by before she turned to him again and asked, "Where are we going?"

"Where no one will find us."

She glanced at Bobby before leaning toward John. "Do you mean we're leaving now?"

He heard the panic in her hushed tone. He glanced at the rearview mirror. Bobby's head dropped forward as he fell asleep. "No. That situation is going to be delayed," John replied quietly while changing lanes.

She sighed, and he'd noted the relief in her eyes. She was still holding onto hope. She didn't want to leave her home. Eventually, her heart would be broken, if they didn't get this ring busted.

"I'm taking you to my cabin, in the mountains. Remember, I told you about it. We'll be safe there until…"

"Until what?"

"Until we get them. We were on the right track, Steph. Maybe Victor will trip over himself trying to find you. Make a mistake. He's frightened. He knows we have the files."

"But the files burnt, and we still don't know who he is."

"No, but once it leaks out our bodies aren't found, he'll know we escaped. When a new set of files aren't ordered he'll assume we still have them."

"His picture had to be in the last envelope."

"Right." John nodded. "We were close. We'll get him." He wanted to touch her, reassure her, but he didn't dare. Feeling her soft skin would ignite the desire he was trying to forget. He gave her an assuring smile instead.

Steph visibility relaxed against the seat. She watched the passing mountains silently for a moment. Combing her hair away from her face, she faced him. "How did they find the safe house, John?"

"I don't know. There's got to be a mole leaking information back to Victor. Only a handful of our people knew of our location. The agents assigned to guard the house, Ben, Alex's superior and Alex, of course."

"Oh, my God. Alex." Steph covered her mouth. "I forgot all about her. Thank, God she left. She was so persistent watching over her sauce. She would've been killed for sure."

"Or she would've heard the attackers." Unless…John's mind whirled. Alex always missed the action. Uneasiness snaked into his gut.

His cell phone vibrated against his hip, jarring him away from his direction of thought. He shifted his weight on the seat and snatched it off the clip. He checked the number before saying to Steph, "Speak of the devil. It's Alex. Don't say anything."

He hit the speaker button. "Dolton."

"John. Thank God." Alex sounded truly relieved. "I was hoping you'd answer and not be inside under the rubble. I came back with the groceries to this. Where the hell are you? Where are Stephanie and the kids? Are they with you?"

"Yeah, the kids are fine. I got them out in time. Steph—" He hesitated for effect, looking at Steph. "She was in the kitchen, checking on your sauce."

"Is she dead?"

Had he recognized a bit of hope in Alex's tone or was it his imagination?

Steph's eyebrow arched. She had heard it too.

Apprehension grabbed him by the throat.

"No. She went to the refrigerator for something. That's where I found her," he said, sounding troubled. "The door shielded her from the blast. She has a broken arm and a concussion. I'm going to take her to a hospital. In a small town. They'll accept a camping accident as a reason for her injuries without asking a lot of questions."

"Where? I'll meet you there."

"I don't know yet. We're headed north on the PA turnpike." He held the phone closer to his mouth so that it seemed he'd raised his voice. "The reception up here is terrible. You keep cutting in and out. I'll call you from a landline." He turned the phone off and snapped it shut without giving Alex a chance to debate him.

Steph brushed her hair back. "We're not headed north. Isn't she going to know? Doesn't this vehicle have GPS system?"

"I disabled it. Shut your cell phone off."

"My battery died days ago. Why did you lie to her? You don't think Alex had anything to do with the explosion, do you?"

He had no concrete proof, but the hairs on the back of his neck stood on end while he'd talked to her. It had been a miracle she'd showed up in time to rescue him and Zohara, and it had been a miracle she hadn't been in the kitchen, stirring her special sauce. Two miracles after one big mistake. Or, had Luke's death been a mistake?

He needed to talk to Ben.

"Do you believe her?" Steph waited for his answer.

"I'm not going to trust anyone but you, me and those two kids back there until this thing is over."

****

Damn. John was onto her. She wasn't a fool. Alex stared at her cell as if she faced John himself. Her jaw tightened. The man thought he was so good. How had he made her?

Her mind raced. She'd played it cool. Left the house. Killed one agent and the other without incident. No witnesses. She'd made it back through the woods with the package of explosives she'd hidden in the trunk of her car without being sighted. She hadn't made a damn mistake.

She whipped the phone shut and stuffed it in her jacket's pocket. Drawing her frame erect, she squared her shoulders and turned to watch the local volunteer firefighters finish dousing the flames she'd ignited.

As far as they knew, there was still a family inside what was left of the charred structure. Up to a minute ago she'd had a sense of triumph. Until she'd hit the recall button on her cell and John had answered.

He was the one who'd screwed up. They'd never heard her outside the house, mounting the package to the propane tank. It didn't surprise her one bit. Over the last few days, it was so apparent how much John and Stephanie were into each other. Last night was the kicker though. Neither John nor Stephanie had seen or heard her while she watched them get it on from the shadows. She clenched her lips together, trapping the chuckle welling up in her belly. John was like every other man—a fool who thought with his dick.

She mentally tisked. Where was the man's integrity?

Alex had to admit, she would've like to have a go at John herself. Watching him suck his way into the bitch's heart had made her own breasts tighten. She could've popped them right then, with one bullet, and walked away. But what alibi would she have had? She was supposed to be guarding the Boyds too.

She had a better plan. One that would leave her cover intact. As a Treasury agent she could do so much for the family.

No regrets. After she got rid of John, Stephanie and her two brats, she and Victor would continue with the plans. Soon she'd be vacationing on the Riviera, screwing whatever *dick* she wanted.

She smiled at the volunteer hunk walking toward her.

Where were Stephanie and John?

He wasn't headed north. She was sure of that. She turned and stalked to her car. John would call his buddy. Her smile widened.

When he did, she'd be standing next to Stover.

~~~~

Chapter Twenty-eight

Stephanie's arm hurt, but she wasn't going to be a wimp about it. She yanked off the last sheet covering the sparse cabin furniture, quickly balled the dusty cloth, and piled it on top of the pine dining table.

And she wasn't stupid.

Victor, or whatever his real damn name was, and his henchmen, had given her no choice. She hated the thought of handling a gun but she didn't intend to be a sitting goose. The slain FBI agent—yes, slain...John had tried to protect her from the fact, but she knew. The agent had stowed an arsenal in his pickup. She would carry a weapon with her at all times, just in case.

The door banged against the wall and she jumped.

Dust particles flittered in the bright sunlight as John pushed through the threshold. He struggled with the limp mattress he'd carried outside earlier to freshen in the mountain air. His strong biceps bulged slightly as he tried to get a good hold on the bed pad.

She'd felt safe in those arms but if anything happened to him, she'd be defenseless against the criminals stalking them. Her hands curled into fists as her shoulders squared. She wasn't going to let them kill her children.

"Let me help you." She grabbed one end of the heavy mattress as if it were the neck of an intruder, lifting it off the floor. Her strength seemingly surprised John because his brow shot up.

"Ah, thanks. I think this mattress gets heavier each time I carry it outside to air. I really should invest in a new one, but I only get up here once, maybe twice, a year, for a day or two." John back peddled into the only bedroom in the cabin—the one she would share with the kids. He intended to sleep on the couch or up in the loft.

After she helped him lift the full-sized pad onto the creaky iron bed frame, she sat down on it. "I need to talk to you while the kids are outside."

"Okay. About?" he mumbled while trying to open a package with his teeth. The plastic bag contained new sheets he'd bought at the little country store they'd stopped at before climbing the mountain. Thinking of such details, the man touched her in ways no one ever had.

She laughed watching him struggle. "Give me that." She snatched the package away from him. "Didn't you buy a pocket knife at the store too?"

"Hey! I was getting it." He posted his hands on his hips, looking really distressed she'd taken his task away.

"Sure you were." She poked her nail through the plastic and slid her finger along the ribbed edge. Standing, she jiggled the combo cotton set free from the wrapper and watched as they fell to the mattress with a thud.

"Show off." He grabbed the fitted sheet, tossed the other pieces to the chair in the corner and snapped the blue fabric across the bed. "What do you want to talk about?"

She gauged his reaction as she looped the sheet's pocket over the mattress's corner. "I want you to teach me to shoot."

John's sprawled hand, smoothing the sheet, stilled mid-mattress. "What?"

She repeated the words slowly holding his intense stare. Bobby and Em's laughter drifted in through the tilted line of small windows above the bed.

After a brief moment, John inhaled and straightened to his full height. "Why? You hate guns."

"We've been attacked twice."

His jaw tightened. He blamed himself for the attacks, which was totally idiotic. "The attacks weren't your fault, John."

"Really? Whose fault were they?"

"How could you possibly know someone leaked information? You couldn't," she argued.

"No, I couldn't. But I should've been on guard every second, protecting you and the kids."

She shook her head while she rounded the bottom of the bed and grabbed the top sheet. "That's impossible and you know it. That is why your superiors posted other agents around us. They knew." She snapped the sheet across the bed. "No man can be on guard day after day, night after night. It's physically impossible."

"You always do that when you're nervous."

"Do what?" She looked up while tucking the material under the mattress.

"Domestic things; dishes, dusting, putting things in place. You're nervous."

She stood and grabbed him by the arms. The feel of his biceps moving under her fingers reminded her of his power. Strength she no longer feared, but longed to have surrounding her.

"I'm not nervous about you protecting us. I feel safe with you. I'm nervous about handling a gun. But I need to be able to defend Bobby and Em," she said softly, looking up into his caring eyes. "I want to help you, John. I want to be able to watch your back. Let me help you."

"What are you going to tell the kids?"

"The truth. We all have to watch each other's backs."

"Aren't you afraid you'll frighten them?"

"After what those kids have seen in the past week, no. They've grown-up. It's about time I do too."

John studied her for full ten seconds before he asked, "When do you want to start?"

She smiled up at him. "As soon as we get this bed made."

****

Stephanie's hand trembled with the light weight of the pistol in her hand. She'd thought it would be much heavier. Holding a loaded weapon was terrifying. But the experience didn't compare to the occurrences over the past week where she had to sweep Bobby and Em away from danger while bullets blasted the air around them.

John moved closer. His warmth wrapped around her like a security blanket. "You can do this," he whispered into her ear, while his hand ran along the length of her arm. "Just focus on your target, keep your hand steady and squeeze the trigger slowly."

He stepped back and she stood on her own. The gun vibrated in her hand as she squeezed the trigger and kicked back as it discharged. The target, a tin can, pinged and flew off the tree stump at an angle.

"All right, Mom." Bobby's yell mixed with Em's shouts of excitement from their safe position on the porch. "You did it."

She sighed, watching the spinning can. "I did it."

"Yes, you did," John said.

Blood raced through her veins as she looked over her shoulder at his smile.

"You're quite good for a beginner. Most novices can't hit a target the size of grizzly bear within the first hundred rounds, but you…ten shots and you got the can."

"I got the can." She stared at the gaping hole in the tin cylinder. "But could I shoot a human being as easily?"

John stepped forward. His hand trailed down her arm and covered her hand holding the gun pointed toward the ground. "You don't have to do this."

"Yes, I do. For them." Her moist gaze darted to the kids and came back to him. "And for you."

He held her troubled gaze. She was being very brave. She hated guns. She loved her kids more.

And him?

She hadn't said the words, but he was pretty sure Steph felt the same way he did about her.

He wanted to pull her into his arms and hold her tight, but he couldn't, not with Bobby and Em watching. Instead he brushed his thumb across the back of her soft hand.

"I think we had enough practice today." He took the gun from her and flipped the safety. With his back to the kids he said, "Tonight, after they're asleep, I'll show you how to load this and where I have the bullets stored."

Her chest rose with her deep intake of air. She squared her shoulders and nodded, understanding the reason for his hushed tone.

Satisfied she was ready to face the kids with a smile, John holstered the gun. "Bobby, why don't we grab those fishing poles and go catch dinner while your mom and Em clean the sweet corn?"

"Yeah," Bobby yelled as he scampered off the porch in the direction of the pickup.

"I want to go too," cried Em.

"No. You and Mr. Blakeslee stay here with me." Steph grabbed Em's hand. "We're going to see if we can make something special for dessert."

As Bobby handed him a pole, John thought he'd heard the word raspberry in Steph's conversation with Em before they entered the cabin. He knew, for all their sakes, he shouldn't think of Steph in any way other than protecting her, but he couldn't seem to help himself. He wondered what the combination of sweet berries and Steph would taste like.

~~~~

Chapter Twenty-nine

The lazy sun perched on the Blue Mountain to the west. Alex swung her car into a parking spot at the State Police barracks and climbed out of the sedan.

Beads of sweat moistened the top of her lip while her stomach knotted as if she'd eaten a pound of Grandmama's raw sourdough. She had to find John and the Boyds before Randall's involvement with the heists was revealed and her cover blown. And walking back into the State Police Station and facing Agent Stover was her only hope.

Papa told her to have guts.

She had to make Ben, John's friend, believe she wasn't involved with the attempt on John's and the Boyds' lives. If she was going to find them, Ben had to trust her.

At least enough to slip up.

This whole situation was Victor's fault. If only he hadn't screwed up by taking Randall along on the heist, she wouldn't have her ass on the line. She loved her cousin, but Papa couldn't possibly consider Victor as his successor. Kisha's husband or even she would make a better choice.

She had guts and brains. Why not her?

Alex's hand hesitated only a second before she yanked the station's door open. At least a dozen armed officers stood in the station's lobby. She couldn't falter again. A mistake could cost her her life.

Keeping her chin high and focusing ahead, she stalked across the gleaming tile floor, knowing all eyes followed her. With her slate-blue pants suit and brand new pumps covered in soot, she reeked of smoke and charred wood. She hoped staying on the crime scene for three hours, doing a walk-through of the burnt house, pretending to search for any evidence that might lead Ben to the would-be assassins would cement the ground work for her lie.

Her fingers trembled ever so slightly as she pulled her badge from her pocket and flashed her credentials at the burly officer sitting behind the front desk. "Treasury Agent Mosely. Where's Agent Stover?"

The bridge of his index finger covered his nostrils before he looked up from his paperwork. His customer service grin faded as he examined her badge.

The man didn't like smoke, well neither did she. She arched her brow. "Well?"

"He's in the back, ma'am." He hooked a thumb in the direction she should take. "I'll let him know—"

Without waiting for him to finish, she headed toward the double doors leading to the back of the station. "Buzz me through," she ordered and stuffed her badge back into her suit's pocket.

A hum resounded as she reached the door. She pushed her way through and past Zohara's dark office. A minute later, she found Ben in a smaller office, toward the back of the building. He was on the phone, apparently with his superiors by the number of "Yes, Sirs" he uttered. The moment he saw her, he cut the conversation short, promising to resolve the mishap pronto and dropped the phone into its cradle.

"What the hell happened out there? We've got two agents dead." Ben chewed on the stump of a cigar which hugged the corner of his mouth.

Still standing in the threshold, Alex shifted her weight from one foot to the other and straightened her stained blazer. "When I left, Peterson and Roth were both fine. I checked on them. They were at their posts."

She had thought to throw in a 'sir' but at the last second decided acknowledging Ben as her superior would be a bit too much.

He pulled the cigar from his mouth and tossed it on the desk. "Get in here. Close the door. Where the hell did you go?"

Alex did as she was told. She ran her tongue across her lips before meeting Ben's hot stare again. "To the store. Supply goofed up. There was barely anything in the house for Em to eat. Initially John was going to go but he decided to stay with Ms. Boyd while she continued to review the pictures the Treasury sent over, and I was elected to go instead. Have you heard from them?" She held up her hand. "No, don't tell me."

Tightlipped, Ben simply stared at her. The man was smart. He'd refused to tell her superiors at the Treasury where the Boyds were too.

"John doesn't trust me as it is," she said. "And I'm sure you have your doubts too. I can't say that I blame either one of you."

"What do you mean by that?"

"First, I shot John's partner." She laced her fingers together and worked them as she paced the small area between the wall and the door. "It was an accident, but I did it." Thanking God for the ability to force tears to her eyes, she turned and faced her adversary. "I killed Luke. Then the attack at the mall happened. I don't think the guy followed me, but hey, I'm sure John has his doubts. And now this." She trapped her trembling lip between her teeth and paced again. "I know how it looks. I leave the safe house and it gets blown up."

Ben sat on the edge of the desk and folded his arms across his chest. "Who said anything about blown up?"

"John did. I talked to him for a few seconds after—" Alex splayed her right hand across her heart for a soul-wrenching effect. "Anyone with half a brain would put two and two together and say I did it, but I swear on my mother's grave, Ben, I didn't do this."

Ben held her glistening gaze for what seemed like forever before he finally said, "What did you find at the scene?"

She dropped her hand to her side. "You believe me?"

"I'm not your judge, Alex, but you're here, where I can watch you."

She was in. She exhaled loudly and dabbed her eyes with the edge of her finger. "Fair enough."

He pushed off the desk. "Tell me what you found and then you can wash up."

A knock at the door turned both their heads. Ben motioned for the female officer standing outside to enter.

"I have the number you requested." The stocky woman wore slacks like the rest of the police officers Alex had seen in this barrack. She carried no gun, however, and had her left thumb hooked in her belt at the buckle. Her right hand held a slip of paper. Alex noticed she demonstrated a slight limp.

Ben glanced at her before he took the paper from the woman. He stuffed the note into his pocket. "Thank you."

"Do you need anything else, Agent Stover?"

"No. No, thank you." Ben remained silent until the door clicked closed and the officer disappeared from his view. Ben rounded the desk and dropped onto the chair. "Go ahead. You were saying." He grabbed a pencil and waited to make notes.

The number meant something, but she couldn't ask. How was she going to get the paper out of Ben's pocket without taking him out? She was surrounded by armed cops.

She spied a letter opener stuck in among pencils held in a ceramic mug and thought, *maybe*. Her fingers itched to grab it and sink it into Ben, but unless she stabbed the agent in the throat, his cry would alarm his fellow officers.

Patience will be rewarded, one of Papa's sayings echoed in her ears.

Alex nodded. "I think they strapped a bomb to the gas line, but I'm no expert. The fire chief at the scene pinpointed the area where the gas meter had been as the point of origin, so that would be my guess. He said it would be a few days until the fire inspector knew for sure what caused the fire." She slumped onto the hard plastic chair next to the desk. Her hand, marked with charcoal, visibly trembled. "John said if I would've been in the kitchen, standing next to the stove like I had been earlier, I wouldn't be—" She turned her tear-streaked face to Ben. "How the hell did they find us?"

"That is what we've got to figure out." Ben dropped the pencil and stood. "Go wash up. Ask one of the officers for a change of clothes—scrubs, something. Your—the smell is giving me a headache." He waved her away from the desk.

"A headache? You?" She faked a weak smile.

"Get cleaned up."

Alex nodded. She was going to stick next to Ben until he slipped up even if it took days. She exited the office and started down the hall when she noticed the woman officer who had handed Ben the note entering the ladies' wash room. It was a chance that might save her days.

She checked the empty hallway and rushed into the restroom. Three of the four stall doors stood ajar. The last door was firmly closed. Alex banged on the door. "Hey, you."

"I'm busy. There are other stalls you know."

"It's Treasury Agent Mosley. You're the officer who just came in and gave Agent Stover the number, right?" Alex shifted around to keep an eye on the entrance door to the restroom and caught her reflection in the brightly lit mirror and cringed. She had to look dirty and distressed, not dirty and coldly calm, in case the woman saw her image through the slit between the door and partition.

"Yeah. So?"

She heard the woman gas off and shook her head. The smell clinging to her wasn't bad enough.

"Men." Alex hissed. "Ben spilled his coffee on the slip of paper and now he needs the number ASAP. Did you write it down anywhere else?"

"No." The officer exhaled loudly and mumbled something about this place was just like home and she couldn't go to the pot there either.

"I'm sorry. I know exactly what you mean. I have two kids at home," Alex lied. "Every time I close the bathroom door, they need something. I wouldn't be bothering you if Agent Stover wasn't my superior in the case we're working. Don't you remember the number?"

"I'll call information again, as soon as I'm finished here."

"He's really in a huff. As if it's my fault he spilled his coffee. You know men. The pencil jumped under the cup as he sat it down." Alex bit her lip, waiting. "Look. I don't want him to come in here. He will. I know him. Do you at least remember the name and area code?"

"Yeah, Hartman's Pharmacy. Five one seven. I think it was in the Mountain Pine area."

Alex smiled. Em needed an Epipen. She recalled overhearing John talking to Steph about a cabin. "Okay, great. I'll call information for you. Thanks. And take your time."

After a grunt and another gas pop, the woman said, "I will."

Alex rushed out the restroom and down the hall. She grabbed her phone from her pocket and pretended to be speaking into it as she stopped in front of the desk officer. "Okay. I'm on my way." She snapped her phone shut. "Tell Agent Stover I got a call to head back to the Treasury Department. If he has any questions, he should speak to my superior, Randall."

The man nodded, but didn't pick up his phone. It was change of shifts. The desk officer had other things on his mind, like clearing his desk for the next guy and what he was having for dinner or his bowling night. He wouldn't call or run back to Stover immediately. By the time he did, she'd be on her way to Mountain Pine.

~~~~

Chapter Thirty

"It took awhile, but they're finally asleep. I'm ready for my lesson." Steph's bare feet padded the planked floor boards as she approached him on his right side. "Hey, isn't that my job?"

"Do you want to do it?" John smiled at her as he finished washing the last dish. Stephanie had showered and changed from her baggy sweat pants and oversized T-shirt to a navy tank top and gray sweat shorts. And from what he could see, no bra.

"Not really." She returned his smile.

He rinsed the sink, hoping the icy water would lower his temperature and douse the rise in his jeans. "You're not nervous."

"Not about learning to load a gun. I've made up my mind. It's something I have to do."

He stared at the black and blue mark on her upper arm. She was right. As much as he wanted to be, he wouldn't be with her every moment for the rest of her life. She needed to be able to protect herself.

"Good." He wrung the dishcloth out and hung it over the drain board before turning and meeting her amused smirk. "What?"

"You. It still kills me to see you do everyday chores."

"Knock it off. I'm just like anyone else."

"No, you're not. You're special, John."

The woman was killing him, standing so close, staring at him with a twinkle in her eye and the peaks of her breasts calling to him. He could easily slip his arm around her waist and pull her against him. He'd loved to linger over her, satisfy her.

He dropped his gaze to her raspberry tinted lips. He could almost taste her sweetness on his tongue. He wanted her but he couldn't take her. Their time together before had been lust and sex. Making love to her now, would still be just that.

He'd fallen for her, and he didn't know how he could stay with her. He wouldn't make promises he couldn't keep. He cleared his throat, willed his restraint in place and said, "I think we better get started, just in case Bobby or Em wake up and look for you."

Her eyes studied him for a moment before she simply said, "Okay. Let's get it over with."

She followed him to the ladder. John flipped the switch turning on the single light in the loft.

"We're going up there?"

He stopped with his foot on the loft's ladder. Steph looked nervously upward. She trapped her bottom lip between her teeth.

"I carried all the ammunition up into the loft so the kids wouldn't see it. You're not afraid of heights, are you? It's only twelve feet."·

"I can handle a six-foot ladder no problem, but when it comes to something taller I, ah… well, sort of freeze up."

"Stay here. I'll go get the guns and ammo and bring them down."

She blew out a sharp breath. "No. It's okay."

Before he could argue, she grabbed the ladder and climbed two rungs. She looked down at him. "It's one thing for the kids to see me learn how to properly handle a gun, but I don't want them to know how to load one. And I don't want to take a chance they might overhear either."

Her arm extended upward, jutting her breast forward at his eye level. John's blood rushed as the curves of her body passed by him. Even her damn bare toes were sexy.

He looked up.

Her hips called to him. Her long legs disappeared into the hem of her shorts, driving him nuts. He couldn't watch. He couldn't think about the patch of heaven between them.

He peeked.

As she rose higher, her steps slowed. She made a mistake and glanced down at him. "Okay, I can't do this. I really thought I could, but I can't. Help!" Steph whimpered while she clutched the ladder.

"Stay there." John scurried up the ladder. He pressed his chest against her backside, supporting her, reassuring her and igniting a fire deep in his gut.

"I feel like a damn fool," she cried.

"Take a deep breath and just focus on the next rung. No higher. I'm right behind you. You can't fall."

With visibly shaky legs, Steph climbed the remaining four steps. Her rump wiggled as she crawled on her knees away from the edge. John felt his reaction below his belt grow hard. Maybe this was a mistake.

She turned and sat on his sleeping bag, sweeping her hair back from her flushed face. Her tan legs curled under her.

No. There was no maybe about it. The kids were asleep. They were alone. This was a mistake.

John climbed through the gap in the railing and stood in the long but narrow loft. Quickly he turned, hiding his growing interest. "Over here is a cubby-hole where I stored the ammo for now. All you need to do is press on the left side and the door swings open."

"Got it. My problem will be to get up here." She forced a chuckle. Her heart still pounded wildly, mostly because of John. She didn't like heights but his hard body sliding up her backside and pressing against her had done more than to make her feel safe from falling. The action had sent her blood pressure skyrocketing.

And if questioned, he couldn't deny he hadn't enjoyed their closeness too. She felt his reaction to her, and she'd bet the last four dollars and seventy-seven cents in her purse his erection was the main reason he immediately dodged for the corner.

She smiled while staring at his back.

Stephanie inched back and stood on wobbly legs. The floor felt solid beneath her feet. She was okay. Turning, she kept her feet planted and looked around three sides of the loft, avoiding the area where there was no wall, just a rail.

There wasn't much up here. A small table with a lamp, a straight-backed chair, several sleeping bags rolled up and stacked in one corner, and one spread out on the floor near her feet on top of a large braided rug, where John apparently had decided to sleep.

She took a deep breath and forced herself to look past the rail. "I hadn't really noticed the high window in the cabin's wall before."

"What?" John rose from his knees, holding several small yellow and green boxes.

She pointed past the railing, focusing on the narrow but long pane of glass. "I bet during the day you can stand here and have a great view of the lake."

"Yeah, it's great. You'll have to come up sometime and see for yourself."

"Or I could stay."

John froze in mid-step for a second. Ignoring her comment, he walked to the back of the loft, switched on the small lamp on the night table and placed the boxes next to it. "Do you want to get started?"

"Yeah, why don't we," she said seductively.

His gaze met hers.

She couldn't help herself. Every night since they'd made love, she'd lay in bed longing for his touch, wondering if he was thinking about her. She needed to know.

She looked around and located the switch to the blaring light above them. With her heart pounding, she padded across the plank floor toward the railing and turned off the light. A soft glow from the little lamp behind John was enough. This time she wanted to see him.

All of him.

She waited for his move.

His gaze drifted over her, stopping briefly on the bruise coloring her upper arm.

Her blood rushed, warming her, making her ready for him. She shifted her weight, parting her legs.

His tongue crossed his lips. "Steph, I…"

"I know you don't have the answers, John. I don't either. Right now, I don't want to think about tomorrow or the next day. I just need to know how you feel."

Steph reached down and grabbed the hem of her shirt and pulled it over her head.

Desire grew in his eyes as his gaze fluttered over her bare breasts.

"Don't say anything, just show me," she said.

In two quick strides, he stood before her. He gathered her in his arms. As their kiss deepened, she melted against him. His right hand palmed her ribs before sliding to her breast. He rolled her tight peak between his fingers. She moaned as his touch sent delicious painful charges all the way to her toes. John's mouth left hers and trailed down her throat until his hot tongue teased her nipple. She pushed her chest forward to meet his mouth. His warm, moist tongue licked and sucked until her breasts ached with desire and she bit her lip for fear of crying out. Her fingers wrapped into the soft material covering his back. She tugged his shirt from the waistband of his pants.

As if on fire, he stepped back and yanked his shirt over his head and threw it to the floor. In the soft light, he was beautiful, his body etched from hours of workouts.

She hungered to touch him and, without hesitation, combed her fingers through his coarse chest hair. Strong muscles flexed beneath her hands. The wild beat of his heart gave away his excitement and added to her own.

His hands circled her waist and hastily, he pulled her shorts over her hips in one swift motion. She stepped out of them. Totally unprepared for his next move, she squealed softly as he swept her off her feet and carried her to the back of the loft. There, he lowered her gently onto his sleeping bag.

She leaned on her elbows, enjoying the view as he shrugged out of his jeans and jockey shorts, exposing his erection thick with need.

He dropped onto his knees beside her. "This is much better than the last time."

"How's that?"

"I can see you."

She blushed while agreeing with him. She could see the passion in his eyes and his desire made her feel sexy. And she loved the look of him, hot and ready.

Reaching out, she wrapped her fingers around his shaft, teasing his glistening tip. A moan escaped from John's lips as she playfully pumped him.

The very moment she thought she might bring him to climax, he pulled back and sat on his thighs. He visibly shook while fighting for control. She ran her tongue seductively across her lips, teasing him.

He leaned back, grabbed his duffel bag and rifled through it, coming up with several foil wrappers.

"Where did you get those?" Surprise laced her tone.

His eyebrow cocked. "At the store, when we stopped for supplies. I'd hoped I might need them."

"Here with me or later?"

"I don't want to think beyond here, with you."

Seeing into his soul, Stephanie's heart melted.

John's hands trembled as he tore open a packet and sheathed himself. Ready, his hand drifted down over her stomach. Her skin tingled with excitement where his rough fingers slipped beneath the silken material of her panties and grazed across her sensitive mound. Under his touch, a whimper escaped her lips.

She reached for him again. He clasped her hand with his free hand and held it while he slid two fingers between her moist lips. He slipped into her again and again, while his thumb rubbed her sensitive nub. Her body clasped him, wanting, needing to intensify the sensations.

Her breaths came faster and faster. He was driving her insane. She needed more. "John, please. I need you, now."

He rose on bent knees and tugged the last piece of material she wore down her legs and tossed it to the side.

"God, you're beautiful," John whispered as he settled between her thighs. The head of his cock teased her mound while his fingertips traced along her cheeks, her lips, across her pounding heart, feathering her fluttering stomach, to her flamed center.

He leaned down and blew on her slippery opening. A shiver spiraled up her spine. She couldn't stand the teasing any longer. Grabbing his shoulders, she dug her nails into his hard muscles and pulled him onto her. "Now!"

His gaze, glazed with desire, locked with hers as he entered her.

Stephanie's hands traveled over the thick muscles of his back to his taut buttocks, enjoying the feel of his weight on her and his thickness spreading her wide. He smoothed her hair and feathered kisses across her eyes as he made his entry into her soul.

She arched her back and drew him inside, deeper. His groan commanded her to continue her rocking movements. Higher and harder, he thrust into her, until they could no longer stop their shattering releases.

Afterwards, when the room gradually came into focus, Stephanie looked into John's hooded gaze and he kissed her softly.

"Is that what you had in mind when you asked me up to loft to see your gun?" She smiled up at him.

John laughed. "Not exactly, but it'll do."

She smacked his ass.

He chuckled again as he rolled from her and stood. She admired the broad span of his shoulders, the flex of his thighs and the tightness of his buttocks as he crossed to the wastebasket where he peeled off his protection. He grabbed a handful of tissues from the box on the stand and strode, without modesty, toward her. He handed her the tissues and gave her privacy while she cleaned herself of their juices.

A moment later, he lay beside her, under the cover of a thin sheet, cradling her. Silently, he brushed her arm with his thumb. She loved being with him, and in a little more than a week, she'd fallen in love with him. Her heart broke every time she thought about the moment she'd have to say goodbye to him.

She didn't want to let John go. She wanted Victor captured, now. Maybe she and John could go on seeing each other.

But before she could ask John if he wanted too to see her, she had to be honest and tell him about Gene. "John, I need to tell you something."

"Hmmm." He sounded sleepy.

She needed to look at him, gauge his reaction. She moved out of his embrace and pushed up on her elbow.

Lazily, he studied her. His hand brushed back her hair, causing a tingle to run along her shoulder. "What is it?"

"I was going to tell you at the safe house, but before I could, all hell broke loose. It's about Gene."

"What?"

Suddenly, feeling as guilty as Gene was, Stephanie sat up, pulling the sheet with her. She ran her tongue across her dry lips. "I wasn't completely honest with you. I want you know why, first. I didn't tell you because of Bobby and Em. I didn't want them to know—"

"That their father was involved with the heists?"

She sat back as if she'd been sucker punched and stared at him. "How did you know?"

"Ben ran checks on every member of the Mt. Laurel force. Suspicious activity popped up on both Morse and Gene's accounts, or rather accounts using the social security numbers of their family members."

"Are you telling me he used Bobby and Em?"

"Yes. And his parents."

What the hell had Gene been thinking, involving

Bobby and Em in his crime? And her. As their legal
guardian, what kind of trouble could she be in? Surely,
John didn't think she had anything to do with the heist.
"You've got to believe me. I didn't know about anything."

"I believe you." He squeezed her hand.

"If Gene were alive, I'd, I'd…How long have you
known?"

"Two days?"

"Why didn't you ask me about it?"

"I knew you would tell me."

"You did?"

"Yes." He nodded.

"I have another question. If…" She wet her lips and
started over. "I mean when this is all over, will I see you
again?"

"I'm hoping."

"But you're not sure." Panic gripped her stomach. The
threat of having to enter the Federal Protection Program
still loomed as a possibility for her future. He knew it, and
she had to face it. How was she going to say goodbye to
him when the time came?

"I don't know what's going to happen." He rubbed her
leg.

It was an act of comfort, but she didn't feel appeased at
all. Suddenly, she felt naked and vulnerable to pain she
didn't know if she could handle. She pulled her knees up
and tucked the sheet tighter around her, exposing John's
hairy legs.

He shifted back and moved to sit beside her. The sheet
skimmed his lap, but his strong chest was completely
exposed. He kissed her shoulder and she bit her bottom lip,
keeping her attention focused on a knot in the wood railing
in front of her while she fought the tears that threaten to

spill.

John leaned forward, catching her eye. "If Victor and everyone involved are apprehended, you'll be able to go home," he said quietly. "When I call you, will you think about going out to dinner with me?"

A smile formed on her lips as she thought about the best case scenario. "Maybe."

His brow arched. "After all I've done for you tonight, I get a maybe?"

"You've done for me?"

"Okay, we've done for each other." He chuckled. John wrapped his arm around her and pulled her closer. His forehead met hers. "I'm a waste."

"Why do you say that?" She looked at him through her damp lashes while her heart danced a waltz in her chest.

"Because every time you're near me, I lose all track of responsibility. I smell you and my mind turns to one thing and one thing only."

A trembling need built in her belly. "What's that?"

"How much I want to make love to you all over again."

~~~~

Chapter Thirty-one

Alex cut the rented SUV's lights. She wasn't sure, but she thought she saw a single light ahead. She squinted through the rain-streaked windshield. The wipers did little to swipe away the downpour. She waited.

Maybe she should have brought Victor with her. But she wanted to take care of John on her own. Besides, business continued. Her cousin was pulling another heist tonight.

Thunder rumbled low overhead. The truck vibrated in its quake. Lighting streaked across the sky, allowing a glimpse of how low the trees lining the mud-sodden road bowed.

There!

Her blood rushed hot through her veins as the white beam of hope appeared in the darkness ahead. She had to make sure she hadn't made a wrong turn and this cabin was the one John had told Stephanie about. They hadn't seen her standing just inside the glass door, listening, while they'd shared soft drinks and heartbreaking stories from their pasts. Boohoo.

She jammed the SUV into reverse and backed along the road until she got to a spot where it was safe to swing the vehicle into the thick bush. The metal screamed as thicket and laurel bit into the sides. She didn't care. Tomorrow, after she'd taken care of these loose ends, she'd ditch the SUV anyway. Right now, she didn't want to get stuck out here in no-man's land.

In the dim overhead light, Alex grabbed a poncho off the seat next to her and slipped it over head. After checking her Colt 45, she snatched up the flashlight she'd stashed in the cup holder and forced the door open just enough to slip out of the SUV.

Torrents of rain bombarded her. Her jeans below the poncho immediately clung to her legs. Alex cursed under her breath as thorns grabbed at her legs and arms. The road was slick and mud stuck to her hiking boots, sucking her to the earth. Holding her head low, she peeked toward the light. Soon, she'd know if this was at the right place.

Cold droplets dripped from her nose. Impatience caused mistakes. She couldn't afford any slip-ups. This time John, Stephanie and her two kids wouldn't escape. They would die.

As she drew closer, the rattle of the tin roof covered her steps. The clatter gave her confidence and she simply stalked to the window and peered inside.

A grin bloomed on her lips. She had been right.

John lounged on an old sofa with the little brat, Em, tucked in between him and Stephanie. The other brat, Bobby, lay on the floor in front of the fire. It was a freakin' Norman Rockwell picture.

Alex fumbled under her poncho and clasped her Colt. She could easily blow John's head off and when Stephanie jumped she'd nail her too. The kids would be easy. She could walk right in the front door and pop them both while they cried over their mommy. A mommy whose arm wasn't broken.

Her jaw tightened with anger, knowing John had lied to her, again. But her smile soon lifted the corner of her lips. It would be days, maybe weeks, until they'd be found. The wildlife would have a feast.

John stretched his arm across the back of the couch. His fingers twirled a lock of Stephanie's hair and the smile the action brought to her lips was affirmation that their affection for each other had grown.

Alex pulled back her gun. John was so weak. He thought with his cock. No government should have such a weak man working for them.

She'd give this pathetic man one last chance to show his strength. She'd tell him the truth about the operation and how his partner died. She'd give him the opportunity to face death with dignity and honor.

Sliding her Colt into the holster, Alex backed away from the window. She recalled her grandfather's words as she trekked to the vehicle, *"Savor the chase, my little pumpkin."*

She would wait until tomorrow.

~~~~

Chapter Thirty-two

"Good morning. The coffee smells great." The porch boards creaked a moment before John felt Steph's soft hands on his shoulders, and her warm lips kissing the back of his neck. "Did you sleep well?"

After a week, her touch was familiar. His heart melted. He grabbed her hand, holding her in place as he turned and smiled down on her. Her nipples pushed against her white T-shirt. He gently brushed a knuckle across one peak. "No. It was hell without you."

"Mmmm. Same here." She pulled back and lifted his arm around her, curling into him. Looking out over the lake, she sighed. "I could stay here forever, if you'd let me."

"I wish we could." He gathered her closer and kissed the top of her head. "But eventually Bobby and Em would have to go to school."

"I could home school." Her pain echoed in her strained chuckle.

Drawing in a breathe of her sweet scent, his heart wrenched. He would like nothing more than to forget about the world and stay here with her and the kids. But they couldn't. "Sooner or later Ben will call. We'll have to go back."

"I know."

Steph moved away, leaving a cold void in her place.

She drifted to the other porch column. Leaning against it, she folded her arms across her chest. Her lips pressed together as if she was forming the right words behind them. "I know I said that our time together was going to be enough to last me a lifetime, but—" Tears brimmed her lids. "I was wrong."

John stepped toward her. "I don't know what—"

"I know… You don't know how we can be together. So, Ben will call. We'll go back, and I'll identify Victor. You'll toss him in jail and throw away the key. You'll drive off in pursuit of the next bad guy and me…Well, I'll go home and wonder where you are. Wonder if what I felt was love."

The woman knew how to make a guy feel like a heel.

John pulled her into his arms. She buried her head in his chest and cried softly against him. He kissed her head and smoothed her hair. "Steph, I didn't think I'd ever love again," he whispered softly, cupping her chin and tilting her face up until she looked at him. "Like a bomb, you dropped into my life. Every defense I'd put up to protect myself from ever being hurt again came tumbling down. You opened up my heart. As much as you don't want to live without me, I don't want to live without you. I love you."

He kissed her gently. Her arms wrapped around him and held on. "Somehow, we'll figure this out. I promise," he assured her.

From inside the cabin, they heard Em yell at Bobby to leave Mr. Blakeslee alone.

"Sounds like the kids are awake." He wiped a tear from her cheek.

"Yes. And hungry." She smiled up at him. "I'll trust you, Agent Dolton, to find the answer."

He didn't know how, but he wouldn't stop thinking until he came up with a way for them to remain together.

He pecked her lips. "I'm going to go down to the lake to wash up."

"Why not use the shower?" She pointed toward the cabin the same moment Em screamed at Bobby again.

"I feel like the lake this morning."

She wiggled her hips against him and smiled openly. "I understand. The water is colder."

He backed away from their embrace and grabbed the towel he'd hung over the railing earlier. "Exactly."

A smile played on her lips. "Did you want breakfast?"

"Just leave the pan hot. I'll scramble a couple of eggs when I get back."

"Okay." She disappeared inside.

John heard an immediate change in her tone, from lover to mother, as she stopped the war between Bobby and Em. He couldn't stop a grin from forming on his lips. With determination in his step, he headed toward the lake, thinking about what Steph had said. She trusted him.

****

The pan sizzled again as Stephanie dropped another strip of bacon onto the hot iron. Tired of their constant bickering, she'd placed Bobby and Em at separate ends of the table.

"Where's John, Mom?" Bobby slumped over the table, his head propped in his hand.

"He went down to the lake to wash up."

Bobby's back straightened. "Can I go too?" His eyes lost the bored, sleepy look and danced with excitement.

"He's not fishing without you." She couldn't see her son actually wanting to take a cold bath, but Bobby was beginning to follow John's lead on quite a few manly habits. "He's probably on his way back by now."

Bobby scampered off his chair. "I'll go see."

"Me too," Em whined.

"No, you stay." Stephanie pointed the spatula she held at Em.

"Bobby, tell him I just started breakfast. Ask him if he wants bacon," she called after him, but he was gone.

She shook her head. "Men."

~~~~

Chapter Thirty-Three

The man was making it easy for her. Alex walked fearlessly out of the forest and perched on a log where John would clearly see her when he surfaced from the water. She held her Colt 45 across her lap and waited.

He emerged with a gasp.

She could easily make it his last, but she'd wait. As much as she longed to end his life, she also wanted to have some fun with him too.

He swung his head back. Droplets created a rainbow arch over him. Once his hands wiped over his face, his eyes widened with surprise.

Alex grinned. "Good morning, John."

"What are you doing here? Did Ben send you?"

She noted his hope and laughed. "No. I found you on my own. Come out of the water, John."

Confusion creased his brow. "I'm not wearing anything. Turn around."

"No." She stood and aimed her gun at his heart. "Come out now."

The lines of John's face hardened as reality set in. "You're the mole."

She couldn't stop the grin lifting the corners of her lips. "Very good. You met your goal, John. You solved your case before you died, just like your partner."

"What's that supposed to mean?" He stared back at her.

"Luke knew the truth before I pulled the trigger."

Under the water, John's hands balled into fists. He'd been right all along. "You murdered him."

She chuckled. "Of course I did. You read the reports. Just one little detail was missing. It wasn't a mistake."

"You bitch." John trembled with the urge to charge out of the lake and kill Alex with his bare hands. But he had no defense. He was nude. One wrong move and he'd get himself killed. Alex would go after Steph and the kids next.

His gut wrenched. He had to think of some way out of this mess.

"I see your mind working. Stop. In a few minutes, it will be over. Now, be good and get your ass out here. I don't want to make you fish food. I'll be kind and let you say goodbye to Stephanie Boyd and her brats." With her free hand, she wiggled her index finger at him to come.

He had to protect Steph and the kids. He had to play it smart. Slowly, he moved forward, watching Alex's every blink. Her gaze drifted over him while he walked onto the shore.

"Mmm, I see now why Stephanie enjoyed her ride out in the backyard so much." Her brows arched. "Oh, don't look so surprised. If you're going to screw out in the open, there's a possibility someone will see. Let's go." She waved her gun toward the path.

His clothes were draped across a fallen tree about ten feet from him. His Sig was under his jeans. If he could get to it, maybe he could surprise her. "Can I at least put my pants on?"

She glanced at his clothing.

"The kids," he lied holding his hands in front of his privates.

A smile played on her lips. "Stay where you are."

She circled around him, wide, leaving a distance too far to reach her in two quick steps. While pointing the gun at his chest, she tossed his shirt onto the ground and grabbed his pants from the log. The exposed Sig glistened in the sunlight.

"Never go anywhere without your weapon. It's the first thing they taught us in training. You won't need this any longer." She picked up his pistol by the butt and flung it into the thicket, yards away.

John's heart sank. Even if he could make it to the gun, he'd have trouble untangling it from the thorny undergrowth.

Alex skimmed his pants under her arm, checking for other weapons before tossing them at him. "There you go."

Dread pooled in John's gut as he picked his way along the path barefooted toward the cabin with Alex a safe distance on his heels. Hopefully, Steph would see them coming and get her gun. If she shot one round, Alex could flinch and he might have a second of opportunity to grab her and wrestle the weapon away from her. However, as they drew closer and closer, the scent of bacon frying filled the air and he heard Steph talking to the kids. His hope slipped into his tightening gut.

She said he made her feel safe. She trusted him and yet, he was letting her down again.

Short of the porch, he stopped and turned on Alex. "Take me, Alex. Let Stephanie and the kids go."

Her icy stare darted toward the cabin for a split half-second and then knocked him back on his heels. Her lips thinned into a wicked smile. "I don't think so, John. She can identify my cousin."

"Victor is your cousin?"

"Yes. If he goes down, so will our operation. Move."
She nodded. "Stephanie's waiting for you."

When John walked through the door, Steph turned from the stove. The smile she wore was short-lived. She paled and dropped the fork she held as Alex pushed him into room.

"We're home, honey." Alex chuckled. Her weapon poked John's shoulder blade. "Get over there."

He moved to stand next to the table.

"You too," she ordered Steph. "Where are the kids?"

He took Steph's hand in his and gave it a squeeze. He wasn't giving up. God help him, he'd die before letting Alex hurt Steph or the kids.

"Where are the kids?" Alex shouted. "I'm not going to ask again." She pointed her Colt at Steph.

John's blood pounded in his temples. Steph's troubled eyes met his. He gave her nod.

"They're washing up."

Alex glanced toward the closed door. "Okay. I'm sure they'll coming running soon enough. In the meantime, I told John, out of the goodness of my heart, I'd let him say goodbye. Since you two have grown so close."

The scent of burnt bacon rose from the iron pan. He had to do something and quick. The grease would catch on fire soon. The whole cabin would go up in a matter of minutes. If Alex shot him and Steph, the kids wouldn't have a chance to get out in time.

John stepped in front of Steph. "Let them go."

Alex's hand jerked, and she aimed at him again.

"You're trying my patience. Now, do you want to say goodbye to her or not? It doesn't make a damn bit of difference to me."

John held Alex's cold glare. There was no reasoning with her. He had no choice. He turned to Steph and cupped her face in his hands. He wanted to tell her he loved her and that he wished they had a lifetime together, but he couldn't choke out the words. He hoped his eyes said it all. He kissed her tenderly.

Steph's arms wrapped around his neck and their kiss deepened. Trembling in his arms, she cried his name against his lips. His heart broke knowing he'd failed her and the kids. He had to do something. He wasn't going to go out without a fight. While their lips were locked, he scanned the immediate area for any kind of weapon.

"Come on. That is enough," Alex ordered.

With his mind whirring, John slowly let Steph go and stepped away from her. Their fingertips parted. Alex's gun remained on him just as he'd hoped. His gaze darted toward the smoking frying pan. Stephanie's followed.

"Oh, my," Steph cried.

Alex glanced toward the stove.

It was all the time he needed. Quickly, John darted to the left, away from Steph. He dove across the floor and rolled, knocking over a side-table and lamp. Alex fired at him. Feathers flew from a pillow and into the air above him. Alex had missed him by inches.

He dove behind the couch and peeked around its corner. Following his lead, Steph had darted to the right and rolled under the kitchen table.

The bedroom door creaked open. John's heart jumped to his throat. Em stood in its threshold.

Alex honed in on the little girl.

Another shot blasted the air and the floorboards next to Alex's foot splintered. Wide eyed, she spun around.

Bobby stood in the entry. The boy must have followed him and had found his Sig after Alex forced him up the path.

Bobby's jaw dropped as Alex aimed her Colt at him.

Out of the corner of his eye, John saw Steph scramble from under the table, grab a hot pad and then the iron frying pan's handle.

John yelled hoping to draw Alex's attention. Like a caged animal, Alex turned on him.

Without a thought to her own safety, Stephanie raced toward Alex and flung the hot bacon grease into her face.

Alex's wail echoed off the walls as she swiped at her blistering flesh.

"You bitch." Wildly, she aimed the gun.

Even in horrific pain, Alex intended to take them out. She clicked off a couple of wild rounds at the couch, sending batting flying into the air and making John hit the floor. Then she turned her weapon on Steph.

John leaped over the coach.

Alex squeezed the trigger as he tackled her from behind.

Steph bellowed, dropped the frying pan and crumpled to the floor, hitting her head on the pan.

"No!"

"Mommy!" John and the kid's cries mingled in anguish. Blood trickled down Steph's forehead and pooled around her stomach. Bobby and Em rushed to her side.

"Don't move her." John wrestled Alex's Colt from her hand, flipped her onto her stomach and sat on her back while he yanked the cord from the lamp he'd knocked over. "Steph, I'm here. I'm coming."

He barely heard Alex's pain-filled whimpers as he roughly tied her hands behind her back. His blood thundered in his ear drums as he strained and prayed to hear anything, a whisper, from Steph.

Alex cursed him as he scampered over her and crawled on his knees to Steph's side. Her shirt was soaked with blood both in the front and back. It looked like the bullet passed through her. "Bobby, get a towel from the bathroom."

Bobby returned within seconds. John grabbed the hot pad off the floor and placed it over the wound in Steph's back. "Get me the other hot pad."

"Mom is not going to die, is she?" Bobby handed him the pad.

Tears ran down Em's cheeks.

"I hope the bitch burns in hell for what she did to me," Alex yelled.

Em sobs grew louder.

Bobby's hands curled into fists. "Shut up, you—you, witch."

"Ignore her," he said to Bobby and to Em, "I'm not going to let your mommy die." Quickly, John wrapped the towel around Steph, lifting her as gently as he could. She winced as he tightened the cloth and curled the edges of the towel under itself.

Satisfied he had packed the wounds the best he could, he rolled Steph over and assessed her head wound. She was going to need stitches. "Bobby, can you climb up to the loft and get my cell phone? It's on the table in the corner."

"Yes, sir." Bobby raced to the ladder.

From the corner of his eye, John watched him climb. "Your mommy is going to be okay, Em. I promise. Can you get me a clean hand towel?" The little girl nodded and dashed away. "Make it damp."

Gently, John cradled Steph in his arms. He swiped her hair back and ran his fingertips along her pale cheek. Even at death's door she was beautiful. His teeth ground together as he swallowed the pain and fear rising in him. He wasn't going to let her go. "Sweetheart, can you hear me? Open your eyes. Come on, stay with me." His throat thickened with emotion. "Steph, please. I can't lose you. I love you."

Steph's eyes fluttered. A weak smile pulled at the corners of her lips before she slumped in his arms.

Alex continued to curse in her native tongue.

~~~~

Chapter Thirty-four

John's stomach twisted into a baseball-sized knot. His mouth tasted like horsehide, too. He rifled his hand through his hair as he stared down at Steph. She'd come through surgery with flying colors, or so the doctor said. John wasn't so sure.

Steph was as white as the crisp sheets covering her. A huge bandage with a visible blood stain plastered her hair to her head. She was hooked up to a half dozen wires, which ran to machines that clicked and beeped in rhythm. Tubes pumped fluids into her arm and drained infectious matter from her belly.

She'd been asleep for two days and he wondered how many more would pass before he could look into her sparkling eyes and tell her how he felt about her.

How had the Zosimoskys pulled this scenario off? After her capture, Alex's prints and ID pictures in Philadelphia Treasury's records were reviewed with the Treasury's main dossier. They didn't match the file from the department in Denver. John curled his fingers around the bed's side rail. Randall had protected her. The traitor had no rights as far as he was concerned.

The door behind him swung open. John caught a glimpse of the armed agent guarding the door before Ben filled the threshold and entered the sterile room. "How's she doing?"

A cigar tip peeked from Ben's coat's pocket.

"As good as can be expected, considering she's lost a lot of blood. The good news is, the bullet passed through with no serious internal injuries. It nicked her intestine and grazed her lower rib, broke it. The doc said they closed up the intestine. Both will heal."

"Good."

"Did we get Randall?"

"Yeah. He rolled like the dog he is. In exchange, his family will be put into the Federal Protection Program. He knows he's a dead man. Wherever we stash him."

"Does he deserve anything less?"

Ben shook his head. "Not in my book."

"He tell you how they pulled this off?"

"Apparently the real Alexandra Mosely had been intercepted and disappeared nine months ago. Three months before the first trailer heist. The real Agent Mosely was never reported missing by her family, because they'd received official notification from the Treasury department, via Randall, that she had gone uncover. Once in a while they received notes from her, stating she was still unavailable, but safe. Again the communication came through Randall. The family had no reason to suspect anything was wrong."

Alex hadn't pulled this job off alone. "And Victor?"

"He's still out there. Neither Alex nor Randall is saying, but you know this was a mob job. Right?"

John nodded. The complexity made it so. "Three people didn't have the resources to pull off what they did."

"They won't rest until Steph is dead or Victor is caught," Ben said quietly as if he didn't want Steph to hear.

Thus the decision. It was the only way to protect Stephanie and the kids. "I know."

"Well, everything is set. The sooner we get this act going, the sooner we'll have Victor. I hope, for her sake."

John faced Ben. "I don't like this. She is defenseless."

"Look, if you have a better plan, tell me now."

John's jaw clenched. He didn't have a better plan and that was the problem. The only chance to save Steph and give back her life was to take out the one person she could identify. Perhaps the mob would leave her alone. He hoped. But he didn't like using her as bait.

He turned back to Steph and covered her soft hand with his own. "No. I don't."

****

Did the FBI think he was stupid?

Holding a bouquet of daisies, Victor leaned against the counter while a nurse checked for the room number of a Myrtle Haupt and glanced down the corridor checking where Steph Boyd was roomed. The room was easy to spot. An armed guard barricaded the door.

"Keeping track of patient's names day in and day out is almost impossible," Nurse Lillian Michaels said, glancing up at him with a shy smile.

"I'm sorry to take up your time. I'm sure you are very busy." Victor smiled back. He knew the woman was impressed with him and planned to use her innocence to the fullest.

"Here she is. Mrs. Haupt is in room D133." Her gaze dropped to the flowers. "Beautiful flowers."

"Yes. My great aunt's favorite. I know she might not know me but I'm hoping the flowers will help. She used to help me pick wild daisies for my mother when we visited at my grandfather's farm." Victor inhaled as if the memories were almost too much for him to bear, straightened and with a mask of confusion said, "D133. Which way is that?"

"I can show you. I'm going that way." She grabbed a tray filled with paper cups which held tiny pills.

"That would be so kind of you." They strolled down the hall, chatting. The agent gave them a minute amount of attention as they passed by, but Victor knew if the agent was worth anything he'd memorized a full description of him.

After checking the sleeping Mrs. Haupt's vitals, Victor took the nurse's hand. "Lillian, thank you. I hope I shall see you again. Perhaps dinner?"

Blush traced the mid-age woman's cheeks. "I'm married, Mr. Haupt."

"Ah." He pursed his lips with disappointment. "Your husband is a lucky man."

"Yes, he is. I tell him all the time."

Victor laughed at her lame remark.

"If you need anything, just call." She bid him goodbye and left him alone in the room with the old woman. Victor placed the vase of daisies on the nightstand where Mrs. Haupt could see them and enjoy them. His grandparents had installed in him a deep root of respect for the elderly. Besides, beautiful things shouldn't go to waste.

Victor edged toward the door and cracked it open.

The FBI really did think he was stupid. They were laying a trap for him.

He chuckled. Little did they know he had other plans.
****

"I'm here," Ben said.

John rubbed the back of his neck and spun the chair away from the makeshift desk and the laptop. In the room directly below Steph's, they'd set up surveillance. They were far enough away so the agents coming and going wouldn't be easily detected, yet only twenty steps from her door. The stairwell was monitored as well. So far the only ones to use the stairs were the maintenance people. "It's been three days. Where the hell is he?"

"Patience. We're not dealing with some street punk here. He knows where Stephanie is and he will come. I can feel it in my gut."

John turned back to watch Steph via the laptop. His gut said the same thing. That was why he wasn't going anywhere. Victor would only need a few seconds and Steph would be dead.

Ben nudged his shoulder and handed him a cardboard cup.

"Thanks. How are the kids?"

"Fine. They're happy to be with their grandparents, but they miss Stephanie, and you."

"I'll call them later. Steph's mom and dad enjoying the hotel?"

"Yeah."

John flipped the plastic cover from the cup, tossed it toward the waste can and missed. Like an old man, his back and leg muscles ached as he rose. He picked the lid off the floor and dropped it into the trash. He put the cup to his lips and smelled what faintly resembled coffee. "Why doesn't Starbucks set up shop in hospitals? They'd make a mint."

"Why don't you go get some sleep? You're getting grouchy."

After swallowing a gulp of the lukewarm liquid, John arched a brow and replied, "Me?"

"Harmen doesn't want to work with you any more." Ben took a sip of his own brew and nodded toward the door. "Go ahead. You haven't been out of this room in days. I'll watch the monitor."

"I slept."

"In that chair. Go. That's an order."

"You're not my boss."

"No. I'm your friend. Take a walk. Loosen up. Get some fresh air, something to eat and then sleep. I'll call you if a dusty bunny moves in her room."

John stared at the laptop's screen. The doctor had Steph drugged to keep her immobile. She was sleeping soundly.

Ben was right. His reflexes were getting sluggish. Even with a shot of adrenaline he wouldn't be his best and he needed to be, for Steph's sake.

He placed the half-full cup in the garbage. "Ok, but no more than a couple hours. You wake me."

"You got it."

Before he changed his mind, John grabbed his jacket and headed out. He circled the sixth floor, twice, before stopping at the bank of elevator doors and punching the down button. With a ping, the doors opened and, miraculously, the elevator was empty. He relaxed against the wall and drew in a deep breath while listening to the rumble of the lift as it lowered. What if Victor didn't show? Steph and the kids would have no choice but to go into the Federal Protection Program. How could he let her go? He couldn't. But what choice would he have? He'd give up his career in a minute, but the bureau would never allow him go with her.

He pinched the bridge of his nose. Why worry? That scenario wasn't going to happen. Victor would show and when he did, John intended to make sure he'd never come after Steph or the kids again.

The elevator's bell rang and the door slid open. John pushed off the wall, through the opening and into a guy carrying a bunch of flowers. "Pardon me."

"It is not a problem," The man said while pushing white petals from his leather jacket.

John sidestepped the guy and headed outside for that walk Ben suggested.

****

Victor stepped off the elevator. He entered the public restroom, did his business and exited to the room. "Good Morning, Lillian," he said passing the nurse's station. "How is my aunt today?"

"She slept well, Mr. Haupt. I see you brought more daisies."

"Auntie seems to enjoy them. At least I think so," he answered, back peddling down the hall. He spun on his heel with a lighthearted step as he passed the oaf of a FBI agent, throwing him a nod. "Morning."

Inside Myrtle's room Victor greeted the mindless woman and patted her hand. He followed the routine he'd done the last three days, with the exception of placing the fresh daisies in the vase. He retrieved fresh ice, poured Myrtle more water, relaxed onto a chair and had a one-sided chat with her while she stared at a late morning game show. And he waited.

****

John swallowed the mouthful of burger he ate while he grabbed his cell phone from his hip pocket. His heart skipped a beat looking at the display. "What is it, Ben?"

"Where are you?"

"Down the street. Wendy's."

"You better get back here."

"What's happening?"

"I think your lady is waking up."

"I'm on my way." John stuffed his cell into his pocket and trashed the rest of his chili-mega meal. He entered the hospital elevator just as the fire alarm sounded. The couple inside with him stopped the door from closing and exited the lobby. The hospital staff directed others toward the hospital's front exit. Victor. It had to be. With his blood jetting through his veins, he jabbed the seventh floor button and willed the doors to slam shut. He had to get to Steph.

****

Feeling a prick in her arm, Steph jolted. She grabbed for covers that eluded her fingers. Her head throbbed. She wanted to sleep, but it was time to get up, get the kids ready for school and head out to work. Her eyelids were weighted. She struggled to open them. She tried to lean forward but she couldn't.

"Lay still, Ms. Boyd," a gentle voice cautioned her while a steady pressure held her in place.

At the sound of the stranger's voice, she threw all her effort into forcing her eyes open. A very tall man in a lab coat looked down at her with concern. His hand lay on her shoulder and held her in place. "Where am I?"

"You're in St. Mary's hospital. I need you to lie still."

A tray of instruments, including a used needle, laid on the nightstand. Steph heard a toilet flush. A moment later a nurse carrying a tube and plastic bag entered her view. The nurse dropped the items into the trash can.

"Hospital. Why am I in—" Her words drifted off as the memory of Alex's attack played out in her mind. Right up to the moment Alex had fired her gun. After that, she couldn't recall a thing. Her breath caught around her racing heart. The machine monitoring her began to beep franticly. "John? My children?"

"I've been instructed to tell you they're all fine. Now please, relax. I just gave you a pain killer. It should help in a few minutes," he said calmly while pushing gently on her side.

Above the small incision was a bandage. She immediately became aware that another bandage clung to her back. She'd been shot. She felt different, like someone had played around with her insides.

Steph studied the doctor's profile. What if he was lying to her and the kids weren't fine, but also in a room, shot by Alex? "I need to see my kids and John. Please, where are they?"

"I don't know. Remain still. I just removed a PJ drain from your side and I need to check the incision and bandage it. It'll only take a moment. Afterwards, Nurse Michaels will get you some breakfast."

How could she eat not knowing what happened to her family? She tried to sit up again. "Can you at least tell me if they were shot, too?"

The doctor sighed and straightened while holding a piece of gauze to her side. "No. I mean, you're the only one that was brought into this hospital." He pursed his lips, apparently putting himself in her position. "I'll make you a deal. You lie still for a few minutes and I'll have the nurse tell the agent guarding your door to contact his superior. Deal?"

She nodded and rested against the mattress. She tried to work up a bit of moisture in her mouth while the doctor worked on her side. If Alex had harmed John or the kids, and she wasn't already dead, Stephanie would hunt her down and kill her.

An alarm blared.

Steph's eyes popped open. "What's that?"

The nurse was already heading for the door.

****

John shouldered between the opening elevator doors. Smoke clung to the hallway ceiling in eye-stinging, bellowing waves. Doctors and nurses raced between patient's rooms, calling and responding to orders. Teary-eyed personnel directed people toward the stairwell.

With his hand over his mouth and nose, John sprinted toward Steph's room. He rounded the corner and hit the entry button to the wing when he heard Ben call his name. "John, over here. We've got the son of a bitch."

Ben waved above the heads of the crowd moving toward the stairs.

Relief and joy mixed with the adrenaline already pumping through his veins. John rushed to Ben's side. "Victor? We got Victor?"

"Yeah. We caught him going into Steph's room."

"Are you sure it's him?" Because of the crowd noise, John leaned into Ben.

"He says he is. Matches Steph's description and he's carrying ID." Ben coughed. "The guy didn't think he'd get caught. He set a fire in the restroom as a distraction. He expected the agent guarding the door to help put it out. He didn't know we had the room monitored. So we saw him enter."

"The agent left his post?"

"Yeah, for about thirty seconds and he was only thirty feet away. He checked the situation status with the head nurse and rushed right back. Victor had to be lying in wait somewhere close by."

"Not in the stairwell?"

"Not the one we're monitoring. Come on. Let's get away from this stink."

"In a minute. I want to check on Steph," John said, stepping back.

"She's fine. The doctor is with her."

"What about the fire?"

"It's out. He set a trash can in one of the stalls and apparently filled it with paper before starting it on fire."

"Seems like a lot of smoke for that type of fire."

"He set off a couple smoke bombs with it."

Anger boiled in John as Ben led the way back to the elevators. He was finally going to get his hands on the guy who had concocted the plot to steal millions from the Treasury Department. The plot that had stolen his partner's life. The plot that had almost robbed him of Steph and the kids.

In under three minutes, they had descended the seven floors and made their way through the crowded lobby to the hospital's office of head of security. An agent stood outside. Two more were on guard over a man wearing a leather jacket who sat in a hardback chair. The guy's hands were cuffed behind his back.

Victor.

John's fingers curled into fists at the sight of the killer. He wanted to look the thug in the eyes and tell him exactly what justice was going to be dealt him. John rounded the man and slowly let his gaze trail over him. Victor's boots were just as Steph had described. Leather cowboy style with silver-tipped toes.

Seeing John's interest in the boots, Victor picked his foot up off the floor and twisted his ankle left and right as if modeling the boot. "You like them?"

John met his stare. The guy's eyes laughed. They weren't cold, smug.

John's every nerve went on alert. "Who's watching Steph, Ben?"

"The agent is outside the door," Ben answered, standing behind him.

"On the monitor?"

"No one. No need. We got our guy."

The hairs on the back of John's neck prickled. "Stand up."

Wearing a smart grin, the guy relaxed back onto the chair. "Why so you can rough me up?"

"I said stand the fuck up." John grabbed him by his lapels and forced him out of the chair.

Ben grasped his wrist. "I know you want to kick the crap out of him but I can't let you."

"This isn't Victor." John glared at Ben.

Ben's brow furrowed. "What the hell are you talking about?"

"Steph said Victor was very tall, about six-four, six-five. This guy is about six-two with a two inch heel. He's not Victor."

The fire alarms blared again.

John didn't wait for Ben's response. He dropped the imposter and ran.

****

Stephanie felt as light as dandelion fluff floating on a summer breeze. Without opening her eyes, she knew someone was in the room with her. Whoever stood next to the bed. Perhaps it was the doctor or a nurse. But if her dreams came true, John would be standing there when she woke.

She ran her tongue across her dry lips. "John?"

"Nah. I am not your John."

The accent flooded her with horrible memories. Memories that took Gene's life, among others. The drug induced state seemed to vanish as if sucked from her. Stephanie opened her eyes and shot up on her elbows. The IV catheter pulled at her vein, causing her to speak his name in a whimper. "Victor."

The gun he held seemed to grow in size as he stepped closer.

"So you do recognize me."

Stephanie instinctively glanced toward the door.

"There is no help, Mrs. Boyd. Even if you scream, know one will bother. There is too much confusion. You see, someone has set a second fire."

The call button was wrapped around the side rail. She gathered the sheet in her fists. "Someone?"

A devilish smirk traced his lips. "Ya. It seems an elderly woman, just a few doors down, came by matches somehow. She wasn't quite right in her mind and has had an accident. Your guard was the first to hear her screams and smell the stench. Knowing the man who was trying to kill you has been apprehended, he felt a need to help."

"What do you mean apprehended? You're here."

"Many men want to move up in our ranks. They do anything I ask."

A death chill ran down her spine. She was alone. What had Victor done to the old woman? To think he had a conscience would be a grave mistake. She shivered and pulled the sheet higher, covering the call button. If Victor noticed she'd pressed the button calling for help, he'd kill her instantly.

Where was John?

She needed to buy time until someone answered her call. "What do you want?" She prayed she wasn't putting anyone else in danger.

"I want nothing. I only need to erase the mistake that your husband made."

"What mistake?"

"Involving you." He moved to the bottom of the bed.

Stephanie heard the click of his gun. Her thumb tingled with numbness as she continued to depress the call button.

"I know what you're trying to do, Mrs. Boyd, but with all that is going on, I doubt anyone is answering calls for soft drinks."

Knowing he was onto her, she let go of the alarm and pulled her hand out from under the sheet. She wasn't going to give him the satisfaction of seeing her fear. She would die with courage. Stephanie raised her chin. "Well, what are you waiting for, you coward?"

Victor laughed.

The door burst open and, in a blur, John shot across the room, tackling Victor.

The gun discharged. Stephanie dropped back onto the mattress. The bullet had whizzed by her head.

John knocked the weapon from Victor's hand.

While the men wrestled for control of the other, one of them kicked the gun and it skittered across the shiny linoleum floor.

Steph slid off the bed. She grabbed the side rail to steady herself as the room seemed to shift under her feet. John and Victor's actions appeared to be slowing down. She knew that wasn't possible. Each man was fighting for his life. And for hers. John to keep it. Victor to take it away.

She had to get help. Stephanie yanked back the tape and removed the IV from the stint in her hand. On shaky legs, she struggled toward the door, only to be stopped by John's cry. She looked back. Victor had wrestled John to the floor and was on top of him. Suddenly, the floor seemed to rise up to meet her. She grabbed for IV pole as a means to steady herself. Sweat beads pelted her forehead. She couldn't succumb to dizziness. John needed her help.

Victor slammed his fist into John's jaw and, for a split second, John was still. Victor took the opportunity to scramble to his feet and dove for the gun.

With gun in hand, he rose. He aimed at John and pulled the trigger.

Stephanie blinked. Nothing happened. The gun jammed.

Victor struggled with the hammer.

Planting her feet, she gripped the IV pole and, with all her might, swung and smacked Victor across the face. The gun discharged into the floor and Victor dropped like a century-old oak, landing at the feet of an out-of-breath Ben.

She slumped to her knees.

"Sweet. Did you see that?" Ben kicked the gun away from Victor.

"That's my girl." John got to his feet while rubbing his jaw. Reaching her side, he gathered her up in his arms. "Good to see you back."

She smiled and then everything went black.

~~~~

Chapter Thirty-Five

She missed the kids, but they were safe with her parents.

Stephanie didn't notice the splinter of light cutting the darkness. She was barely aware of the tropical breeze which carried the scent of salt water and exotic flowers along with the beat of a steel drum and laughter as it bellowed the sheer drapes. She knew, below the balcony, torches basked the pool area with shimmering light while a calypso band entertained guests. But at the moment, she was far away.

She stood before a mirror. A single lamp, turned low, lit the room. Through the silken material of her nightgown, her fingertips traced the outline of the scar near her waist. A mirror image of it marked her back. She didn't want to remember how her life had come to this point. The memories caused fear to wrap around her heart, tainting the joy she'd come to know.

In the glass, she noticed movement behind her. A second later, he was there, staring at her. The man she'd die for.

"You have the devilish look," she said.

"You look beautiful in red, Mrs. Dolton."

Smiling, she turned. Her breath caught. The plush towel he wore hung low on his hips. His broad chest, glistening with moisture from his shower, rose and fell steadily. She longed to feel the strength of his body under her hand.

John closed the short distance between them. His fingers traced her nightgown's thin strap. The strap fell from her shoulder. The shimmering material draped her breast.

She saw John's tongue trace his lips. Warmth pooled between her legs, knowing he wanted her, again.

Her shoulder tickled under his touch as the other strap fell.

Her nightgown slipped to the floor.

She heard the catch of his breath. His lingering look heated her skin as it traveled up from her toes, across her belly and breasts, until it locked with hers.

She arched a brow. "Are you happy?"

"Oh yeah. Are you?"

Her breasts jutted forward while she pulled out the clip holding her hair in place. "I'm going to be." She combed her fingers through his coarse chest curls, tugged the towel from his waist and tossed it to the side. "For the rest of my life."

About the Author

Award-winning author Autumn Jordon is a quiet nut who has earned the title of 'trouble' by her family and friends. Even her pets look at her with a cautious eye, at times. Life is never dull in her valley surrounded by the beautiful Blue Mountains of northeast PA.

She loves to travel with the man who is not only her husband but also her best friend. They love to learn about the areas they visit and make new friends.

She's never bored as she has a long list of hobbies.

No matter what Autumn is doing, she is always busy dreaming up ideas to put her very believable characters of her romantic suspense novels in grave danger while falling in love.

Visit her at www.autumnjordon.com

Made in the USA
Charleston, SC
08 December 2013